The Cobbler's Kids

Rosie HARRIS

arrow books

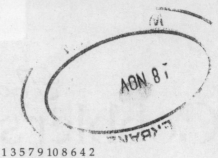

AON 8

13 5 7 9 10 8 6 4 2

Arrow Books
20 Vauxhall Bridge Road
London SW1V 2SA

Arrow Books is part of the Penguin Random House group of companies
whose addresses can be found at global.penguinrandomhouse.com

Penguin
Random House
UK

First published in Great Britain by William Heinemann in 2005
First published in paperback by Arrow Books in 2005
This edition reissued by Arrow Books in 2019

www.penguin.co.uk

A CIP catalogue record for this book is available from the British Library.

ISBN 9781787463226

Typeset in Palatino by Palimpsest Book Production Ltd, Falkirk UK
Printed and bound in Great Britain by Clays Ltd, Elcograf S.p.A.

MIX
Paper from
responsible sources
FSC
www.fsc.org   FSC® C018179

Penguin Random House is committed to a
sustainable future for our business, our readers
and our planet. This book is made from Forest
Stewardship Council® certified paper.

The Cobbler's Kids

Rosie Harris was born in Cardiff and grew up there and in the West Country. After her marriage she lived for some years on Merseyside before moving to Buckinghamshire where she still lives. She has three grown-up children and six grandchildren and writes full time.

For Ken and all the Harris family

Acknowledgements

With many thanks to Georgina Hawtrey-Woore and her many colleagues for all their help and to Caroline Sheldon for her tremendous support.

Chapter One

'If you don't shut that squealing little brat up I'll come in there and wring his soddin' neck!'

Michael Quinn's voice rose to an angry roar that penetrated every corner of the room at the rear of his cobbler's shop in Scotland Road which served as the main living room for him and his family.

In the prime of life, Michael Quinn was a man whose appearance commanded attention. Handsome, with a head of thick, curly jet-black hair and piercing blue eyes, he stood head and shoulders above most people. He carried himself well – shoulders back, chin up – almost as if he was still a corporal in the Liverpool Irish, the regiment he'd served in during the Great War which had not long ended.

Almost six foot tall, he filled the doorway; he was a scowling, threatening figure dressed in dark trousers and a grey flannel shirt, with a knee-length black leather apron over the top.

His anger made Annie Quinn tremble. In one hand he was holding the heavily studded boot he'd been mending, and for a moment she was afraid he was going to hurl it at her.

She dropped the poker she was using to try and stir the dying fire back to life and rushed to pick up the baby and hold him protectively in her arms.

'What the hell is he bawling about this time?' Michael Quinn snarled. 'I've never known a kid that could howl like he does. Night and day he's at it, the miserable little bugger.'

'He can't help it, Mike. It's not his fault. He's hungry.'

'Then feed him!'

'On what?' she asked wearily. 'The larder's bare, I'm still waiting for you to give me some house-keeping money. Young Eddy and Vee will be hungry when they get home from school, too. The only difference is they know better than to complain,' Annie told him bitterly.

'Watch your tongue, woman. You'll get some money when I'm good and ready to give it to you, and not before.'

'Then you'll have to put up with Benny crying because there's nothing in the house that I can feed him on.'

'If you'd kept him on the titty you'd be able to shut him up any time you wanted to,' he snapped.

'How on earth could I do that? Benny is over a year old!'

'Why the hell does that matter?'

Annie rocked the child, trying to soothe him, then held him over her shoulder and rubbed his little back as he belched noisily from hunger.

Michael watched her impatiently, then he dug down into his trouser pocket and pulled out a handful of coins. He sorted out two florins and slammed them down on the scrubbed wooden table that dominated the room.

'There you are. Plenty enough there for you to

buy food for the lot of us. Make sure that mine is a pork chop, and see that it's nice and lean, with a kidney thrown in as well. Mind you buy it from Wardles, the butcher on the corner of Dryden Street, not from one of the meat stalls in Paddy's Market. Have you got that?'

Annie nodded, but made no comment. She grabbed up the two coins and slipped them into the pocket of the print apron she wore over her blue cotton dress. In her mind she was already working out whether she could persuade the butcher to give her the sort of chop she knew Michael liked as well as some scrag-end of mutton to make a nourishing stew for the rest of them for less than a florin.

If so, she'd be able to buy vegetables and a tin of Cow & Gate for the baby with the rest of the money. With any luck she might even be able to stretch to a loaf of bread, a couple of pennys worth of tea and some margarine.

A hearty helping of scouse would be a nice treat for Edmund when he got in from his delivery rounds. He was a growing lad so he'd be hungry all right, ravenous in fact. There hadn't been any bread left for him and young Vera to take even a jam butty to school for their midday meal because Michael had eaten the last of the loaf when he'd come home from the pub the night before.

She'd send Vera to Paddy's Market to get the veggies the minute she came home from school. They'd be able to afford spuds, carrots, onions and perhaps even a swede. She'd tell Vee to buy herself an apple to keep her going until the stew was cooked.

Her own belly rumbled at the thought of the feast that lay ahead. She'd pop along to the butcher's herself right away, then she could pick up the tin of Cow & Gate for young Benjamin. If she fed him first it would pacify him while she got on with the cooking.

As she scraped back her hair into a bun, pulled a shawl round her shoulders and tucked Benny into his battered pram, Annie wished she could go back to the days when Michael had been in the army and she'd only had the children to look after. Her army allowance had come through as regular as clockwork and she'd been free to plan how she would spend every penny of it. She'd been able to keep the children well fed and decently clothed and buy coal to keep their home lovely and warm.

She could remember so clearly the wonderful sense of freedom she'd enjoyed. There had been no one telling her what she should and shouldn't do, and no violence. Michael's favourite form of punishment for poor Eddy these days was thumping him across the top of his head with a bunched up fist.

They'd still been living in Wallasey then, in a lovely little house in Exeter Road. It was a quiet, respectable area and she'd been on friendly terms with her neighbours. All the children played together so well that they'd been like one huge happy family.

Even when the war came and Mike had responded to Kitchener's call 'Your Country Needs

You', she'd managed her life with no real problems at all.

At first she'd felt lonely, but with three young children – ten-year-old Charlie, seven-year-old Edmund and four-year-old Vera – she'd been kept so busy that she soon adjusted. It had helped, of course, that her parents lived only a few streets away, and were always ready to lend a hand if necessary.

In fact, looking back, she realised that those were the happiest days of her life. She'd had no worries then. Her life had been plain sailing until the war ended, and then it seemed as if every misfortune possible had hit her at once.

The traumatic memories brought tears to her eyes and a deep ache to her heart. She'd led such a happy, sheltered existence up until then, so why did it all have to change so suddenly? It was a question she asked herself over and over again.

To the outside world, Michael Quinn was still the perfect gentleman and the ideal family man. Whenever he went out he was always immaculately dressed in a perfectly ironed white shirt with a stiff collar, a well-pressed suit and polished black shoes.

'Your husband looks more like a bank manager than a cobbler,' Iris Locke, who ran a sweet and tobacco shop with her husband a few doors away in Scotland Road, told her admiringly.

Michael was always charming, polite and helpful, doffing his trilby and even offering to carry heavy shopping bags for their neighbours. He was so ready to give helpful advice to all and sundry that many people thought he deserved a more rewarding career than mending boots and shoes.

Annie Quinn sometimes thought he should have been an actor. He was so polished when he was out but, these days, such a bully within his own home. Domineering, selfish and harsh were the words she would use to describe him since he came home from the army.

Sometimes she wondered what her own parents, if they were still alive, would have said about the change in him.

Annie's mind went back to the days when Michael had first come courting her. They'd met at the Tower Ballroom in New Brighton. It had been the New Year's Eve ball, Thursday 31st December 1903.

She'd been with a crowd of girls she had known at school. It was the first time that most of them had been allowed to go there and she'd felt really grown up and excited to be one of them. She'd been wearing her very first dance frock in a gorgeous pale blue taffeta with a heart-shaped neckline and puff sleeves. Her long fair hair had been caught back in the nape of her neck with a silver hair slide.

Michael had been next to her when they all joined hands on the stroke of midnight to sing 'Auld Lang Syne', and he'd asked her later if he could walk her home.

She'd refused because she'd promised to stay with the crowd of girls she'd come with. He'd followed them home and, the next day, he'd called at her house with some flowers.

When she'd asked him in, her mother had been

quite taken by him. She'd even felt sorry for him when she'd learned that he'd been born in Ireland but had grown up in an orphanage in Liverpool and knew nothing at all about his family. Ever since he started work, he told them, he'd been living in a hostel.

In the months that followed, Michael Quinn became a regular visitor to the Simmonds' home and Annie noticed that her mother would even go out of her way to cook the dishes she knew he liked best.

'Poor lad, he looks as though he needs feeding up, and he enjoys my cooking so much,' she would protest if her husband commented.

'Yes, I know he does, but remember young Michael has Irish blood in him so you should take his honeyed words with a pinch of salt.'

His other reservation about Annie's new friend was that, despite Michael's good looks and charming manner, he was only an apprentice cobbler. Although they hadn't said as much, Annie sensed that her parents would like her to find a boyfriend who had better prospects.

At fifteen, headstrong and completely innocent, she had chosen to ignore any cautions about her boyfriend. Michael was so good-looking that she had fallen in love with him. He was full of promises for their future and she believed every gilded word he uttered.

Throughout the spring and summer of 1904 she'd existed in a blissful, dreamlike trance. She adored everything about Michael and she devoted every spare minute to being with him.

Michael was so wonderfully attentive that he made her feel like a princess. When he took her to the cinema it was always to see the picture she requested. When they went dancing at the Tower Ballroom it was to the strains of the band she liked best. On her sixteenth birthday in June 1904 he took her on the ferry boat across to Liverpool and treated her to a special meal at the State Restaurant in Dale Street.

As the weather became warmer they walked along the seafront at New Brighton, or wandered amongst the sand hills in Harrison Drive. She was so infatuated by him that she made no protest whatsoever when he wanted to make love to her whenever they were alone. She was head-over-heels in love with him.

She was the envy of all the other girls at the hairdresser's, where she was an apprentice, when she told them he wanted to marry her.

'You can't get married until after your next birthday,' her friend Ellie warned her.

'That's less than a year away!'

'Maybe it is, but you won't be able to marry then unless your parents give their permission, will you?'

'They will,' she told Ellie confidently. 'They think the world of Michael.'

When she discovered she was pregnant, though, she was scared stiff about what her parents would say.

They were shocked by the news when she finally told them. Her mother was in tears and her father was so angry he could hardly bear to talk about it.

'Michael has promised there will be no scandal. As long as both of you are agreeable he says we can be married before anyone knows there is a baby on the way.'

Instead of being pleased, as she'd expected, they'd tried to persuade her to finish with him there and then.

'We'll take care of you and we'll arrange for the baby to be adopted as soon as it is born,' they told her.

Michael had dug his heels in when she told him what her parents had said. 'It's out of the question! I love you, I want to take care of you and our baby. If we get married right away no one will be any the wiser.'

'How can you possibly manage to conceal such a thing when my daughter's already over four months pregnant?' James Simmonds demanded when, hand-in-hand, they went to him and begged him to let them marry.

'We'll elope if we have to! It's simple enough, Mr Simmonds,' Michael told him.

Annie could remember to this day the look of horror on her father's face. She was their only child and he'd saved each week for her future since the day she'd been born.

He had set his heart on her having a fairy-tale wedding when the time came. She'd be dressed in a beautiful white dress with a long flowing veil and would carry white roses, just like her mother had done on their wedding day.

Her mother, Emma Simmonds, had been heart-broken, too. Michael Quinn could say what he liked, but she knew full well that her friends and neighbours would guess why he and Annie had married in such a hasty, secretive way.

Respectability was an important facet of life in the middle-class area where they lived in Wallasey. Tongues would wag behind the lace curtains at each of the semi-detached Victorian houses in Trinity Road. Even if nothing was said openly, they'd be counting the days to when Annie's baby was born. When it happened only a few months after the wedding ceremony they'd draw their own conclusions and it would be hard for any of the Simmonds family to hold their heads up again.

James Simmonds' position as a teller at the Liscard branch of Martins Bank might even be jeopardised. He'd certainly never be promoted to manager once the scandal got out.

They accepted the inevitable, however, and James Simmonds used the money he had carefully saved up for his daughter's white wedding to buy his new son-in-law a partnership in a cobbler's business in Wallasey's busy King Street. He also found them a small house to rent in Exeter Road, only a short distance away, and furnished it from top to bottom.

Having a child at seventeen was a tremendous shock for Annie. She had barely needed to lift a finger at home, but now, instead of being the one who was waited on, she found she not only had to look after a new baby, but a husband and home too.

Charlie was born in April 1905, a bouncing seven and a half pounds, with his father's dark hair and vivid blue eyes. Annie found that her mother, despite her earlier qualms, was a tower of strength and did all she could to help.

Emma's delight in her grandson turned to recriminations against Michael, however, when she learned that Annie was expecting again when Charlie was barely seven months old. She seemed almost relieved when Annie miscarried when she was only three months pregnant.

Charlie was not quite two and a half when Edmund was born in October 1907. He was a sickly baby and Annie knew that without her own mother's devoted care he would never have survived. Edmund also had his father's vivid blue eyes, but his hair was a shock of curls as golden as freshly churned butter.

'Given time, we'll have our own little football team,' he announced proudly when, a year after Edmund was born, Annie was pregnant once again.

This time it was a little girl. Vera Quinn was born on 1st May 1909. A plump, contented baby, she had her mother's fine features, but her father's eyes and jet-black hair.

'She'll be a real beauty when she gets older,' Michael announced happily.

There was no doubt at all that she was the apple of his eye. He picked her up and nursed her the minute he came in from work. He would even carry her down the street in his arms, showing her off to anyone who expressed the slightest interest.

Annie worried that the two boys might become jealous, but they seemed to accept her arrival in their lives. They had each other to play with and

Annie made sure that they had plenty of attention from her whenever Mike was cuddling Vera.

She was expecting again when war was declared, but the shock of Michael dashing off to serve his country caused her such distress that no one was surprised when she miscarried.

'You mustn't worry about it, Annie. You've got quite enough on your plate as it is with three youngsters, my dear,' her mother told her.

She didn't fret; in fact she felt a sense of relief. She silently agreed with her mother that three children were quite enough to cope with, especially with Michael being away in the army.

As the years passed, despite a great many shortages as a result of the war, the children seemed to be happy enough and to grow apace and Annie felt quite contented with her life. With all the children at school, and her own mother willing to be there for them when they came home, Annie was even able to go back to work for two days a week. She saved this extra money, hoping that they could have a family holiday when Michael was eventually demobbed.

It was early 1919 before he was discharged, though, and by that time an influenza epidemic was sweeping across Europe, so a holiday was out of the question. Charlie, as well as both her parents, were ill.

She still found it hard to believe that all three of them died within days of each other. At the time she'd felt as if her entire world had collapsed. In a way, it had. The happy days with her own mother and father supporting her had gone for ever.

She was in such a daze that she left it to Michael to settle up her parents' affairs. When he told her that they were moving to Liverpool, and that he was setting up his own business, she made no protest at all.

What did it matter where she lived. Her parents were gone and so, too, was one of her little boys. There seemed to be so much sorrow in her life that she didn't even ask Michael where he was getting the money from to rent his own shop, or even care that it was in Liverpool on the other side of the Mersey.

It wasn't until many months later that she realised that in order to set up on his own Michael had sold all her parents' possessions, every single thing they had ever owned. He hadn't even kept a picture, an ornament, or a piece of her mother's jewellery for her to have as a keepsake.

Chapter Two

No one knew better than Michael Quinn how much the army had changed him since his days as a raw recruit in 1914.

When the other men in his unit found out that he came from Merseyside they immediately wanted to know if he was a Wallasey boy. He couldn't understand the jeers, the laughter and the nudges when he readily admitted that he was. It was only later that he found out that being termed a 'Wallasey Boy' meant they thought he was homosexual.

He had lived through a similar scenario because of his good looks when he'd been in the orphanage. He didn't relish a repeat of the torment he'd endured then so he tried to blend into the background.

The moment he completed his square-bashing though, he started working hard to gain his stripes. It had taken six months to get his lance corporal tab, but from the moment he did he was relieved to find that he had earned himself a degree of respect. There were no more jibes, at least not within earshot.

When he was finally made a full corporal his life changed completely. He was in charge. No one could sneer or guffaw after that. Those who had already done so quickly felt the weight of his authority. He handed out so much punishment that he was the most feared NCO in the regiment.

After that, there was no turning back. He'd heard the saying that 'power corrupts' and he supposed that in a way it had that effect on him.

He could still charm his superiors when it suited him to do so, but he was no longer the easy-going, smiling chap he'd tried to be from the moment he'd met Annie.

Being away from his wife and kids had put that relationship into perspective as well. The world was a harsh place. He was living in dangerous times, balancing on the knife-edge of survival, experiencing hunger, pain and fear. He'd seen his comrades die. Having survived the mud and bullets of battle he vowed that in future he would put himself first, even before his family.

Once he was back home, he was annoyed to see how protective Annie was, how she coddled their children. Edmund, in particular, irritated him so much that he couldn't bear to look at him. He was such a short, skinny kid, and, what was worse, he always had his nose in a book or comic. He was not the sort of lad he could be proud to say was his son. He wanted his boys to be tough enough to hold their own in the school playground or out in the street. Boys should know how to use their fists to defend themselves.

He intended to knock Edmund into shape, even though this meant he'd have to fight with Annie as well. Not long after Michael had arrived home he'd tried to teach Edmund to box, but he just hid behind his mother's skirts.

'Leave the lad alone! It's not his nature to be aggressive,' Annie had told him sharply.

'He'll need to learn to stand up for himself now he's living in this area. The lads in school will pick on him, especially when they hear he's from Wallasey.'

He'd tried to explain to her what was meant by the term 'a Wallasey boy', but she'd been disgusted and gave him a right earful.

From that moment on their relationship had turned sour. She'd learned over the past years how to bring up her children without a father. Michael had been away for over four years, and now she felt that she no longer needed or even wanted to listen to him, nor did she welcome his attentions.

When, within a couple of months of his home-coming, she found she was pregnant again, she expressed such anger that he'd seen red and slapped her across the face almost without thinking.

Instead of cowering back, she had turned on him like an alley cat.

'Don't you ever do that again,' she'd hissed. 'This is the last baby you're going to foist on me, understand?'

Sensing danger he'd turned on the charm. 'What about that football team we were going to produce,' he joked.

'This is my last baby and I don't care whether it is a boy or a girl, you won't be fathering any more. You've changed so much that I hardly know you. You're no longer the man I married. There's no tenderness or kindness left in you. You're drunk with your own power and nothing but a great bully. You might be able to browbeat Edmund and Vera, but you'll never intimidate me.'

Her tone was icy and the look of hatred in her eyes scared him as much as anything he had experienced in his very worst moments in France. He knew she was right. His whole attitude to life and to other people, even his wife and children, was different.

To this day he didn't truly understand what had happened to him when war was declared in August 1914. All he knew was that he couldn't wait to join up. It was as if he had waited all his life for this moment. He felt needed, eager to be in the thick of the fighting. He thought he could take on the enemy and sort them out, single-handed if necessary. It seemed he'd reached a crisis point. He'd blindly abandoned both his job and his family, and rushed along to the recruiting office.

He'd been confident, of course, that Annie's father, James Simmonds would keep an eye on Annie and the children. He was far too old to be called up and so he'd be there for them whether the war took a month or even a year.

He'd never expected it to be more than four years until he was back home again. Or that he would undergo a complete change in his outlook on life, indeed, a metamorphosis of his entire personality.

From the Liverpool recruiting office he was sent off with about fifty others to the training barracks, kitted out in khaki and drilled by a bullying sergeant until he marched automatically and jumped to attention almost before an order was bellowed out. He would never forget the pride he had felt when they were sent by train to London and marched five-abreast through the city to Victoria station on their way to embark for France.

By October 1914 he was at Ypres, living in a muddy trench and experiencing first-hand what it meant to 'go over the top' when every nerve in your body was screaming with fear. The casualties were alarming. Later on there was an even greater hazard to be faced when the enemy started using gas.

His family was rarely in his thoughts; he was too busy concentrating on his army duties and his own survival. Verdun, the Somme, and then back again to Ypres.

Whilst the majority of his companions were maimed or killed he came through the many campaigns virtually unscathed. It was as if he had some invisible form of protection. The only thing he suffered throughout those terrible years of war was a change of personality. He was no longer the mild suburban family man. He'd reverted to the hard, wily character who'd learned to face the hardships of growing up in an orphanage and to fight for his place in life.

He built up such an inner reserve of strength that, unlike others in the same campaigns, he was never sent home for falling victim to stress, shell shock or war fatigue. The greater the bombardment, the more resolute he seemed to be. Everyone told him, his 'luck' would run out one day. He'd be another statistic. He proved them all wrong.

He was still on active service, proudly wearing his two stripes, when peace was finally declared on 11th November 1918.

He was moved around and delayed so much prior to his final demob that he'd not heard from Annie for several months. It hadn't worried him. It was only a matter of time before he would be home for good, then he'd be able to do all the catching up necessary.

Returning to Merseyside would be an anti-climax. Having been in charge of other men he knew he could never stand being servile to a boss ever again. It wasn't going to be easy explaining to Annie that he wanted to be his own boss so the longer he could put off doing so the better.

He certainly hadn't expected to become embroiled in the tragic situation that faced him soon after he arrived home. He'd known that the influenza outbreak that had swept right through Europe at the end of 1918 had reached pandemic proportions, but he hadn't realised that any of his immediate family had been caught up in it.

After seeing so many men die in battle he would never have believed that he could feel so devastated. He was sorry that Annie's parents, James and Emma Simmonds, had died, but they were getting on in years so it had to be accepted that they would have died sometime in the near future. It was Charlie's death that affected him so badly. Charlie! His first born. The boy he was so proud of because he was the spitting image of himself.

Annie was so distraught by her parents' and their son's death that he'd automatically taken charge. The skills he had developed from handling difficult situations while he'd been in the army stood him in good stead for sorting out a new future for them all. By ruthlessly disposing of all of his in-laws's possessions, and most of their own furnishings, he raised the capital to start up in business as an independent cobbler.

It was as if all the dreams and ambitions he'd built up in his mind while he had been in the trenches in France were coming to fruition. It was a challenge, of course, and one he felt should be tackled in new surroundings, so that they all made a complete break from their past.

Crossing the Mersey to Liverpool seemed to be an ideal solution. As a result of the police riots that had centred in Scotland Road during the summer of 1919, there were plenty of vacant shops with living accommodation which were being rented out very cheaply in that area. It meant that there was enough money left to buy stock to set himself up as an independent cobbler.

His war years had accustomed him to living rough so he never stopped to think that Annie and the kids might find it a hardship to move from their quiet little backwater in Wallasey to a place like Scotland Road.

At the time, Annie had showed little interest. 'I don't care where we live,' she had said dismissively when he'd told her their new address. 'No matter where it is Charlie won't be with us, nor will my mother and father.'

He'd tried to be sympathetic, but he'd seen so many of his mates die over the past four years that he was now hardened to such things. He was still alive and so was she and so, too, were Edmund and Vera.

One of the biggest problems was Edmund. He wasn't the sort of son he wanted. He was so quiet and withdrawn. Michael frequently wished that it had been Edmund, not Charlie, who'd succumbed to the influenza epidemic. Charlie had taken after him whereas, in many ways, Eddy took after Annie's family. He was far too reserved. Whether Annie liked it or not he intended to toughen him up, ready to face the world.

Living in Scotland Road should help put that right, Michael thought. It was the opposite of where they'd lived in Wallasey. He liked it there and felt quite at home. There were nineteen pubs in Scotland Road alone and no matter what time of the evening he went into one of them for a drink there was always someone willing to listen to his tales about what had happened in France.

Annie had made it clear right from the moment he'd returned home from the war that she hated him going drinking, but he told her it was something she'd have to get used to. He'd become accustomed to living with men and he needed to be with them, swap yarns and enjoy their company.

His feelings for Annie had changed. The closeness and tenderness they'd known in the old days was no longer there. He was still prepared to bed her, of course. He'd proved that by putting her in the club almost the moment he'd got home. He regarded that as being providential since a baby would help fill the gap that Charlie's death had left. A woman is always happiest when she has a youngster to care for because it fills in their day for them, he thought wryly. He hadn't, of course, expected the baby to be such a whingeing little bugger.

He realised that Annie didn't like living behind their shop in Scotland Road, but there wasn't very much he could do about that. It was a bit rough after the little house they'd had in Wallasey, but the Simmonds had furnished that place for them and he'd sold most of it to buy the stock and machines he'd needed to get started.

He knew he often kept Annie short of money, but it was taking time to build up a steady flow of customers. In his view she wasn't the best of money managers. They'd lived far beyond their means when they'd been in Wallasey. James Simmonds had always been ready to slip Annie a couple of quid to buy clothes for the kids, or for a pretty dress or a new hat for herself.

She'd also grown used to her mother dropping by most days with home-made cakes, or some other treat for the children. She missed all that help now that there was no one to indulge her.

He kept telling Annie that the kids didn't need all that sort of rubbish and she must use her house-keeping money for the basics. She accused him of spending too much on beer, but at the end of a long working day a man deserved a pint to wet his whistle, and the chance to have a gab with other men. The sooner she got used to his new way of living the better, as far as he was concerned.

Chapter Three

The moment the bell signalled the end of afternoon lessons at St Anthony's School in Newsham Street, Vera Quinn hurried to collect her jacket from her peg in the cloakroom, anxious to get home.

'Hey, wait for me, Vee!' Her friend Rita Farthing caught up with her as she hurried across the school yard towards the iron gate.

'Come on then, slowcoach, get a move on.'

Linking arms, they hurried out into Newsham Street. Two best friends: one plump, round-faced, with straight brown hair and brown eyes, the other as skinny as a beanpole with jet-black hair and bright blue eyes.

They turned left into Scotland Road and then ran helter-skelter towards the biscuit factory on the corner of Dryden Street.

'I hope he's saved something special for us today, I'm starving!' Rita exclaimed as they reached the gatekeeper's booth. She waved cheerily at her grandfather who controlled the barrier to the factory.

He waved back to them, a broad smile on his whiskered face, then dived under the counter and emerged holding a brown paper bag.

'I wonder what he's got for us,' Rita exclaimed excitedly. She disentangled her arm from Vera's and ran forward to reach up and take the bag from her grandfather, shouting her thanks to him as they ran off down Dryden Street.

When they came to the corner of Louis Cohen Place and turned back into Scotland Road they stopped to peer inside the bag. Their eyes widened with delight when amongst the mass of broken biscuits they spotted three whole ones which were all coated on one side with chocolate.

'One each!' Rita squealed. 'My granddad must have put those in specially. Come on.' She closed the bag again and grabbed at Vera's hand. 'If we hurry we'll be able to catch your Eddy before he starts out on his delivery round.'

Vera pulled back. 'No, you go and meet Eddy, I ought to get home.'

'Must you?' Rita frowned.

'If Mam's had a bad day with Benjamin you know she'll be waiting for me to give her a hand and look after him,' Vera reminded her.

'OK. Here, take your choccy biscuit then and a handful of the broken ones for your Benny. I'll share the rest with Eddy when I find him.'

'You sure?'

'Course I am! We always divide everything between the three of us, don't we?'

'Well, you do.' Vera grinned. 'I don't often have very much to share with you.'

'Yes you do, we share your brother,' Rita reminded her with a cheeky grin.

As she hurried towards her own home at Quinn's Boot and Shoe Repairer's further along Scotland Road, Vera compared her own life with that of her friend Rita Farthing.

Rita had lived all her life in Ellenborough Street just off Scotland Road and they'd been friends from the very first day Vera had started going to St Anthony's School.

Vera had been nine years old at the time and had dreaded having to go to a new school because she knew everyone would have their own special friend or belong to a gang, and she'd be left out of everything. She wished she could stay with her crowd in Wallasey, especially with Jack Winter who'd been her special friend.

She'd been told to sit next to Rita Farthing and the teacher had told Rita to keep an eye on her. Rita had done more than that. She'd never left her side. She'd introduced her to everyone else and made sure she was included in everything they did.

From that day on she and Rita had been inseparable. Rita's father, Stan Farthing, worked as a stevedore at the docks. Vera wasn't sure what that was, but she did know it meant that the Farthings always had plenty to eat. Millie Farthing, Rita's mother, loved cooking and usually she packed so much into Rita's lunch box that there was plenty for Rita to share with her and Edmund.

Sometimes Vera wondered whether Rita would have become her best friend if Eddy hadn't been her brother. The moment she'd heard that there was a new boy, Edmund Quinn, two classes higher than them, and realised that he was Vera's brother, she'd wanted to know all about him.

'Come on,' she'd demanded as soon as school ended on that first day, 'you can introduce me to your brother.'

Vera hesitated. Edmund was walking down the road with two or three boys of his own age and she wasn't sure it was a good time to approach him.

Rita insisted.

Eddy had scowled when she tapped him on the arm, but when he heard the reason why she'd stopped him he had managed to smile and say hello to Rita before moving on with his new friends.

'He's not a bit like you!' Rita exclaimed in amazement.

'He looks like my mum, except that her hair isn't curly like his. I take after my dad, only my dad's hair is curly.'

'You're nearly as tall as your brother!'

Vera frowned. She was tired of hearing her dad say that Eddy was a runt. 'He's only twelve, he's still got time to grow,' she said defensively.

'Not too much, I hope,' Rita grinned. 'I like him as he is. I hate it when boys tower over me.'

At first Eddy had been completely uninterested in hearing about Rita and had given Vera black looks whenever she mentioned her friend's name.

'Why do you have to keep going on about her, she's only a kid, the same as you are,' he told her huffily.

When he discovered that the tasty wedges of pie or hunks of fruit cake that she passed to him now and again during their lunch break came from Rita he began to pay more attention.

Within a few months he was as interested in Rita as she was in him. He plied Vera with questions about where Rita lived and what she did after school until, in the end, she'd told him to go and ask Rita himself.

He'd turned as red as a beetroot and didn't mention her name once over the next couple of weeks. Rita hadn't talked about him either. The reason why that was had suddenly dawned on Vera one evening when she'd spotted them talking together on the corner of Ellenborough Street.

After that they often went round in a threesome and both Vera and Edmund enjoyed Rita's generosity with the contents of her lunch box. The bag of broken biscuits that her grandfather gave her once a week, which she always shared with them, was an added bonus.

At first Vera thought she would never get used to living in Scotland Road. Liverpool was so different from where they'd lived in Wallasey. Yet, within a few months she felt as if she had lived there all her life, and she hardly noticed the trams clanging up and down right outside her bedroom window, or the loud shouts and general noise that went on in the street from early in the morning until late at night.

Even so, she didn't like Scotland Road very much. Their main living room was at the back of her dad's shop. It was dark and dreary and not nearly as nicely furnished as their living room in Exeter Road had been. The bare wooden floor had only a rag-rug in front of the fireplace and there was only one comfortable armchair and that was kept for her dad. The rest of the space was taken up with a scrubbed wooden table and an assortment of upright chairs.

She didn't know what had happened to all the other furniture that they'd had in Wallasey and her mam refused to talk about it. She knew her mam wasn't happy, though. Sometimes she could see she'd been crying, but she didn't think it was just because she didn't like her surroundings.

So much had happened since he'd come home from the war. Losing both her grandparents as well as her brother Charlie in the influenza epidemic had been terrible. She'd loved them all so much and she knew her mother still hadn't stopped grieving.

When Benny had been born she hoped he would fill the gap in their lives, a kind of replacement for Charlie, but he didn't. Benny wasn't anything like him. Charlie had been a strapping fourteen-year-old and he'd taken after their dad with dark, curly hair and bright blue eyes. He'd just started an apprenticeship at Cammell Laird's and cycled across the Penny Bridge to Birkenhead each day as proud as punch to be a wage earner at last.

Vera was sure that there was some deeper reason for her mother's unhappiness and that it was something to do with her dad. She'd only been four years old when he'd gone off to war, but her memories of him before then were quite different to what he was like now. In those days he'd been so friendly, he'd always been ready to play with her and her brothers and, as far back as she could remember, her dad had always made a tremendous fuss of her.

Whenever they went for a walk, the moment she complained that her legs were tired, he'd pick

her up and sit her on his shoulders and then pretend to be a horse.

Sometimes they used to chase Charlie and
Edmund. Once, when they'd been on the shore at
New Brighton, he'd carried her right into the
Mersey until the water was almost up to his knees.

Now, he never even seemed to smile. He picked
on Edmund, hitting him across the top of his head
with the knuckles of his clenched fist if he didn't
jump to it when he asked him to do something.

He seemed to have no time for the baby, either.
Benny cried a lot, but that was because he was
always hungry. Mam never said anything to Vera,
but she often heard her mam and dad arguing
about money because her mam claimed he kept
her short and yet Vera felt sure that there had
never been any problems like that in the past.

When her dad had been away in the army there
had always been a hot meal waiting for them when
they came home from school. Every morning their
lunch boxes had been packed ready for them and
inside would be a jam butty, a piece of home-made
cake and an apple. Nowadays they were lucky if
there was anything at all in them. Most days both
she and Eddy relied on Rita to share her lunch
with them.

Vera tried her best to help her mother by running errands and looking after Benny as soon as
she came home from school. At weekends she
always took Benny out in his pram. Sometimes
Rita came with her and they took him to see the
flowers in St John's Gardens.

Edmund was usually expected to help in the

shop, sorting out the studs and nails into their right boxes, or putting the leather soles into pairs. It was something he hated doing. With the new leather being so shiny on both sides it was difficult to tell which side up was the correct one and so he could never work out which was the sole for a right shoe and which one was for a left.

Their dad insisted that it was because Edmund was stupid and, after thumping him across the skull with his rolled up fist, he would fling the whole box of soles onto the floor and make him pick them all up and start again.

Whenever this happened, Vera would sneak into the shop while her dad was busy talking to a customer, or working on the polishing machine with his back towards her, and scrabble up a pile of soles and take them through into the living room and sort them out for Edmund.

It was risky because they both knew that if he ever spotted what was going on, Edmund would get another crack across the skull.

Neither of them ever breathed a word about this to Rita. Only their mam knew what went on. She did her best to protect Eddy, but she also knew that if she was seen to be making too much fuss of him he would be punished again.

He was hit so often across the top of his head that it was a mass of raised bumps. Sometimes he complained that it sounded as if there were 'bells ringing inside his ears'.

'You should tell the school nurse next time she comes to examine us,' Vera told him.

Eddy shook his head. 'She wouldn't be interested.'

'She might be. She makes you raise your shirt and lower your trousers so that she can look at your back to make sure you're not being beaten, doesn't she?'

'I know, but I couldn't tell her about my head, Mam would be too upset if I let on,' he declared stoutly.

'She'd understand.'

Eddy shook his head. 'Dad might turn on her if I said anything about it. He's so bad-tempered these days you don't know where you are with him. He only picks on me because I'm so small,' Eddy grumbled. 'I can't help it if Charlie was six inches taller than me when he was my age.'

'You still might grow,' Vera told him hopefully.

'I shouldn't think so,' Eddy muttered gloomily.

'Well, don't worry. Rita Farthing likes you the way you are. She thinks you're absolutely perfect,' she teased.

Chapter Four

Eddy Quinn struggled to balance the loaded delivery bike as he wheeled it along Scotland Road. It was the first time he had ever taken it out and he was wishing that the boss at Steven's Hardware Store didn't expect him to do so many deliveries at once. There was so much packed into the big wire basket on the front that it made the bike top-heavy, and he could hardly see over the top of it. It was far too dangerous for him to ride.

He waited for a break in the traffic so that he could wheel the bike across the intersection with Juvenal Street. He had three deliveries to do in Aldersley Street and one in Nicholas Street. That would hopefully lighten his load so that he'd be able to ride the rest of the way.

If he was lucky he'd manage to get to Ellenborough Street and meet up with Rita Farthing before she got tired of waiting for him and went indoors.

It was the thought of seeing Rita that made him want to try and get as many of his deliveries completed as he possibly could before they met. The less that remained to be done then, the more time he could spend talking to Rita.

She often had an apple, or a snack of some kind, for him and he wondered which it would be tonight. Her mam was a smashing cook and her currant scones were the best he'd ever tasted. Rita's grandfather also gave her a bag of broken biscuits each week, which she usually shared with Vee and him. Vee normally took hers back home for little Benny, but he was always so hungry that he ate whatever Rita gave him right there on the spot.

As he struggled with his heavy load Eddy wondered why his parents had had another baby. They were so hard up these days that another mouth to feed meant that the rest of them had to go short.

He wondered what Charlie would have thought about the change in their way of life if he was still alive. He'd never had to get a part-time job while he was at school. In those days their mam had never seemed to be worried about money, not even when their dad had gone into the army.

Of course, Gran and Granddad Simmonds had been alive then and they'd always been popping round with treats of one kind or another. At least once a week they would invite them all to their house in Trinity Road for a meal.

Granny Simmonds had loved cooking, just like Rita's mam seemed to. His own mam never seemed to dish up anything better than scouse these days, probably because she was always short of housekeeping money, he thought morosely.

She'd looked so pleased when he'd told her that he'd got a part-time job as a delivery boy and would be getting two shillings and sixpence each week. She'd told him he could keep the sixpence for himself, but his dad hadn't agreed with that.

'You don't smoke or drink so what do you want

that much money for?' he scoffed. 'You'll only spend it on sweets and they'll rot your teeth.'

'I want the sixpence so that I can go to the pictures,' he explained. Instead of agreeing that he could have it, his dad had thumped him across the top of his head for answering back. He'd hit him so hard that he'd had a headache for two days afterwards.

He didn't know what his dad would have said if he'd told him that he wanted to take Rita to the pictures, as a way of saying thanks for all the scoff she gave him.

He should have expected his dad to say he couldn't keep the sixpence from his wages; he'd never let him keep any of the tips he was given for delivering boots and shoes. In the end he'd worked out a devious plan: whenever a customer gave him a penny, he told no one and hid it behind a loose brick in the back jigger wall before he went indoors.

When his father intercepted him, which he did without fail, he was able to hand over the money he'd been told to collect and say quite truthfully that that was all he had.

Eddy was pleased that he'd got this job as a delivery boy and he intended to work hard and keep it to prove to his dad that other people didn't think he was thick.

He was always telling him, 'You're too bloody short and weedy to ever amount to anything. You'll never be a man because you're such a wet little sod. A spell in the army is what you need, but they'd never take you because you're such a little squirt.'

He used to get upset about this. His dad's caustic

remarks would bring tears to his eyes. Nowadays, however, he just moved away as quickly as he could before his old man reached out and battered him across the head.

'I'll thump your bloody skull,' seemed to be the only thing he ever managed to say to him these days, Eddy mused.

Charlie had never been treated like that, he didn't live to see how much the war changed their father. When Charlie was alive, their dad had been a wonderful sort of fellow. He'd always been ready to kick a ball about or play some game or the other with them. Vee was his favourite, then, but he and Charlie didn't mind. Their dad had always explained to them that you had to make a fuss of girls, so they'd accepted it.

Vee had been such a pretty little girl, with her bright blue eyes and thick black hair that framed her elfin face. She generally wore dainty dresses, trimmed with ribbons and lace, and a matching ribbon in her hair. She never seemed to get grubby like they did, or run and jump and climb onto walls when they went for a walk. Instead she walked along holding their dad's hand. The moment she said she was tired, he'd pick her up and sit her on his shoulders.

The war had changed all that. Their dad had gone away a happy smiling man who'd loved them all, and he'd come back a miserable old grump who was mean and hard, and had no time at all for any of his family, not even Vee.

It could have been the shock of Charlie dying as well as Gran and Granddad Simmonds. Their mother had been so upset she'd cried for days and said that life would never be the same again. She'd been right about that, though their dad had come out of it all right in the end, he reflected.

He'd taken charge, because Mam had been so upset, and handled all the settling up that had to be done. Out of all the chaos he'd ended up with a business of his own. It was a pity he couldn't have managed to provide them with a decent home to go with it. Their mam was used to a nice place with pretty things about her.

Mam was also used to having enough money to live on without having to scrimp all the time. Now they seemed to live hand-to-mouth with every penny having to do the work of two. There never seemed to be enough food to go round or enough coal to keep the place warm. He was fed up with patched clothes and seeing his mam trying to make do and mend everything. Even little Benny was dressed in things she made for him out of their old clothes.

The only one who didn't seem to mind the change in their affairs was his dad, but then he wasn't going short like the rest of them. Mam always made sure that he had a good plateful, and she even bought chops and bacon and stuff like that especially for him. Even when all they had was scouse he'd look round as soon as she'd dished it out to see if there was any meat on his or Vee's plate; if there was, he'd spear it with his fork and put it on his own plate.

'You two aren't working so you don't need feeding up,' he'd state.

Mam would look angry, but she'd signal with her eyes to say nothing. Nowadays, she usually kept back a piece of meat for each of them hidden away where he wouldn't find it. If there was any bread left at the end of the day, she'd make it up into butties and put them in their lunch boxes for the next day.

Mam didn't look happy any more, he reflected. Dad spoke to her as if she was a skivvy. He dictated orders as if he was still a corporal in the army and he wasn't above shouting 'jump to it', or 'get a move on then woman, I haven't got all day like you', if she didn't do what he asked right away.

He hoped his dad wouldn't start on Benny when he was older. Poor little sod, he'll probably turn out to be even smaller for his age than I am since he's always hungry, he thought gloomily.

When he'd mentioned this to Rita she'd given him one of her wonderful smiles and squeezed his arm.

'Well, I like you the size you are,' she told him. 'You're taller than me and that's all that matters.'

Eddy grinned to himself at the memory. 'Make sure you don't grow any more then and spoil things,' he'd told her.

He liked Rita a lot. For a girl she had so much sense, which was probably why she and Vera were such good friends. He liked the fact that she didn't show off, or put on any airs and graces, even though her family was better off than his.

More often than not she was the one who provided the tickets when they went to the pictures.

She'd always say that her granddad had got them for free, or her mam had been given them and didn't want to see the film.

The thing he liked about her most was that she didn't try to chat him up at school. He'd already warned Vera not to speak to him unless she absolutely had to. He didn't want the other boys teasing him because, whatever Rita might say about his size, he knew he was the smallest boy in his class and he didn't want to attract attention to himself. He'd seen what could happen when the rest of the class picked on a boy.

His classmates were a pretty tough bunch who lived in and around Scotland Road. A lot of them had dads who'd been out of work for years, or who worked on the docks and drank all their wages away the moment they got them.

Most of them came to school in patched-up jackets and trousers, some had no socks, and some had newspaper stuffed in their shoes because there were holes in the soles. In summer there were often some kids who were barefoot, or wore canvas plimsoles that were either miles too big, or had the toes cut out because they were too small.

They thought nothing of thieving from the stalls in Paddy's Market, or from the counters of the sweet shops or the bakers, because they were hungry and had no money. Eddy was often hungry too, but he couldn't bring himself to become a petty thief. That was why he had found himself a delivery job. It was hard work but it was honest.

Keeping back any coppers he received in tips was also honest as far as he was concerned. It wasn't all that often that people gave him a tip, anyway. Most of them didn't have any money to spare themselves. Friday night was best because most of the men had just been paid.

He'd found that out when they'd first moved to Scotland Road and his dad had sent him to take back boots and shoes he'd repaired.

'Don't pass them over until they give you the money for the work I've done,' his dad would warn as he handed him the freshly soled boots.

He'd only done so once. That was when the woman who'd answered the door had been old, and slightly deaf, and he hadn't been able to make her understand a word he was saying. She'd taken the boots from him and then slammed the door in his face. He'd banged on the door for ages, but she'd refused to open it again.

His dad had been livid when he'd eventually gone back to the shop and admitted what had happened. Unfastening his leather belt he'd given him such a thrashing that he hadn't been able to sit down for days.

He'd kept a tight hold on his deliveries after that and as soon as he was thirteen, and old enough to do so, he'd gone looking for a paid job as a delivery boy. He'd been lucky, the chandler's on the corner of Lawrence Street had a vacancy and were willing to give him a try.

He'd been afraid to tell his dad in case he expected him to deliver boots as well as do his new job and he knew he couldn't do both no matter how hard he tried, especially on Friday nights which were busy for both of them.

'Why don't I ask Dad if I can deliver the boots and shoes?' Vera suggested.

'He probably won't let you because you're a girl.'

'Things have changed. Dad's not the same man as he was when we lived in Wallasey. He treats me differently now,' Vera reminded him. 'I'll tell him I want to earn some pocket money. Let me do it before you tell him about your new job.'

He'd waited in the passageway behind the shop where he could hear everything that was being said and watched round the half-open door.

At first it seemed hopeless because their dad had laughed, telling her she was too young to do something like that.

'I'm ten!' she reminded him, 'and if I can run errands, and go to Paddy's Market to buy veggies for Mam, then delivering a couple of pairs of boots and shoes is nothing.'

'I don't know about that. It's not just a matter of handing them over to whoever answers the door, you know. I expect you to get the money for them as well.'

'I know that. And I know what will happen to me if I come back without it,' she told him with a cheeky grin.

For a moment, as he saw the scowl on his father's face, Eddy thought he was going to slap her, but then he'd laughed and ruffled her hair.

'All right, you can give it a go. Twopence a week, but only if you do it properly. It will teach that lazy little bugger Eddy a lesson if you take over his job. Here you are,' he held out a pair of boots, 'you can start right away by delivering these.'

40

Vera tucked the newly repaired shoes under her arm, and Eddy held his breath, expecting an outburst, as he heard her say, 'Eddy won't mind. He's already got himself a job as a delivery boy at Steven's Hardware Store.'

Slowly he let it out again as he saw she was out of the door and skipping down the street before it had dawned on their dad exactly what she had said.

Chapter Five

Annie Quinn hurried down the jigger between Penrhyn Street and Scotland Road and let herself in through the back door, shutting it quickly behind her as soon as she'd manoeuvred Benny's pram inside. She hated having to use the back entry. It was so dark and threatening with its high walls on either side, but Michael had forbidden all of them to come in through the shop during the day.

'It looks bad,' he told her. 'The shop is a business and the only people I want to see coming through that door are customers with a pair of boots or shoes in their hands that they want to have repaired.'

'Surely your own wife, with a pram loaded down with shopping, can walk through,' she declared in an irritated voice. 'After all, we do live in the room at the back.'

'I know. It's bad enough that people in the shop have to stand and listen to that brat screaming his lungs out all the time without seeing you parade him through the shop, too,' he snapped back. 'Anyway, if I let you come in that way then Eddy and Vee will want to do the same when they come home from school, and in next to no time there will be a horde of snotty nosed kids wandering through looking for them.'

'I very much doubt it! They haven't managed to make many new friends even though we've been living here for almost two years now.'

'And whose bloody fault is that? You've probably discouraged them from doing so because you don't get on with any of our neighbours.'

Annie didn't answer. It was quite true that she didn't like the area. Scotland Road had a bad name and those on either side seemed rough and uncouth to her after the people she had lived next to in Wallasey.

Michael seemed to revel in mixing with them. When they'd lived in Wallasey, before he'd gone into the army, he had stayed home and kept her company in the evenings. Now he spent less and less time with her, preferring to go out most nights to the local pubs, often not returning home until throwing out time.

He made no bones about the fact that he found her dull and boring. There was no longer any tenderness in his love-making. He was no longer considerate about the way he treated her or spoke to her. He didn't trouble to keep his temper in check and when he arrived home the worse for drink her heart was in her mouth until he finally fell asleep.

She supposed she was partly to blame because she was always bewailing the fact that he didn't give her enough money to feed them all properly, let alone buy them decent clothes. She hated seeing Eddy going off to school in patched trousers and darned jumpers, but she simply couldn't afford to replace them. As it was she'd had to cut down two of her own dresses to make new ones for Vera so that she had something decent to wear.

She struggled constantly to overcome the depression that had enveloped her ever since she'd lost her parents and her darling Charlie. He'd been such a fine-looking boy, and on the brink of manhood. He'd been so proud of the fact that he had an apprenticeship with Cammell Laird's. He had been taken away so suddenly. What started as a cough and a cold had developed into a high fever within hours. Even though he was a big, strong lad he'd no more been able to fight it than her frail aged parents had.

She had to try to look on the bright side and be thankful that Eddy and Vee had survived, and that they were both still fit and well.

Edmund was growing into a handsome boy with his thick flaxen curls and sensitive face, but she knew Michael resented the fact that, physically, he took after her side of the family.

'Puny little weed,' he declared scornfully. 'At thirteen he should be twice the size he is! He's got no guts either! Always stuck indoors instead of being out in the street kicking a ball around.'

When Michael had tried to teach Edmund how to box, he'd ducked away the moment he saw his father's curled fist coming towards him. He hated being hurt. Michael had flicked him hard on the chin, sending him reeling backwards and then laughed uproariously when Eddy had caught his shoulder against the edge of the table and burst into tears with the pain.

From that day on a knot of hatred towards

Michael became lodged inside her chest. Silently, she vowed to do her utmost to keep Edmund out of his father's way.

Michael still doted on Vera. He was forever saying, 'With that black hair and those blue eyes she takes after me. She should have been a boy!'

Now, turned ten, she was as tall as Edmund and far sturdier than he was. She was afraid of nothing, not even of her father when he was in one of his violent tempers.

It frightened Annie the way Michael had changed since his time in the army. When he recounted his experiences in the trenches in France the stories were of such nightmarish quality that she was sure this was the reason for his change in personality.

She hated the way he had become a tyrant. He acted as if he was still a corporal, and they were the lower ranks. He barked the orders and expected them to obey. Sometimes he even made Edmund and Vera stand to attention for inspection before they sat down to a meal. If they weren't dressed properly, or if he decided that their hands didn't look clean, then he would rap them sharply over the knuckles with the back of his knife or poke them viciously in the ribs.

He'd become terribly impatient, as well. He expected them all to obey his commands instantly, and flew into a temper if his meal wasn't put in front of him the moment he sat down at the table.

Every night Annie was on edge, wondering whether he would come straight through for his meal when he closed the shop at seven o'clock, or whether he would go out to the pub first. She didn't know which was worse. If he went to the pub straight away then he usually didn't come back until closing time. No matter what time he turned up, though, he expected to find his meal on the table, freshly cooked and piping hot.

If he ate his meal first, he'd certainly not come back home until chucking out time. In all probability he'd then demand some bread and cheese, and a pickled onion, before he turned in.

Whatever he decided to do the evening would end the same for her; it always did. Unfortunately, he was different from most other men in that he never suffered from brewer's droop; it was quite the opposite, in fact.

She'd meant it when, after Benjamin was born, she'd said there would be no more babies. It might be against the law, but if she fell for another then she'd have an abortion, even if it killed her. But if it did, she reflected, it would be hard on the children. Vee would be expected to look after Eddy and little Benny, but at least she would stop another poor little soul being born into such a harsh existence. Every time she thought about the future that lay ahead for Benjamin she cried inwardly. What hope was there of him growing up fit and strong when half the time he was hungry?

She had never in her life felt so lethargic and she was sure that was because she could never afford decent food for herself. She had to try and make sure that Eddy and Vee had their bellies full. She hated it when Michael pinched the meat from their plates, or snatched away their butties.

Before the war he'd always been so kind-hearted, so concerned that the children had the very best. She'd seen him cut up his own meat into tiny slivers for them when they were small. He'd always made sure that he shared the top off his egg, or he'd dip a piece of bread into the yolk and hand it to one of them as a little treat.

Although Vee had always been his favourite, and treated like a precious doll, he'd been proud of Charlie, and Edmund when he was younger. He'd enjoyed nothing more than taking the two boys down onto the shore at New Brighton to kick a ball around. Often he would ram some sticks down into the sand and improvise a game of cricket for them.

Eddy had been too small to wield the bat, but he'd run after the ball when Charlie batted and throw it back to his father so that he could bowl it to Charlie again.

Those had been such happy days. Thinking back, she always remembered the sun shining and the entire family smiling.

Even when the war came, and Michael had dashed off to be a soldier, life hadn't been anywhere near as demanding as it was nowadays. Of course, she reflected, she'd had her own mam and dad to help her. They'd been growing old, but they'd been full of energy and had loved the children so much.

She was glad in some ways that they hadn't lived to see the change in Mike. They would have been so shocked and worried. She recalled how apprehensive they'd been when they had first met him.

'It's a pity that we know nothing at all about his parents,' her mother had said worriedly. 'I'm not saying that he isn't a nice young chap, but having been brought up in an orphanage since babyhood means he hasn't had the same caring background as you have had, my dear.'

Annie had been so cross with her mother and told her she was bigoted and prejudiced. Now, with hindsight, she wondered if her mother had intuitively seen something in Michael Quinn's make-up that she had overlooked.

Today he kept his flattery and charm for his customers. Women, especially, thought he was a perfect gentleman, so handsome and charming that they flirted with him outrageously. She would feel her insides curling in embarrassment at the amused, supercilious way he responded to them, yet they never seemed to take the slightest offence.

She often wondered what they would think if they could hear him rant and rave when Benny was crying from hunger, or see the callous way he treated Eddy. Would they still think he was the perfect gentleman if they overheard the way he spoke to her or the names he called her when he was in one of his foul moods, she thought bitterly.

She smiled sadly as she remembered one of her own mother's favourite sayings when things weren't going as well as she hoped. 'What can't be cured must be endured.'

Well, she reflected, that was all she could do now. Endure what was happening and pray that things would get better. Perhaps when the business picked up a bit more, and they had more money, then life would be easier, she thought hope-fully.

But deep in her heart she knew that would never happen, because the more he earned the more Michael Quinn would spend in the pubs up and down Scotland Road.

Chapter Six

'You won't be fourteen until October so you are not entitled to leave until the end of the following term at Christmas. That means, Quinn, that you have to return to school again in September.'

Eddy Quinn fidgeted uncomfortably as he stood in front of the headmaster's desk. Mr Clark was not making it very easy for him, but he was determined to convince him that he should be allowed to finish school at the end of the summer term, which was in a few days' time.

'I know that, sir, but I've got the chance of working at Sunbury's Bakery. If I can't start right away, when school breaks up at the end of next week, then I'll lose the job.'

'Surely you can go and work there during your summer holiday and then return to school in September.' Mr Clark frowned.

Eddy shook his head. 'That wouldn't be playing fair, though, would it, sir. They want someone for the job permanently; if I did that, they'd have to find someone else as a replacement again in a few weeks.'

'Mmm,' Mr Clark looked thoughtful.

'You are really keen on becoming a baker, Quinn?'

'Yes, sir!'

'Is your father a baker?'

'No, sir. He's a cobbler.'

'So why don't you go and work for him?'

Eddy shook his head violently. 'I don't want to do that. I'm not interested in that sort of work.'

'So why are you so keen to become a baker. Plenty of cakes to eat? Is that the great attraction?'

Eddy's cheeks flamed. 'It is important,' he admitted reluctantly.

Mr Clark stared at the small nervous boy in front of him, noting his neatly patched clothes, and then nodded understandingly. 'I can believe that at your age. From the size of you, Quinn, I'd say you've gone hungry a great many times in your life.'

Eddy bit his lip, but said nothing.

'You have a younger sister, Vera Quinn. Is that correct?'

'Yes, sir, and a little brother, but he's not old enough for school, he's not two until September.'

Mr Clark walked across to the window and stared out, deep in thought. The silence in the room as he waited for the headmaster's reply almost choked Eddy. He clenched his hands into fists, digging his nails into the soft flesh of his palms. He could hear his heart thumping and there was a tightness in his chest as he tried to breathe slowly and evenly.

'All right, Quinn.' Mr Clark swivelled round on his heels. 'Off you go and tell the boss at Sunbury's Bakery that you can start immediately after school breaks up. Not before, mind. You've still three days left and I expect to see you at your desk every day. Understand?'

'Yes, sir. Thank you, sir.'

Eddy felt as if he was going to burst with relief. He'd told Mr Chamberlain, the boss at Sunbury's, that he'd be able to start work on Monday 25th July 1921, and now he could. He'd have to work every week day, from seven in the morning until six at night, except on Saturdays when he'd finish at one o'clock.

He couldn't wait to tell his mam. He'd be earning a proper wage, not two and sixpence a week like he was paid for doing the deliveries for Steven's Hardware Store. Mr Chamberlain had promised him twelve shillings a week for the first six months, and then a rise of two and sixpence, provided he worked hard.

He'd do that all right. He couldn't wait to get started. Mr Chamberlain had said that he could have a bread roll and a cake every day for his lunch. He had also hinted that at the weekend he'd get a bag of cakes to take home, if there were any left over. It sounded smashing to him.

He knew his mam was going to be pleased when he told her. He'd been on the verge of doing so for days now, but he'd kept quiet because he hadn't been sure if Mr Clark would let him finish school at the end of the summer term.

Vee already knew all about it, of course, because she'd been the one who'd told him that Sunbury's were looking for someone.

'I don't know anything about baking,' he'd told her.

'That's the whole point,' she'd said. 'You'll learn everything there is to know. It'll be much better than working for a chandler's where all you've learned is how to wheel an overloaded delivery bike up and down Scotland Road.'

'Yeah, but look at these,' he'd flexed his muscles. 'I've built them up from pushing that bike, haven't I!'

'Learning a proper trade is the first step on the ladder to a better life,' she told him gravely. 'Remember, if you don't get a proper job then the minute you leave school Dad will expect you to work full time in the shop with him and you wouldn't like that, would you!'

'You know I'd hate it! It would be hell! I'd never do anything right, and he'd order me about from morning till night, and cuff me over the head every time I made a mistake.'

'Well, make sure you don't make any mistakes when you start at Sunbury's then or someone there might clip you round the ear.' She grinned.

Now that he had actually got the job, and knew when he would be starting work, he'd ask Vee not to say a word to their mam until he'd got his first week's pay.

He could see it now, handing his wage packet over to Mam unopened, watching her eyes widen in surprise when she saw how much there was inside it. From now on they'd all have enough to eat, every day of their lives. There'd be sausages, bacon, eggs, chops, even roast meat. Benny would grow up big and strong, not undersized like he was.

His mam would have to give him back some pocket money out of his wages, but he knew she'd play fair. He'd ask her if she could spare a few pennies each week for Vee as well.

When Vee had taken over his task of delivering boots and shoes Eddy had warned her about making sure she hid any tips that the customers gave her before she got back to the shop. He'd even shown her his secret hiding hole behind a brick in the wall in the back jigger. He'd told her that she could use it as well if she liked, but she'd never done so. For some reason their dad never bothered to ask her if she'd been given anything.

Whether that was because he'd fooled him for so long into thinking that customers never gave any tips, or whether it was because his dad liked Vee more than him, Eddy wasn't sure. It didn't really matter one way or the other, he told himself, but he couldn't help feeling puzzled about it.

Vee never told him if she did pick up any tips. If she did, he had no idea what she spent the money on, and he never asked. He suspected it mostly went on treats for young Benny. She really seemed to adore their little brother. She was always the one who got up in the middle of the night when he started crying, or calling out. Usually, she took him back into bed with her.

'It's easier than hearing Dad having a nark with Mam about the noise Benny makes when he whinges,' she'd told him when he'd commented on it. 'It only makes Benny howl even louder when Dad starts shouting. It terrifies me when he does, so I know it must frighten the wits out of poor little Benny.'

Young Benny looked frightened most of the time, Eddy thought grimly. He had such big, sorrowful blue eyes and he seemed to toddle round in a wide-eyed daze, usually with a dummy, or his thumb, stuck in his mouth. He never seemed to have the energy to play, not even with the big coloured ball that Vee had bought for him.

Eddy found his first week at Sunbury's a bewildering experience. When he'd been working at the chandler's all he'd had to do was collect his loaded bike, do the deliveries on the list he was given, and then return the bike to the shop.

In his new job there were a hundred and one tasks to be done.

Although the jobs were all simple – like sweeping up flour that had been spilled on the floor, washing out the huge mixing bowls, or helping to bring in bags of flour and sugar from the storeroom out in the yard – the two men who worked in the bakehouse behind the shop often asked him to do different things at the same time.

He enjoyed the work, though. The job he liked best was clearing up the bowls after the baker who made all the cakes and pies had finished with them – especially those that had been used for cakes! Before he plunged them into water he surreptitiously ran his finger around the sides, licking up any traces of the sweet mixture. He'd never be hungry as long as he could do that, he thought gleefully. Sometimes, when it was fruit cakes or buns that were being baked, there would be the odd currant or sultana left in the bowl as well.

After an enormous batch of baking there would be the trays to clean. These would often have tiny bits of cooked cake or pastry stuck to them and he wished he could scrape them into a bag and take them home for Vee. As he worked he picked bits off to eat, and even when they were slightly over-cooked he thoroughly enjoyed them.

On Saturday, when Mr Chamberlain handed him his first wage packet, Eddy thought he would explode with happiness.

'These are for you,' his boss told him, handing him a brown paper bag bursting with doughnuts, iced cakes and jam tarts. 'Do you want a couple of loaves to take home with you as well?'

Eddy could hardly believe his ears. He already had a feast that would fill them for days.

'They're yesterday's, mind, so they might be a bit stale, but your mam can always toast them, or use them to make a bread pudding.'

When he reached their own shop in Scotland Road he was about to hurry past and go down Penrhyn Street, and in through the back jigger, when his dad stepped out into the roadway and confronted him.

Grabbing him by the ear he hauled him into the shop and slammed the door shut.

'What's all this then? Been thieving have you?'

'No, Dad, of course I haven't! I . . . I earned it!'

'Oh, yes? Then you'll have some wages as well, if I know anything about it, so hand them over.'

Eddy looked at him defiantly. Giving his first real wage packet to his mother unopened had been something he was looking forward to doing, and now it was all going to be spoiled.

He saw his father ball his fist and knew that at

any moment he would be hit across the top of his head if he didn't do as he'd been asked.

'Give me your bloody wages or I'll thump your skull. Understand?'

The familiar threat made him so angry that he resolved to stand his ground. He wasn't a kid any more. He had a proper job now, so he shouldn't be threatened or beaten, he told himself.

'What makes you think I've got any wages?' he asked boldly.

'You better bloody have, seeing as you've been working all week at Sunbury's!'

For a fleeting moment Eddy thought Vera must have let on about his job, but when his dad spoke again he felt guilty for ever doubting her.

'Word gets round, you know. That fellow Chamberlain who's in charge there drinks in the same pubs as me, and I heard him say he'd taken on a weedy little runt because he felt sorry for him, so I knew it must be you.'

Before Eddy could speak, his father had clenched his fist and had swiped his knuckles across the top of his head. The pain made Eddy cry out, and he darted towards the door that led into their living room.

Annie, hearing all the commotion was already opening the door as he reached it.

'What on earth is going on?' she asked in alarm.

Eddy stumbled past her and dropped his big bag of cakes and the two loaves of bread onto the living-room table before turning to face his father.

'I said no and I meant it,' he shouted. Pulling his wage packet out of his trouser pocket he shoved

57

it into his mother's hands. 'This is for you, Mam. My first week's wages and I want you to have them, not him.'

Roughly, Michael Quinn pushed his son to one side and tried to snatch the pay packet from his wife's hand.

'Give it here, woman! Any money that comes into this house is mine,' he growled angrily.

Annie shook her head. 'I don't think so. Our Eddy has worked all week to earn this money so he has a right to say what he wants to do with it.'

Mike Quinn's vivid blue eyes glinted nastily. With a deep growl he lunged towards her, intent on grabbing the wage packet. When she still resisted he slapped her across the face so hard that she was sent reeling backwards.

Pandemonium reigned. Vera came into the room and found Benny howling with fright in the armchair. Her mother was half lying on the floor, sobbing uncontrollably. One hand was held to the rapidly swelling red weal on her face, and the other was still tightly clutching Eddy's wage packet. Mike was standing over her, looking livid.

As he reached out again to snatch at the wage packet Eddy darted into the shop and picked up a hammer lying on the workbench. As he raised it threateningly, Vera screamed a warning, and Mike swung round in time to catch hold of Eddy's arm. He twisted it savagely until Eddy, sobbing with pain, was forced to drop the hammer.

Then, without a word, Mike Quinn walked back into his shop slamming the door so hard that the whole building shook.

Chapter Seven

The fight over Eddy's wages caused such bad feeling between him and his father that they didn't speak to each other for several months. This resulted in tension between everyone else in the family all over Christmas, except Benny, as he was too young to understand what was happening.

Vera made it her New Year resolution to get them to talk to each other again, but it was no good, Eddy sulked and Michael scowled.

'Leave them alone, luv,' Annie warned her. 'You'll only set them at each other's throats otherwise. Give it time and they'll both simmer down and forget about it.'

Vera sighed. 'I suppose you're right, Mam. Anyway, the important thing is that you now get Eddy's wages!'

Her mother gave a wry smile. 'Yes, but your dad's cut my housekeeping back. He doesn't think he needs to give me as much now that Eddy's working and turning up some money each week.'

Vera didn't know what to say. In silence she hugged her mam, vowing to herself that when she started work in a few years' time she wouldn't tell her dad how much she earned. What was more, she'd also make sure that her mam got every penny that was in her wage packet.

It had been tough luck on all of them that her dad had twigged who it was that the boss at Sunbury's had been talking about when he'd been in the pub.

With extra money in his pocket, Michael Quinn spent even more time out drinking. Always worried about what mood he would be in when he came home, Annie tried to make sure that Vera and Eddy, as well as little Benny, were safely in bed.

Lying upstairs in the dark, afraid to light a candle in case it might enrage their father, Vera would listen in dismay as the rows went on in the room below. More often than not there would be the sounds of a scuffle, of furniture overturning, or a hastily suppressed scream from her mother.

Sometimes the noise would waken Benny, so Vera would tiptoe to his cot and try to quieten him before their father heard him crying. Quite often the only way she could comfort him was to take him back into her own bed.

Frequently she found Eddy crouched on the landing, listening to what was going on downstairs. She would warn him that if he went down and tried to interfere their mam would only get more of a beating.

'I'd sooner he was hitting me than her.'

'Don't tempt him. He'd half kill you.'

'Would he, though? He'd be afraid of what his mates down the pub would say if I turned up for work covered in bruises.'

Vera shook her head. 'He'd tell some cock and bull story about what you'd done so that you'd end up being the one in the wrong. If that happened your boss might sack you and then Mam would be worse off for money than ever.'

'I sometimes wonder if we ought to go to the police and report him,' Eddy said gloomily.

'It wouldn't do any good if we did, because Mam would deny it,' Vera pointed out. 'You know what she's like about keeping things like that secret.'

'Yes, but she couldn't, could she. They'd see the bruises!'

Vera shook her head emphatically. 'No they wouldn't. He never hits her where it shows.'

'Her arms are covered in bruises.'

'Yes, and she keeps them hidden. She always wears her sleeves down to cover them.'

'I bet she's got bruises all over her body as well. I know for a fact that he punches her in the ribs because I've seen him do it.'

'You are probably right, but no one can see the marks, can they, and the last thing she is going to do is show them to anyone.'

'I'll tell you something else, Vee,' Eddy said worriedly. 'He's started betting, on the dogs.'

'Are you sure?'

'Yes, and he's had some good wins. I heard some of the chaps at Sunbury's talking about it. One of them uses the same runner as him. Do you think we ought to tell Mam?'

'What good would that do? Only give her more to worry about, since it's illegal.'

Two weeks before Christmas 1922, Michael Quinn

61

broke his silence and spoke to his eldest son. It was the first time he'd done so since Eddy had started work eighteen months earlier.

'I got something for you today,' he told Eddy as they were sitting having their evening meal.

Eddy looked at him startled, wondering if he really was speaking to him.

'I've bought you a chicken. A big black and white one. It's outside in the backyard inside a wooden crate.'

Vera watched Eddy's reaction nervously. She was so afraid that he was going to refuse the gift and upset their dad that she felt sick.

'You can feed it on some of the bread scraps you bring home from Sunbury's or we can buy it some corn,' she said quickly. 'You never know, it may lay some eggs for us.'

Their father laughed snidely. 'So he hasn't told you that he's handed in his notice at Sunbury's.'

Annie looked shocked. 'Eddy is leaving Sunbury's?'

'Probably just as well before they sacked him. The boss there thinks he's too puny for a job like that.'

'Oh Eddy! If you've handed in your notice then you won't get any dole money!' Annie said, dismayed.

'Don't worry, Mam, I've got another job. Apprentice engineer at Cammell Laird's, the same as Charlie had.'

'You won't hold that down for long,' his father sneered. 'That's man's work.'

Again he laughed loudly. Vera kicked Eddy

under the table, and signalled to him with her eyes, not to answer back as it would only rile their dad even more.

She exchanged looks with her mam and saw that she, too, was bemused by what was happening.

'Go on then, take young Benny out to see the bloody chicken and mind you don't let it peck him.'

The chicken was plump, with glossy feathers and sharp beady eyes. It cocked its head on one side as Eddy held out a handful of crumbs, but kept its distance.

Benny was enchanted. He crouched down at the side of the crate, poking his little fingers through the slats, trying to touch the hen and chattering to it excitedly.

Eddy dropped the crumbs he was holding onto the floor of the crate and Benny clapped his hands in delight when the hen quickly, and hungrily, pecked them up.

'It may be your pet, but I think Benny's going to be the one who gets the most fun out of it,' Vera smiled. 'We must stop him putting his hand inside the crate, though, in case it pecks him; he certainly won't like that!'

'Give it a couple of days and I'll have it tame enough to eat out of our hands,' Eddy assured her.

For the next few nights, the moment he got in from work, the first thing Eddy did was to go out into the poky backyard to make sure that the chicken was all right.

'It's not right keeping it shut up in that crate all

the time,' he told Vera worriedly. 'It should have a proper run so that it can move around.'

'If you let it out in the yard then a cat, or a dog, will have it,' she pointed out. 'The best thing you can do is tame it so that it likes living like that.'

Reluctantly Eddy agreed with her. From then on he spent every spare minute he had talking to it, stroking its glossy black and white feathers and calming it, until finally it boldly took crumbs from his hand.

Benny wanted to try and do the same so Eddy took him outside and gave him a piece of bread to hold out for the hen. The rest of the family, even their father, watched to see what would happen. After one or two delicate pecks, the hen finally took the lump of bread and they all told Benny how clever he was.

For one wild moment Eddy thought they'd achieved a breakthrough, and that, at long last, they were once again a proper family. Was it his imagination or had their dad changed back into the kindly, happy man he'd known and loved when he'd been Benny's age? Perhaps he was over whatever it was that had been troubling him since he'd come home from the army, he thought hopefully.

His dad still seemed to be in the same benign mood when he came home from work the next night. He even accompanied him and Benny into the yard with some food for the chicken, and stood there watching them feed it.

Even though he changed into a newly laundered white shirt and his smart navy blue suit and went off out to the pub as usual immediately after-wards, Eddy still felt things were improving. He had settled into his new job and his dad had at last stopped telling him that he would never be as good as Charlie. It would soon be Christmas, so he hoped they could put all their troubles behind them and start the new year with a clean slate.

Two days before Christmas, Eddy felt he had never worked so hard in his life. He was so tired that he'd almost nodded off on the boat coming home from Birkenhead. As soon as he'd finished his evening meal he went upstairs for a nap, and the minute he lay down he drifted into a deep sleep.

He thought he was still dreaming when he felt someone hauling him out of bed by one leg. Still drowsy, he crashed heavily onto the floor. Blinking awake he saw that his father was standing over him, a look of rage contorting his face.

'What the hell do you bloody well think you are playing at, whacker,' his father snarled, viciously jabbing him in the ribs with the toe of his boot.

Bewildered, Eddy shook his head to try and clear his mind as the fumes of beer and tobacco, that were coming from his dad, almost choked him.

'What d'yer mean? What have I done wrong?' he stuttered.

'You may well ask,' his father snarled. 'I bought you a chicken as a present and you've bloody well neglected it. You've cleared off to bed and left it without food or water. Is that the thanks I get?'

Eddy struggled to his feet and began pulling on his boots. 'Sorry!' he mumbled. 'I was so tired I couldn't stay awake. I'll see to it now.'

'Don't worry, Eddy, I'll do it,' Vera told him, as she appeared in the doorway.

Michael Quinn swung round and pushed her away from Eddy's bedroom door. 'Keep out of this,' he thundered. 'It's got nothing at all to do with you. Mind your own bloody business. Stay indoors with your mother and young Benny while I sort this out. Understand?'

Not waiting for Eddy to finish dressing he grabbed him by the arm and roughly dragged him down the stairs. Opening the door into the yard Michael thrust him out into the cold, frosty night leaving the door wide open. Eddy shook his arm away. 'I'll have to go back inside, I haven't got any bread,' he protested.

'You won't need bread, whacker! Now, lift that bloody chicken out of the crate. Go on, do as I tell you!' Michael Quinn roared as Eddy hesitated.

Shivering, partly with the cold, partly with apprehension, Eddy did as his father ordered. The light from the open doorway streamed across the backyard. The chicken struggled for a moment then settled against Eddy's chest, its bright eyes eager as if it was expecting to be fed.

'Grab it round the neck with both hands,' his father ordered.

'What for? I might hurt it if I do that.'

'Do as you're bloody well told before I grab you round the soddin' neck.'

Gingerly, still cradling the chicken in one arm,

Eddy placed both his hands on its neck as he'd been ordered to do.

'Not like that, you bloody idiot. Hold your hands so that you can twist them one against the other. Go on. Now, twist! As hard as you can.'

Bile rose up in Eddy's mouth as he realised what his father was telling him to do.

'I can't do that . . . it will kill it,' he gasped.

'Of course it bloody well will. Best thing that can happen to it if you can't be bothered to feed it, though, isn't it!'

He suddenly moved closer, his large calloused hands closing over Eddy's, forcing the boy to twist one hand against the other. There was a panicked squawk from the chicken as it tried desperately to break free, but Michael Quinn increased the pressure of his own hands over those of Eddy's. When he released his grasp the chicken was limp.

Tears blinded Eddy's eyes as he held the lifeless body, and white feathers drifted down onto the yard like a sprinkling of snow.

Before he knew what was happening, his father had taken a penknife from his pocket and slit the chicken's throat. As hot blood gushed out over his hands Eddy dropped the bird in horror. Picking it up, his father tied its legs together and suspended it upside down from the edge of the crate. 'No point in wasting it! We'll have it for our Christmas dinner,' he said complacently as he turned on his heel and went indoors.

Chapter Eight

Vera was quite sure that none of them would ever forget Christmas 1922. Except perhaps little Benny who, since he had had only just turned three, had very little idea about what was going on.

The tension as they sat down to eat their Christmas dinner was palpable. Their father was the only one who seemed relaxed enough to pick up his knife and fork and attack the food on his plate with relish.

Vera had helped her mother to do the cooking, although neither of them had any stomach for what should have been the most enjoyable meal of the year. The beautiful black and white chicken that Michael Quinn had told Eddy he had bought for him as a pet, lay in a big serving dish that occupied the centre of the table. It was surrounded by roast potatoes, Brussels sprouts, carrots and parsnips. There was another dish full of boiled potatoes and a smaller one with peas in it.

A mouth-watering feast, better than anything they had sat down to all year, but none of them had any appetite for it. Each of them knew, though, that if they refused to eat what was put on their plates it would incur Michael's wrath, and they dare not even think about the consequences if that happened.

The moment they were all seated, Michael picked up the carving knife and fork and signalled to his wife to place the loaded serving dish in front of him.

'Nice looking bird,' he commented, as he pierced the crisp, brown outer skin with the fork, and plunged the knife into the crevice where one of the legs joined the carcass.

He licked his lips as juices spurted out. Calmly, he severed one plump leg and laid it on his own plate. He selected a generous helping of the vegetables that surrounded it on the serving dish and arranged them on his own plate. Carving off a thick slice of creamy breast meat he laid that on top. Reaching out, he picked up the gravy jug and lavishly covered the food on his plate.

'Any of the rest of you want any?' he asked staring at each of them in turn.

The silence seemed to amuse him.

'How about you, Edmund, since you did all the hard work fattening this bird up?'

Eddy looked away, covering his mouth with his hand as his stomach churned.

His father shrugged 'Please yourself.'

He sliced off another thick piece of breast and put it straight into his mouth. Chewing noisily, he replaced the carving knife and fork onto the platter and pushed it towards Annie.

'Yer mam'll cut you some if you want it, after she's helped herself and put some out for our Vera and young Benny, of course.'

No one moved or spoke as he tucked into his own huge serving with enthusiasm.

'Get on with it, woman, before it bloody well gets cold and is ruined,' he instructed. 'Dish some out to all of them, Eddy as well.'

He continued to devour his own meal, but watched closely to see that his wife did as he'd ordered.

As she was about to pass a plateful to Eddy, he held her arm and scrutinised what was on the plate.

'That won't do at all!' He shook his head firmly. 'That's not a decent meal for a lad! No wonder he looks more like a scrawny eleven-year-old than fifteen. Anyway, since he was the one who spent so much of his spare time with the bird he deserves a king-size share of it. Give it here, woman!'

He snatched the plate out of Annie's hands, spilling some of the vegetables and gravy as he did so. Picking up the carving knife again he hacked off one of the wings and piled that on top of the other food on Eddy's plate.

'Now eat! I only want to see a pile of bones left! Understand?' He looked round the table with an amused smirk on his face. 'That goes for the lot of you. No one gets down until their plate's clean.'

They ate in utter silence, pushing the meat around, trying to hide it. It was as if each mouthful was choking them. What should have been a happy, joyous occasion was an unbearably tense experience that seemed to go on for ever. All of them kept glancing sideways at each other, peeping to see how much was left on everyone else's plates.

For once, both Vera and Eddy wished that their

father would do his usual trick of reaching out and spearing the meat from their plates, telling them that they didn't need it.

Only Benny seemed to enjoy his meal. Annie had mashed up vegetables, cut a slice of breast into tiny slivers and moistened them with gravy, so he was tucking in with great gusto.

The rest of them managed to eat their vegetables, but none of them could bring themselves to touch the chicken. They'd all tried to hide it under the gravy that was now cold and congealing on their plates.

Their father watched with growing anger and they knew he was not prepared to leave it at that.

'I said clean plates and that was what I meant. We're not wasting one scrap of that bird!'

'It's all right I'll make it into a really nice soup for tomorrow,' Annie said quickly.

'You'll do no such thing! I'm not agreeing to that,' Michael sneered. 'Get eating, the lot of you, and that goes for you in particular,' he snarled, prodding Eddy's arm sharply with the prongs of his fork.

Belching loudly, he pushed back his chair and slouched over to the armchair that he regarded as his own. 'Get on with it, the pubs won't be opening tonight so I'm in no hurry. You can bloody well sit there until tomorrow morning for all I care.'

They waited until the surfeit of food lulled Michael Quinn into a sleep that was punctuated by grotesque snores. Annie and Vera swiftly took each plate and scraped the meat from the bones. They then dropped it inside the jug that still held enough gravy to cover it.

'Stay where you are for a minute,' their mother told them as she put the bones back on their plates. She stood up, moving away from the table and deliberately brushed against her husband's leg as she did so.

He woke with a startled grunt. 'What the hell are you doing? I said no one was to move from the table until they'd cleared their plates.'

'You don't expect them to eat the bones as well, do you, Mike?' she asked sarcastically.

He sat up and looked across at the table, a smirk of satisfaction on his face. 'No, they can leave those. Use them along with the carcass for that bloody stew or soup you said you were going to make. Remember to cut all the meat off the carcass for me first.'

'Oh, yes, I'll do that,' she promised. 'I'll slice it off, cover it with gravy so that it won't dry out, and then I'll warm it up for your meal tomorrow.'

As he gave his approval and sank back into sleep, Annie picked up the gravy jug. She signalled to Vera to start clearing the table, then she carried the jug of meat and gravy out to the scullery.

'There's pudding and custard, so you can all fill up on that,' she told them. 'I'll put it into dishes and you can take it up to your bedrooms and eat it there.'

Benny was unable to understand what had happened to the chicken. In the days that followed he spent endless hours looking for it even after they tried to explain to him that it had flown away.

Vera did her best to distract Benny by taking him out to the park as often as possible, as well as taking him with her whenever she had to go and deliver boots or shoes for her father.

Although this saved her mother from having to look after him, it also meant that she wasn't helping as much around the home as she felt she ought to.

Anyone could see that Annie Quinn had lost weight. She was beginning to look as if a puff of wind would blow her away. Although she never complained, Vee couldn't help noticing that she seemed to have no energy for tackling the everyday jobs, and very little interest in what was going on outside their home.

Her mother's main concern was making sure that Benny was all right, and keeping Eddy out of his dad's way. Vera helped as much as she could on both counts, but it was Benny's welfare that concerned her most. Eddy, she reasoned, was big enough to look out for himself, but Benny was too little to understand if he was being bullied or to do anything about it.

To be fair, she had to admit that she'd never heard her dad raise his voice directly at Benny. For the most part he ignored him, as long as he wasn't crying. And, now that he was older and able to ask for things, Benny didn't cry anywhere near as much.

She knew her mother spoiled him. He never went hungry, in fact he was always given the best bits of whatever they were eating. As a result he was growing into a very sturdy little boy. Vera often found that when Benny was with her when she was doing deliveries, with his huge blue eyes, thick blond curls and winning smile he was the one who was given a penny or two, not her.

Usually she saw that he spent the money on a cake or a bun on the way home. She was afraid that if her dad saw him clutching his pennies he might take them off him.

She enjoyed the way Benny prattled on about everything they saw when they were out, and she marvelled at his boundless energy. He never seemed to be tired, or ask to be carried, and his little legs somehow always managed to keep up with her, even when she was in a hurry.

'You'll never find yourself a boyfriend, Vee, as long as you've always got Benny in tow,' her friend Rita told her.

'I'd sooner have his company than that of most of the boys we know,' Vera countered.

'He's lovely, but I'd rather go for a walk with his big brother than with him,' Rita laughed.

Eddy had matured a great deal since working at Cammell Laird's and being in the company of older men who treated him as an equal. Since the episode with the chicken at Christmas he had avoided his father whenever possible. If he found himself in the living room alone with Michael, he quietly went out or up to his bedroom. Vera knew that it was a sensible way to behave, but she found herself missing Eddy's company.

He and Rita were closer than ever. They spent a considerable amount of time in each other's company. But Vera often felt deprived of her friend's company, too, and sometimes felt quite isolated.

Because of his new life, Eddy didn't spend very much time with Benny, either. As the days became warmer, and the evenings lighter, Vera often wished Eddy would play with him or take him for a walk. In the end, one Sunday, she suggested that perhaps he and Rita could take Benny out.

'It will give me a chance to tackle the ironing that's piled up all week because mam hasn't felt well enough to do it,' she told him.

'Oh, Vee, any other time of course I would, but we've made plans to go out with a crowd of friends,' he said apologetically. 'I'll do it next week, I promise.'

'No need for you to trouble yourself. You can bugger off and I'll take Benny for a walk.'

Vera jumped in surprise. She'd had no idea that her father was within earshot. 'It's all right, I'll manage,' she said quickly.

'I'll take Benny for a walk so go and get him ready!'

'Very well.' Quickly Vera dressed him in clean clothes and put on his outdoor shoes.

'Ready?' Michael Quinn held out his hand to the toddler. 'Come on then.'

Vera felt concerned. Benny was sturdy, but he wasn't yet four years old and she wasn't sure if her father appreciated that fact.

'You won't walk too fast or too far, will you Dad,' she begged. 'If he starts to lag because he's tired you will carry him won't you?' she pleaded.

'I always carried you when you were his size didn't I?'

'Yes, Dad, you did. Always!' She smiled at the

recollection. Those moments were still bright jewels in her memory. Sometimes she wondered if they had ever happened. Those halcyon days, when they'd lived in Wallasey and played on the shore at New Brighton, seemed like remnants from another life.

Her father had always been laughing and happy in those days, and her mother had been full of life and had joined in their fun. Why had he changed so much, she asked herself, as she watched her father set off down the street, Benny clasping his hand tightly, his little legs going like pistons as he tried to keep up with his father's long strides.

From then on, it became routine for Michael to take Benny for a walk on Sundays whenever the weather was fine. The fact that Benny came back so tired that he could barely eat his meal before falling asleep worried Vera. When she asked him where they'd been she couldn't make any sense of his answers. From what little she gleaned, as he prattled on about water and boats, it seemed that her father must be taking him down to the Pier Head.

Finally, overcome by curiosity, and concerned about Benny's exhaustion, she decided to follow them.

It was a beautiful hot, sunny day in late July. She'd dressed Benny in a bright blue sailor suit she'd bought from the market, and with his white socks, and little black shoes, he looked angelic.

Tentatively, without revealing what she intended to do, she suggested to her mother that they should go for a walk, but to her relief her mother declined.

'I find this heat exhausting,' she sighed. 'I'd much rather go and have a lie down.'

Vera gave her father and Benny time to reach the corner of the road before she began to tail them. She knew she had to be careful in case Benny turned round and saw her. If that happened she would have a job explaining to her father what she was doing.

To her surprise they boarded a tram, and for a moment she thought she had lost them. Then she realised that it would be going to the Pier Head so all she had to do was catch the next one.

When she reached there it was so congested that she was afraid she wouldn't be able to find them. But then she caught sight of them walking down the floating roadway onto the Wallasey ferry boat.

Making sure they didn't see her, she followed them onto the boat. When they finally reached Seacombe her father and Benny were amongst the first off the boat and they were again lost in the crowd. The next time she caught sight of them they were heading towards the Seacombe Ferry Hotel.

Vera watched in disbelief as he sat Benny down on the steps outside the pub and left him there while he went in. She was torn between rushing over and picking Benny up and waiting to see what happened next.

Minutes passed and she could see that Benny was becoming fractious. She was about to walk over to him when her father came out, grabbed Benny by the hand, and began marching along the promenade towards Egremont.

Vera followed in their wake and saw them stop at Mother Redcap's, and then again at two more pubs before they reached New Brighton. Each time her father went in and left Benny outside. He never once brought him out a drink and, since Vera was gasping from the heat, she knew that by now Benny must be feeling exhausted.

When they reached New Brighton, her father began walking smartly along the Ham and Egg Parade towards Perch Rock. He was almost dragging Benny off his feet, so she felt she had to do something.

Jostling her way through the crowds of holidaymakers she reached their side as her father was about to go into the Mariner's Arms on the corner of Victoria Road. But she was so breathless that she couldn't speak. As she saw the startled look on her dad's face she knew there was no need to say anything, her reproachful stare had said it all.

'Here,' he pushed Benny towards her, 'take him home, he seems to have had enough.'

'It's a wonder he hasn't come to some harm being left outside so many pubs,' Vera exploded furiously as she picked Benny up in her arms and cuddled him. 'I know now why he's always half dead by the time you arrive home after one of your Sunday walks.'

'Less of your lip!'

She stared defiantly back at him, her blue eyes dark with anger. 'Dragging him around all day on a pub crawl without anything to eat or drink, and you call that looking after him! It's enough to give him sunstroke in this heat!' she fumed.

'Take him back home like I've told you to do and think yourself lucky I don't belt you one right here in front of everybody,' he growled.

'You wouldn't dare,' she said scornfully. 'There's a scuffer on the corner watching us and he's itching to come over here and find out what's going on. One whiff of your beery breath and he'll arrest you, especially when I tell him how you've been mistreating little Benny!'

Chapter Nine

May 1924 couldn't come soon enough for Vera Quinn. That was when she would be fourteen and able to leave school to earn some money. There was only one drawback, though, she couldn't find a job.

Rita, had already been promised work on the assembly line at the biscuit factory where her grandfather worked. Vera had gone along to see if they would take her on as well, but she'd been told the list was closed, and that they were now fully staffed.

'You could try at Lyon's Corner House in town,' Rita told her. 'That's where I would have liked to work really but factory work is better paid.'

'Work as a Nippy and have to wear one of them daft little frilly hats? No thank you!' Vera laughed.

She was beginning to think that she would have to go into the centre of Liverpool for a job, or else work at one of the factories at Kirkdale or Wavertree. But by chance she heard about a vacancy for a junior clerk at Elbrown's, the paint and wallpaper merchant's in Great Homer Street.

'I wouldn't fancy having to sit at a desk writing out invoices all day,' Rita commented. 'Anyway, working at that place you'll come home stinking of turpentine and paint.'

'It's not far to go, though, is it! I can cut through Dryden Street and I'm there.'

Vera went straight to Elbrown's when she finished school that afternoon. As she pushed open the glass door a bell jangled noisily and the smell of paint, and a dozen other things she couldn't name, stopped her in her tracks. As she saw that a lot of the display shelves, reaching from the floor to the ceiling, were piled high with cans of paint and varnish she remembered what Rita had said, and she wondered if she would be able to smell it in the offices which were probably above the shop.

A smart young man with ginger hair, wearing a brown coat-style overall over his dark clothes was standing behind the wide wooden counter.

'Can I help you?'

'I ... I've come about the job of junior clerk.' Vera said hesitantly.

'Do you have an appointment?'

Vera felt taken aback. 'No, should I have one?'

'Didn't the letter ask you to come at an appointed time?' the man frowned.

Vera shook her head. 'There wasn't any letter. I heard that there was a vacancy from someone at school. Has the job gone already?'

He looked at her speculatively. 'Wait here a moment.' He disappeared into a glass-fronted cubbyhole, closed the door and picked up a telephone. She watched as he jiggled a handle up and down several times, tapping his pencil against his teeth, until someone answered.

She couldn't hear what was being said, but

when he came back out into the shop a few moments later he directed her towards a wooden staircase and told her to go on up. Mr Brown himself would meet her at the top.

She had never been for an interview before and had no idea what to expect. The grey-haired, rather portly man who was waiting for her led the way into his office and indicated that she was to sit in a chair facing his desk.

'I understand you've come here straight from school, does that mean you haven't left school yet?'

'I am fourteen and I can leave at Whitsun,' she told him quickly.

'In two weeks' time! Hmm!' He looked thoughtful. 'You've absolutely no experience of clerical work or of working with figures, or handling money?'

'I'm good at arithmetic and I always give my dad's customers the right change when I deliver boots and shoes,' she said quickly.

He frowned. 'I don't understand.'

Vera's cheeks burned as she explained that her father, Michael Quinn, had a boot and shoe repair shop in Scotland Road, and that she delivered to his customers.

'Is your handwriting neat?'

She nodded. 'If you give me a pen and a piece of paper I can show you,' she offered.

'Yes! Perhaps you should do that!' He handed her a pad of lined paper and another scrap of paper that had several items written on it. 'Now, this is an order for several tins of paint that someone has brought in. Let's see if you can copy the items onto this invoice pad, work out all the prices, and then total it up.'

Vera found that deciphering the names of the items on the order was the hardest part. She copied them out as neatly as she could, along with their prices, and noted when they wanted more than one tin, and worked out the total cost. Then she added it all up and neatly drew a line under the final total.

'That seems pretty good, although you've made one or two mistakes when it comes to spelling the brand names, but then you've probably never heard of them before,' he murmured.

He leaned back in his big leather chair. 'Can you use a telephone? We have a three-line switchboard, would you be able to operate that?'

Vera's heart sank. She knew how to speak into one, but that was all. She wanted the job so badly that she was tempted to say she could operate a switchboard, but the thought of making a complete mess of things on her very first day stopped her.

'No, I'm sorry I don't know how to operate one,' she said reluctantly. 'I could learn, though. I pick things up very quickly if someone would show me what to do.'

'I see. You've never learned to use a typewriter, either, I suppose?'

Again she shook her head. Her hope of becoming a junior clerk dwindled with every question he asked.

Mr Brown pursed his lips as he studied the invoice Vera had written out.

'Well, you seem to have done this in an accept-able form.' He stood up. 'Come along with me,' he ordered.

He led the way out of his office into an adjoining room where two people were sitting at desks. The younger one, who had straight fair hair and looked about sixteen, was tapping away noisily on a Remington typewriter.

'Miss Linacre,' he addressed the rather formi-dable-looking middle-aged lady, dressed in a neat navy blue costume and high-necked pale blue blouse. 'This is Vera Quinn and she has applied for the position of junior clerk.'

Miss Linacre studied Vera rather critically.

'I don't recall seeing a letter of application from anyone of that name,' she said stiffly.

'No, she didn't apply by letter. She heard that there was a vacancy so she's called in about it on her way home from school. Quite enterprising, don't you think?'

'Indeed!' From her frosty tone Vera was afraid that Miss Linacre thought it cheeky rather than enterprising.

'Now, I'll leave her here with you so that you can have a talk with her. Let me know if you agree that she would be a useful addition to our office staff.'

Mr Brown went back into his own office, closing the dividing door behind him. Vera felt so nervous that she was shaking, and had difficulty answering all the questions that Miss Linacre started firing at her.

'Wait here whilst I have a word with Mr Brown,'

Miss Linacre instructed when she'd finished inter-
rogating her.

Vera nodded anxiously.

As the door closed behind Miss Linacre, the girl
at the other desk stopped pounding the typewriter
and smiled across at her.

'I'm Joan Frith,' she grinned. 'Don't look so
scared, she's not nearly as vinegary as she looks.'

'She's probably very nice,' Vera said quickly.
'I'm not sure she thinks I'm suitable for the job,
though.'

'You'll get it,' Joan Frith told her confidently.
'Mr Brown has shown an interest in you and he's
the real boss. That's probably what's making her
so prickly.'

'What do you mean?'

'Well, she likes to think that she makes all the
decisions when it's anything to do with the office.
She probably thinks that you should have spoken
to her first, and then she could have been the one
to recommend you to Mr Brown. You've done it
the other way round!'

'It's not my fault, the man downstairs . . .' Before
she could finish what she was going to say Miss
Linacre came bustling back.

'Right, Vera Quinn. Mr Brown wants to speak
to you.'

Vera longed to ask if it meant that she had the
job, but Miss Linacre looked so tight-lipped she
didn't dare.

'Thank you, Miss Linacre.'

'Run along then, he doesn't like to be kept
waiting, and close the door quietly behind you.'

Mr Brown greeted her with a smile and motioned her to sit down again in the chair facing his desk.

'We are prepared to give you a trial,' he told her. 'Report to Miss Linacre on the Tuesday after the Whitsun bank holiday. Eight-thirty, half an hour for lunch, and you finish at six o'clock. Half day on Saturday, so we close at one o'clock. Your wages will be ten shillings and sixpence a week and you'll be paid at five o'clock every Friday night.'

Vera could hardly believe her ears. She'd got a job. In less than two weeks' time she would be working and earning money.

'Thank you, Mr Brown.' Her voice was hoarse with happiness, her smile so wide that her face ached.

She walked home on air. Even her father's terseness because she was late to do the deliveries failed to upset her. As she piled the boots and shoes into Benny's battered pram and took him by the hand, her heart was singing.

She hugged her news to herself for the rest of the weekend. She wanted to tell Rita first, since she was the one who had told her about the vacancy. After that she'd tell her mam and Eddy. She'd make them both promise to keep it secret until she actually started work and arrived home with her first wage packet.

'You ought to tell your dad that you've got a job, luv,' her mother cautioned. 'He'll be so proud of you.'

'Yes, and he'll be waiting on the door to take

my pay packet off me the same as he did with Eddy when he first started work.'

'Now, Vee, you know I don't like to hear you talk like that,' Annie reprimanded her.

'Sorry, Mam, but it's not going to be like that for me.'

Michael Quinn did find out, though. As she had feared, Vera found him waiting when she arrived home after her first week of work.

'Hand it over then, girl,' he demanded, stretching out his hand.

'It's for Mam,' she told him quietly, holding on to her pay packet.

Grabbing her hand he tried to twist it from her grasp, but she refused to give way.

'Leave me alone,' she shouted angrily, her blue eyes as bright and fierce as his own.

'If you're earning money then you turn it up,' he bellowed.

'Like you do, you mean?' she retaliated. 'Keeping this family isn't my job, it's yours.'

'So you expect me to go on keeping you when you're working, so that you can line your own pockets,' he laughed cynically.

'I'll pay my way, don't worry,' she flared. 'You tell me how much you want for my lodgings and food and I'll hand it over . . . to Mam, though.'

They stood glaring at each other, neither of them prepared to give way.

'You'll dib up every penny you earn, understand? Even that won't cover what it costs to keep you, or repay me for all the years I've slaved away to buy your food and keep you in clothes.'

Vera ripped open her pay packet and shook out the money in it out onto her palm. 'There you are then, eight shillings and sixpence.'

She counted it out twice. 'Are you going to take it all? Every penny of it?'

'Hand the bloody money over and let's have less gab about it.'

Deliberately she ignored his outstretched hand and passed the coins to her mother.

'Eight shillings and sixpence a week, every week. That's what you want me to pay, right?'

'If that's all they're paying you I suppose that will have to do. If your mother can afford it then perhaps she'll give you back the sixpence for pocket money,' he told her grudgingly. 'You still have to do the deliveries every Friday and any other time when there are any to be done.'

Vera shrugged. 'If you say so. Will I get paid for doing them since I'm only to have sixpence pocket money?'

'Watch your bloody tongue. No you won't get paid!'

She sighed loudly. 'I have to hand eight shillings over to Mam every Friday night and I can keep the sixpence for myself. Is that the deal then, Dad?'

'That's it and if you don't like it then get yourself another job, one where the pay is better,' he snapped.

'Vera, you shouldn't have stood up to your dad like that,' Annie remonstrated as soon as they were alone. 'Now you've ended up with only sixpence a week pocket money.'

'Don't worry about it, Mam. I'm happy to hand over the full eight shillings and sixpence a week, and you don't have to give me back any pocket money. Elbrown's are paying me ten shillings and sixpence a week. This week I didn't get a full week's money because I didn't work on Monday on account of it being a bank holiday.'

Chapter Ten

No one, except her mother, seemed to be interested in all the new things that were happening in her life since she'd started work at Elbrown's, Vera thought resignedly. As far as her father was concerned, she had a job that brought in a regular weekly wage and that was all that mattered. The more money she and Edmund handed over, the less he had to provide, and that suited him fine. He made it quite clear that in his opinion it would have been better if she'd gone to work at the biscuit factory. He didn't see the sense in a girl trying to better herself when in a couple of years' time she would be married, staying at home with kids to look after.

'You'd have earned a damn sight more money on the production line than you will as a junior clerk,' he grumbled.

Her mother listened, but more often than not failed to comprehend half of what Vera was talking about. Such things as switchboards, telephones and typewriters were outside Annie's experience, but she certainly felt proud that Vera had managed to get an office job and not ended up working in a factory like so many girls from her school.

For Vera, her job was the key to a whole new way of life. She was absorbing all the knowledge that came her way like a sponge, and revelling in honing her new found talents.

The weather throughout July and August that year was blisteringly hot so the offices at the top of Elbrown's paint and wallpaper shop were almost unbearable. They were not only claustrophobic, but the smell of paint and varnish hung in the air, making them so stuffy that it was hard to concentrate. Everyone who worked there complained. They couldn't wait for their midday break so that they could get outside for some fresh air.

The moment Vera had eaten her sandwiches, though, she continued teaching herself to type. To her the typewriter was a magic machine. She loved to hear the click-clack of the keys, to see the lines of words appearing, as if by magic, as she picked out the individual letters.

'As soon as you have mastered the keyboard, and practised setting things out, you can do the invoices on the typewriter instead of writing them out by hand,' Mr Brown told her.

Miss Linacre's eyebrows shot up in surprise. 'We need two copies,' she reminded him, 'one for the customer and one for ourselves.'

'That's no problem is it? Carbon paper will work equally well for invoices as it does for copies of letters, surely. In fact, I imagine the flimsy will be easier to read than when it is handwritten.'

'In that case why hasn't Miss Frith been typing the invoices instead of training this new girl to do them? Miss Frith is already a proficient typist.'

'Her time is taken up with correspondence and orders,' Mr Brown said dismissively.

Listening to their exchange, Vera was determined to rise to the challenge and, if possible, to become a proficient typist, too, before her pay review was due.

Miss Linacre was not in the least encouraging when eventually Vera told her that she felt she was ready to try typing the invoices.

'You can't rub out your mistakes, you know,' Miss Linacre told her sharply. 'If you do make a mess of an invoice then remember it means you must cancel the form and report the fact to me. Don't under any circumstances destroy it. They are all numbered and the sequence is important.'

'Yes, Miss Linacre, I do realise that.'

'Well, make sure you remember it.'

Vera took her time and managed to produce six invoices that were more or less perfect. She found the hard part was keeping the extension columns in line. She was almost afraid to press the keys in case the figures weren't in quite the right places.

'We'll all be here until midnight unless you learn to work faster than this!' Miss Linacre told her caustically. 'The idea of having them typed isn't merely for neatness, it is because it ought to be quicker than writing them out by hand. The speed you are working at it is taking twice as long.'

'I'm sure I'll get quicker with practice,' Vera assured her.

'Take no notice of her, you're doing fine,' Joan Frith whispered. 'Let me show you how to use the tab stops, that will speed things up. Anyway, don't worry about getting behind. I'll give you a hand once I've got my own stuff completed.'

'It wouldn't be so bad if I didn't have to break off so many times to deal with the switchboard,' Vera told her.

'It's a pity we don't get more calls so that it was someone's sole job to deal with them,' Joan agreed.

As the months passed the two girls supported each other more and more.

Vera liked Joan and soon realised that she had almost as hard a time keeping in Miss Linacre's good books as she did.

No matter how hard they worked Miss Linacre found fault; she was quick to point out the slightest mistake and if it was something that had been typed then no matter how neat the correction she would make them do it all over again.

Vera was worried in case she didn't get her rise, or, worse still, was told to leave because her work wasn't satisfactory.

'Don't worry, it's Mr Brown who makes those sort of decisions,' Joan assured her.

Vera felt a whole lot more confident once she knew she had a permanent job and somehow Miss Linacre's finicky ways no longer mattered quite so much. As she was given more responsibility she felt more and more that she was one of the team.

At Christmas, she was surprised by Miss Linacre's generosity when she bought both her and Joan boxed sets of soap, bath salts and talcum powder. Mr Brown gave everyone a bottle of Port and even let them finish at midday on Christmas Eve so that they could complete any last minute shopping they might need to do.

Vera felt she was walking on air as she dashed home. It meant she would be able to go to Paddy's Market with her mother for the vegetables and the chicken for their Christmas Dinner.

1925, she decided, was going to be a turning point in all their lives. Benny was happy at school and she and Eddy were both working so her mam need never go short of anything ever again.

Another couple of months and she'd be taking her shorthand and typing exam and once she'd passed that and was properly qualified she could get a job anywhere. Not that she wanted to change her job because she liked it at Elbrow's.

The only worry she had these days, she reflected, was about her mother. She didn't seem at all well. She didn't look it either, although she rarely complained, except about Benny. He still loved school and he was so excited about what he did each day that he insisted on recounting all his adventures the moment he got home.

Most evenings there were boots or shoes to be delivered, so, because her mother complained that his prattling made her head ache, Vera took Benny along with her.

'I do try to be patient when he comes rushing out of school, clutching the picture he's drawn, or is intent on telling me about something he's done in school,' her mother sighed. 'I long for you to be home from work though, Vera, to listen to all his exuberant chatter.'

The first week, Annie had tried leaving Benny in the shop when they got home hoping that Mike would be interested in Benny's news, while she went to make a cup of tea. He had no time for what he termed 'kids' nonsense', though, and speedily sent Benny scurrying back into the living room, threatening to 'thump his skull' if he came in there bothering him ever again.

Vera listened to her mother's complaints about this in bewilderment. 'Why did you send Benny into the shop? You know Dad hates any of us to go in there.'

Her mother sighed heavily. 'Benny's such a chatter-box, Vera. He's bubbling over with energy when he comes out of school and it's more than I can take. By that time in the day I'm so worn out that all I want to do is sit down and be quiet. After walking to the school to collect him, I'm exhausted.'

Vera frowned as she looked at her mother. She did look washed out, and she seemed to have lost so much weight, that she looked quite frail.

'Perhaps you need a tonic, Mam,' she said worriedly. 'Why don't you go and see the doctor and get yourself sorted out before the cold weather sets in. At the moment you look as though a gust of wind would blow you over.'

'I think all the hot weather we've had has taken it out of me,' her mother sighed. 'If it's a nice day on Sunday how about the two of us take Benny over to New Brighton for the day? It's such a long time since we were over there, I think I'd enjoy it.'

Vera shuddered as she recalled the last time she had been on the other side of the Mersey, the day she'd followed her father and Benny. She'd never forget seeing her little brother sitting on one pub doorstep after another in the blazing sun, while her dad was inside enjoying a drink.

'Why don't we all go. A real family outing,' her mother persisted. 'We'd better see what Edmund and your dad think of the idea, but even if they don't want to we can still go,' she said cautiously. 'Don't say anything to Benny, let it be a surprise for him.'

Edmund looked taken aback. 'Sorry, I've arranged to go out for the day with some of my mates from work,' he told them.

Michael Quinn refused point blank. 'Waste of good beer money,' he snorted. 'You must be out of your mind! If it's a fine weekend the place will be packed with people making the most of the weather before winter sets in.'

'That's exactly why I wanted us to make the trip,' Annie told him hopefully.

'What the hell for? You lived over there for long enough, you should know it inside out, so what do you want to go over there for now?'

'You sometimes used to go over there for a walk on Sundays,' Annie reminded him.

His lip curled. 'Yes, until some little bitch started spying on me.'

'I wasn't spying on you!' Vera protested.

'You were following me!'

'Only because I was worried about little Benny. It was such a hot day and ... and ...' But her voice died away as she saw the anger in her father's face. She was suddenly afraid that he was going to hit her.

'My answer is no!' he snapped. 'Understand? I don't expect you lot to go jaunting over there, either. I expect my meal to be on the table on Sunday the same as always.'

Annie didn't answer. She walked out of the room, her eyes bright with tears. She knew it was foolish to cry about such things, but it seemed to her that they had no family life these days. If Vera was willing then they'd take Benny to New Brighton, she resolved, no matter what Michael said.

On Sunday, Annie and Vera waited on tenterhooks, avoiding each other's eyes as Michael Quinn dressed himself up in his best navy blue suit, slipped his gold hunter watch into his waistcoat pocket, and arranged the chain across his chest to his satisfaction. Annie brushed the nap on his bowler and handed it to him as soon as he was ready to leave. Vera cringed inwardly, wishing she could make things easier for her mother. Did marriage have to be like this, she wondered. If they'd stayed in Wallasey and she'd ended up marrying Jack Winter as she'd dreamed of doing, would he have changed like her dad had done?

Michael stopped as Benny came into the room. 'What's he wearing his school clothes for today?' he asked.

None of them could think of a reply. 'Since he's clean and tidy I'll take him with me,' he told them.

'Oh no!' Vera's eyes flashed angrily. 'He's not going to be dragged from one pub to the other, and made to sit on the doorstep while you're inside swilling pints.'

'Who the hell do you think you are you talking to?' her father roared, as he raised his hand threateningly.

Vera faced him without flinching, contempt in her bright blue eyes.

'Michael, do you need a clean handkerchief?' Annie said quickly, anxious to distract his attention.

Savagely he pushed her to one side. 'Stop fluttering round me like some demented old Mary Ellen! Just remember, I expect my meal to be on the table ready for me when I get back,' he ordered.

'It will be,' Vera told him coolly.

He glared at her as if about to say something else, then rammed his bowler hat on his head and stormed out.

The minute he was gone, Vera sent her mother to get ready. 'Go on,' she urged. 'I'll put out a meal for him.'

With lightening speed she spread a white cloth on the table and set out cutlery for one person. Then she went into the scullery and brought out a plate of cold meat and salad, which was covered over by another plate, and put it down on the table, together with condiments and a bottle of sauce.

'That'll do for him,' she stated as her mother came back into the room wearing a navy blue coat over her cotton dress and a navy blue hat on her head. 'Come on, Benny, we're going out for the day.'

As they walked to the tram stop in Scotland Road, Vera was aware of how tense her mother was, and that she was constantly looking over her shoulder.

'Stop worrying, Mam! By now Dad's downing pints in one of the pubs so he's not going to suddenly appear and stop us going.'

'I hope you're right. I won't feel comfortable until we're on the ferry, though.'

The *Royal Daffodil*, was at the landing stage when they arrived at the Pier Head. The moment they were on board, and the gangplank had been raised, Annie seemed to relax.

They went up onto the top deck, and sat on one of the bench seats near the railings, so that they could watch all that was happening as they sailed downriver. Benny was so excited that he couldn't sit still for a minute.

'Keep an eye on him, Vee, we don't want him falling over the side,' Annie said worriedly when he started running from one side of the deck to the other and trying to shin up the safety rails to see more clearly.

'Benny, you come here, and kneel up on this seat, and I'll tell you about everything we see all the way to New Brighton,' Vera promised.

'I can't see over the side when I'm kneeling,' he protested.

'Well you can stand up on the seat then, as long as you keep still.'

Deftly, she manoeuvred him so that instead of being between herself and her mother, he was standing on her other side.

After the first few minutes of excitement he settled down, absolutely entranced by all that he could see. There was a smile on Annie's face as she listened to them chattering away. Vera was a good daughter, she helped to make life bearable. She wondered what the future held in store for her. So far, she didn't seem to bother with boys, yet when she'd been little she'd been inseparable from Eddy's friend, Jack Winter.

When they reached New Brighton, they walked along the promenade as far as Perch Rock, and then went up one of the side streets in search of a café.

Benny enjoyed their meal of fish and chips and Vera bought him an ice cream afterwards whilst she and her mother enjoyed a cup of tea.

Although the beach was packed they managed to find two vacant deckchairs. Whilst Annie lay back with a handkerchief over her face to protect it from the hot sun, Vera helped Benny build a sandcastle.

By mid-afternoon the sun had vanished behind clouds and there was a freshness in the wind blowing in off the river. As the sky darkened, there was a mad stampede towards the pier. Everyone wanted to get back to Liverpool before the threatening storm broke.

Instead of following everyone else, they decided to take a tram to Liscard so that they could show Benny the places where they used to live. Their old house in Exeter Road, and the one in Trinity Road where Annie's parents had lived, seemed very quiet after the noise of Scotland Road.

'Do you wish you were back here, Mam?' Vera asked.

Annie sighed and wiped a tear from the corner of her eye. 'It was a different world, luv. We've all changed, too. Your dad was such a wonderful man in those days, before he went in the army. You've no idea how much he's altered,' she said sadly.

'I have, Mam. I can remember how kind and jolly he was when I was little. He used to carry me on his shoulders when he took me to the shore with Charlie and Eddy.

'Charlie!' Annie sighed. 'He was such a lovely boy. Perhaps everything would have been different if he hadn't died. He had it quite easy when he was alive, compared to poor Eddy.'

'Eddy seems to have made a good life for himself since he left school, though.'

'Mmm! I suppose you could say that. He certainly doesn't have much time for us nowadays,' Annie admitted.

'I blame Dad,' Vera said bitterly. 'He's so harsh with us all, even with you, Mam!'

'Shush!' Annie gave her a warning look. 'Little ears hear a lot, you know.'

As the ferry boat grated against the side of the landing stage back at the Pier Head, and the gangplank was lowered, Annie suddenly seemed to realise that evening was drawing in.

'We're terribly late,' she said worriedly. 'Your dad will be waiting for his cooked meal. Benny has to be up for school in the morning and you have to get your things ready for work.'

Chapter Eleven

It was almost dark by the time they reached home from New Brighton.

'Mind you both go indoors as quietly as you can so as not to disturb your father,' Annie warned them as they walked down the back jigger. 'Benny, you go straight upstairs and get ready for bed. Then come back down in your pyjamas for some supper.'

'Perhaps you'd better take him up and help him, Mam,' Vera suggested, 'he looks tired out. I'll start laying the table and getting things ready for our meal.'

'All right,' her mother agreed, 'but I'll be back down as soon as I can to help you.'

Michael Quinn was in the living room reading the *Liverpool Echo*. He lowered the paper, rustling it angrily as Vera walked in.

'Where do you lot think you've been until now?' he snapped as she started clearing the table and then relaying the white cloth and setting out fresh cutlery.

'We went to New Brighton, like we told you. We asked you to come with us.'

'I told you not to go! Waste of bloody money going over there!' he grunted.

'Well, we enjoyed it. We took Benny to Wallasey

on the way home to show him our old house and where Gran and Granddad Simmonds used to live.'

'And left me here on my own with nothing but a plate of cold meat.' He scowled.

'And a tasty salad. You must have enjoyed it because it's all gone!'

'Bloody rabbit food!' he glowered. 'Where's your mother?'

'Upstairs taking her hat and coat off and . . .'

With an oath, Michael threw down his newspaper and made for the stairs.

Alarmed by the look of fury on his face Vera grabbed at his arm. 'She'll be down in a minute, Dad!'

Angrily he shook her off and bounded upstairs, taking them two at a time. Annie was on the point of coming down, but hesitated on the landing

'What the hell do you think you are playing at, buggering off without a word, leaving me to fend for myself all day,' he exploded, pushing her savagely against the wall.

'We went to New Brighton . . . I told you we were going . . . and I did leave something ready for you to eat.'

'Don't bloody well answer me back!' He lashed out and caught her a back-hander across the mouth.

Taken by surprise she staggered, and her foot slipped over the edge of the top stair. She swayed then lost her balance, and, with a frightened scream, hurtled forwards.

'Mam! Are you all right?' Hearing the

commotion, Vera rushed to where her mother lay in a crumpled heap at the bottom of the stairs. She dropped to her knees, feeling for her mother's pulse, trying desperately to rouse her.

She looked up at her father, who was standing at the top of the stairs, staring down at her poker-faced.

'She's not moving,' she said in a frightened whisper.

Benny came running out of his bedroom and peered through the banisters. When he saw his mother lying prone at the foot of the stairs he ran to his father, clinging on to him, begging him to make her better.

Irritably, Michael shook him away. 'Get back in your bedroom and stay there,' he ordered. 'Now!'

He made his way downstairs, and nudged Annie's body with the toe of his shoe.

'Don't do that!' Vera hissed at him, her eyes blazing.

'You'd better go and fetch some help,' he snapped.

'What do we need, a doctor or an ambulance?' she asked anxiously.

His face was blank. 'How the hell do I know. Get anyone.'

Shaking with fright, Vera ran down the road to the phone box. She was so upset that she had difficulty finding the words to tell the operator what had happened and where she lived. As she reached home again she realised that she had not given their full address only said Scotland Road.

'You'll have to open up the shop door and put

the lights on so that the ambulance can find the place,' she told her father.

She thought he was going to make a fuss, but to her relief he did as she asked without protest. He even stood out in the roadway, waiting to flag down the ambulance when it arrived.

Benny was still huddled on the landing, his face white, his eyes streaming with tears, as he stared down between the banister rails at the inert figure of his mother still lying where she had fallen.

Vera kept on trying to find a pulse, but there wasn't even the slightest flicker. She was equally concerned that her mother didn't seem to be breathing. She longed for the ambulance to arrive although, in her heart, she knew it was going to be too late.

Annie Quinn was dead long before they took her to hospital. Vera cuddled Benny close, trying her best to comfort him, but he was inconsolable.

Edmund was heartbroken when he arrived home and heard what had happened. Bitter and angry, he vowed revenge.

In the days that followed, he did his best to comfort Benny, and distract him by taking him out or playing with him whenever he could. It was the worst time that he and Vera had ever experienced.

At first Michael seemed numb with shock, morose and withdrawn. Then he pulled himself together as rumours abounded as to how Annie had fallen down the stairs. Neighbours, newspaper reporters, even the police, were all asking countless questions. It meant that they found themselves reliving the horror of what had happened over and over again.

On the day of the funeral, Michael Quinn played the grieving husband to perfection. Dressed in his best suit and wearing a black bowler hat, he held Benny by the hand as they followed the cortege.

Vera and Edmund walked behind him, each angry in their own fashion at the way he was exploiting little Benny who, in their opinion, should have been left with one of the neighbours.

As well as the overpowering grief at losing their mother there was the fear at the back of both their minds about what the future might hold for them all. Their mother had been so instrumental in keeping the peace. When their father's temper flared, and he was about to hit one of them, she had tried to placate him, even if it didn't always work.

Vera knew that in future her father would expect her to run the home, and she also knew that her rash, lippy attitude was bound to antagonise him. Somehow, though, she would have to try to please him, if only to make sure that he didn't bully little Benny

Eddy was determined that he would no longer be browbeaten by his father. He was more than halfway through his apprenticeship so, as soon as he was fully qualified, he'd be able to ask Rita to marry him and they could set up home on their own.

He'd make sure that it was nearby, so that he could keep an eye on Vera and Benny, and make sure they weren't being intimidated by his father.

As the eldest he felt it was his duty, and that he owed it to his mother's memory to do so. Vera hadn't said very much about how the accident had happened, but she didn't need to, the weal across his mother's face told its own story.

Some of the men he worked with at Cammell Laird's had told him that his father's moods were a form of shell shock. Many of them had fathers or brothers who'd been on active service and they said that they were the same. They were either moody or bad-tempered, or had frightening nightmares and woke screaming, thinking that they were back in the trenches.

He wondered if he ought to find someone who could talk to his father, and find out if that really was his problem. He never spoke about his army days and Eddy felt sure that something must have happened while he was in France to have changed him so much.

He could never remember him shouting at any of them or even smacking them before the war. Making them go up to their bedroom had been the severest punishment he could ever recall him giving.

True, his father had been younger then, but not all that much. It was only because he was so bad-tempered, and grouchy, that he appeared to be so much older than he really was.

He knew Vera would do her best to make sure that young Benny came to no harm from their dad, but she wouldn't be there all the time. Benny came home from school almost two hours before she finished work at night.

He wondered if it was possible to arrange for Benny to go and stay with one of his playmates until Vera finished work, if their father would allow him to do that.

If Benny was a few years older, streetwise and able to stand up for himself, it wouldn't be so bad. But he'd always been so protected that he wouldn't be safe, not in the area where they were living, with gangs of young ruffians roaming around looking for trouble.

The kids who lived in Scotland Road, and the courts and alleys leading off it, were tough nuts. They'd pick on Benny and make his life a misery, simply because of his big blue eyes and mop of blond curls.

It had all been so different where they'd lived in Wallasey. He and Charlie had never had any problems, but then they'd had each other and he supposed that had made a difference. If anyone had tried to bully one of them the other would have been there ready to take his part.

He could remember what a shock it had been for him when they'd first arrived in Scotland Road. Apart from the dangers of all the traffic, he'd found right away that he was the butt of practical jokes, taunts and attacks from older boys because he was new to the area.

Benny was too pretty by half and also too trusting. He'd smile and chatter to anyone, given half a chance. Perhaps the best thing I can do, Edmund resolved, is to teach him to use his fists.

Vera was dead set against this idea when he suggested it. She didn't approve of physical violence.

'After what happened to our mam I would have thought the last thing you wanted to do was to encourage Benny to be aggressive,' she said angrily.

'Come on, Vee. This is different. We have to make sure that Benny can look after himself. You don't want him to suffer like I did, now do you!'

'Teach him to run then. Run so fast that the others can't catch him.'

'They'll taunt him for being a coward if every time he's involved in an argument he beats it off home.'

'Maybe, but we both know he's too young to defend himself. Isn't there some other way we can make sure he is OK until I come home from work?'

'Well, Rita sometimes does shift work,' Eddy said thoughtfully. 'I suppose I could ask her to collect him from school on the days when she finishes at two and take him home with her, or to the swings, until you finish work.'

Vera smiled with relief. 'If she could manage to do that until I can get something else organised, it would be a terrific help. Do you think she will agree?'

Rita did agree, and Benny accepted that she was going to collect him from school without question. The arrangement lasted for almost two weeks before Michael Quinn stepped in and demanded to know what was going on.

'That can stop right now,' he thundered. 'In future, Benny comes straight home from school. Understand?'

'He's scared to come down the back jigger on

his own. Bigger boys waylay him and tease him, and snatch his cap and throw it over the wall.'

'Then tell him to walk down Scotland Road and come in through the shop.'

Vera was about to argue, but she thought better of it. Maybe her dad was trying to help, she decided. Letting Benny in through the shop was a concession none of them had been granted. The least she could do was give it a try and see how things went. Perhaps if they all pulled together and tried to help each other this terrible cloud they were all living under would gradually disappear.

Even though he hadn't said so, Vera suspected that deep down her dad was as heartbroken about what had happened as the rest of them. He'd let his temper get the better of him, but she was sure he'd never meant to push her mother down the stairs.

Although Benny could now walk down Scotland Road and in through the shop he still seemed very quiet and subdued when she came home at night. He said everything was all right so she put it down to the fact that he was missing their mam. It wasn't until about three weeks later, when Eddy ruffled his hair and he let out a scream, that she realised something was very wrong.

Filled with trepidation she lifted him up onto her lap and wiped away his tears. As she did so she spotted the mass of bumps and bruises beneath his mop of curls. She didn't need to ask him how he had come by them. She remembered, only too well, the way Eddy had suffered the same treatment when he'd been younger.

'Benny, what do you do in the shop until I get home?' she asked gently.

At first he wouldn't tell her. Then, very hesitantly, the whole story came out. He was expected to sort out the new leather soles into pairs, the same as Eddy used to have to do. Like his brother, Benny found it difficult to work out which was a right one, and which was a left one.

Vera didn't need to hear any more. She knew that his dad had been trying to impress on him how it was to be done by 'thumping his skull'.

Chapter Twelve

In the months leading up to Christmas 1925, Vera tried hard to run their home and still do her job at Elbrown's to the best of her ability, because she knew that was what her mother would have wanted her to do.

Some nights when she fell into bed, she felt utterly exhausted, and yet her mind was racing round at such a speed that sleep was impossible. She kept remembering all the things she had forgotten to do, as well as all the jobs that still lay ahead to be done the next day.

All the harsh, sarcastic comments her father made about everything she did also went round and round in her head, filling her alternatively with anger and shame.

'Didn't your mother ever teach you how to iron a shirt properly,' he roared, when he found that the starched collar of his best white shirt had a slight crease in it.

'I did my best, Dad. If the iron isn't hot enough then it won't bring the creases out, and if it is too hot it scorches the collar.'

'So what puts the sodding creases into the collar in the first place then?' he demanded. 'I'll tell you,' he went on before she could reply, 'your slipshod way of doing things.'

'That's not fair, Dad . . .'

'I don't want to hear your silly excuses, or any of your lip, my girl. If your mother could iron my shirts properly then so can you. Bloody slapdash worker, that's what you are. Either that, or you're thick like your brothers. Neither of them can tell right from left.'

It was much the same over his meals. She knew she wasn't anywhere near as good at making scrag-end of mutton, or any other off-cuts, into tasty meals as her mother had been. She did her best, though, and Edmund seemed to enjoy almost everything she put in front of him.

Benny was still moping for his mam, and one of the ways he showed it was by being finicky about his food. Even so, he usually cleared his plate with a little gentle coaxing from Vera because he was afraid that if he didn't he might get a hiding from his dad.

Her father was never pleased with what she dished up. He also made it very plain whenever she ran short of money on a Thursday, and had to serve up scouse made mostly from vegetables and leftovers, that she didn't manage things as well as her mother had done.

'Perhaps it is because you don't give me as much money for housekeeping as you gave Mam,' she pointed out defensively.

His face darkened and his blue eyes turned icy. 'Of course I bloody well don't, you silly bitch! With your mam gone there's one less mouth to feed so you don't need as much money.'

She tried to point out that the housekeeping

money wasn't only for food, but that she had to buy cleaning materials and clothes for Benny out of it, too.

In desperation she had to ask Eddy if he could manage to give her a few shillings more.

'I'm already using all my wages to eke out the housekeeping and I still can't make ends meet. I know you and Rita want to get engaged, and that you are saving up to buy a ring, so once I get the hang of balancing out the house-keeping you can stop giving me extra,' she promised.

She also suggested to Eddy that it would help if he gave her a hand when he came home in the evenings. 'If you could clear away the dishes and wash up when we've finished our meal, I could get straight on with the house cleaning,' she told him. 'It takes me all day on Sunday to do the washing, and then there's all the ironing and mending to do somehow, too. I have to leave changing the beds and all the other jobs for week-days when I come home from work.'

At first Eddy wasn't very enthusiastic, but once he realised how much responsibility Vera had to shoulder he was as helpful as could be. He even encouraged Benny to lend a hand.

'You can help by clearing the table,' he told him. 'You bring everything through to the scullery so that I can wash them. OK?'

Benny treated it like some kind of game to start with, but he quickly tired of it. More often than not, Benny would leave half the dishes on the table. Eddy would keep calling to him to bring the rest through, but usually, in the end, he had to go and collect them himself.

This nightly pandemonium, as he termed it, infuriated their father. When he tried to take his temper out on Eddy by calling him shiftless, Eddy retaliated by telling him it was about time he helped around the place.

The row that ensued had both of them shouting abuse at each other. Vera, who was upstairs changing the beds, came running down to see what was happening.

'What on earth is going on?' she asked, looking at their angry faces.

Neither of them would answer. When Benny, who was cowering under the table, piped up, 'They're fighting over who does the dishes,' Vera had to suppress the urge to laugh, knowing that both of them would be furious if she did.

'You're the one who should be clearing up and washing the dishes,' her father barked, stabbing at her chest with his forefinger.

'I've only got one pair of hands,' she retorted, her blue eyes flaring, 'and there's so many other jobs that need doing that I can't fit them all in.'

'You could do if you stayed home and ran the place properly instead of spending your day in that piss-farting office.'

'Right,' she told him defiantly, 'I'll stay home if you'll give me the same amount of money each week as I'm earning at Elbrown's.'

Michael Quinn didn't even bother to answer. Shoving her roughly to one side he stomped upstairs. Vera and Eddy exchanged knowing looks as they heard him pulling out drawers and banging cupboard doors. He was changing into his best clothes before going out for the night on a drinking spree.

'He's in a terrible temper so we'd better all be in bed when he comes back home tonight,' Vera warned after their father had left the house.

'You can be, I'm off out to see Rita once I've finished helping you,' Eddy told her.

'Then make sure you don't wake Dad up when you come home. You can see the mood he's in, and after he's had a few drinks he'll be itching for a fight.'

'And I'm the very person to take him on,' Eddy boasted, flexing his muscles.

Vera shook her head. 'No, Eddy. It's wrong to fight your dad.'

'It's wrong for him to treat us as his slaves and to speak to us like he does, but it doesn't stop him.'

'I think he's still very upset about Mam dying,' Vera murmured.

'About him causing her death, you mean!' Eddy exploded. 'If he hadn't lashed out at her she would never have stepped back and . . .' He stopped as he caught the warning in Vera's eyes. She put a finger to her lips and nodded at Benny, who was listening to all they were saying.

'Go on, you go out and I'll finish clearing up the dishes.'

Eddy shrugged. 'I know I should do more around the place, but I feel knackered most nights when I get home, especially now that I'm going

116

to night school straight from work. I know you must be just as tired after working in that office all day, so perhaps we should draw up a rota showing which of us is responsible for doing what.'

'That's not a bad idea,' Vera agreed. 'It would save the jobs piling up, or,' she added with a grin, 'me forgetting that they have to be done.'

'And make sure you include Dad on the list,' Eddy added firmly.

Vera laughed. 'I don't think he'd take any notice, do you?'

'He might if you typed it all up on that machine in your office and made it look all official,' Eddy said hopefully.

After she'd finished changing the beds, tidying downstairs and putting Benny to bed, Vera made herself a cup of tea and sat down in her father's armchair. She'd found a piece of notepaper and a pencil, so she began drawing up a list of the many tasks there were to do.

She started the list with the everyday jobs like making the beds, washing the dishes, cleaning out the ashes from the fireplace, making up the fire and preparing meals for them all. Then came all the other tasks which she did weekly, or whenever she could manage to fit them in. Washing, ironing, sweeping the floor, scrubbing the steps, cleaning the windows and getting the shopping.

For once she was glad that their home was so sparsely furnished. There were no ornaments to dust and, since there was only one rag-rug on the bare boards in the living room, it didn't take long to sweep the floor.

When she'd covered both sides of the paper she almost gave up in despair because there were so many jobs. But she found some more writing paper and began to divide the list up into separate columns. There were a great many which she would have to do herself, but also some that Eddy could help her with, or perhaps even her father might agree to do. She also made a list of those that she thought Benny would be able to do.

When she'd finished she put the list to one side. She would look through it again tomorrow, she told herself. She felt far too tired to check through to see if everything was on it. All she wanted to do was go to bed and sleep.

Vera had no idea how long she'd been in bed when she felt someone dragging at the bedcovers and shouting something she couldn't understand.

When she managed to open her eyes she found it was her father who was trying to waken her, and he was shaking her roughly by the shoulder. Her first thought, as she struggled to sit up, was that there must be something wrong with Benny, that he had been taken ill in the night.

'Downstairs! Get downstairs right this minute you lazy little bint!'

Rubbing the sleep from her eyes and pushing her hair back from her face Vera reached out for her dressing gown that she'd spread across the bed for extra warmth. Roughly he pushed her hand away. Seizing her by the arm he began to drag her out onto the landing. The noise as she fell against Eddy's bedroom door brought him out of bed to see what was going on.

In a flash, his hand shot out and grabbed hold of his sister, pulling her into the safety of his room before he faced his father.

'You trying to push our Vera down the stairs and kill her the same as you did our mam?' he asked, his voice hoarse with fury.

'Piss off, you silly young sod, and get back to sleep,' Mike Quinn told him contemptuously. 'I want my supper and that lazy little bitch hasn't left it on the table ready for me.'

'If you want some supper then go and get it yourself,' Eddy told him in a sibilant snarl. 'And make sure you clear up after you as well! Don't think you can leave your dirty dishes for one of us to deal with in the morning before we go out to work.'

With a muttered oath, Michael Quinn's fist shot out and slammed Eddy's head against the door jamb. Vera screamed in terror. She tried to stop Eddy retaliating, but her brother was too quick for her. His punch landed fair and square on his father's chin, snapping the older man's head back.

Michael Quinn responded with a belly blow that left Eddy doubled up, but even that didn't stop him. Fuelled by fury, Eddy hammered at his father with piston-like blows. Some went wide of their mark, but enough were on target to wind the older man and make him retreat. Cursing loudly, he lurched his way downstairs.

Eddy turned to Vera who was shaking with fright. 'Go on, back to your bed. He won't bother us any more tonight. He's probably too drunk to come upstairs again so he'll sleep in his armchair.'

'What will happen tomorrow, though?' she asked anxiously. 'He won't let either of us get away with this.'

'He probably won't even mention it. He wouldn't want the whole world to know that his eighteen-year-old son had managed to give him a good hiding.'

Vera shook her head, not at all sure about this. She was grateful for the way that Eddy had stood up for her, but she was scared that it was going to cause trouble and dreaded what form the repercussions would take.

Suddenly she was seeing Eddy in a new light. He was a force to be reckoned with. He might not be very tall but he was now a sturdy young man. It was obvious from his encounter with their father that the time he'd spent as an apprentice in the Merseyside shipyards had developed his muscles.

Vera saw now that it hadn't been mere boasting when he said that he was as strong as their dad and no longer feared him. He also had the advantage of being more agile and alert than Michael because he was so much younger.

Nevertheless, she was worried. She could only hope that the fracas wouldn't result in too much bad feeling between them. She knew without being told that the moment Eddy was fully qualified he wouldn't think twice about walking out of their home if he had any further disagreements with their dad. The fact that he was planning to get engaged to Rita meant that he was already thinking about an independent future.

She shuddered at the thought of being left at

home on her own to look after Benny and her father. With Eddy gone it would mean that her dad could bully her as much as he liked and make her life, and little Benny's, sheer hell because there would be no one there to stand up for them.

At that moment she missed her mother deeply and longed to be able to turn back the tide of events. If they hadn't defied her dad by going over to New Brighton, if she hadn't persuaded her mother to take a detour through Wallasey instead of coming straight home, then he might never have known they'd been out for the day.

If there had been a hot meal ready for him, if she'd been the one to go upstairs with Benny . . .

The series of events raced round and round in her head like buzzing bluebottles until she thought she would go mad. There was nothing she could do about any of it, she told herself. Her mam couldn't help her now, the future was in her own hands. She had to be strong, she had to do everything she could to make sure that Benny was safe and well looked after and that she didn't end up being browbeaten like her mother had been.

Chapter Thirteen

Early in 1926, after a miserable Christmas, Vera felt she couldn't stand it any longer. Looking after their home, coping with her job, and making sure that little Benny was all right, kept her so busy that she had no time for herself. Even though Joan Frith asked her time and time again to go to the pictures or out dancing, she always had to refuse.

In desperation she asked Eddy if he would give up just one evening a week to be there with Benny so that she could go out.

'It's difficult enough as it is, Vee,' he grumbled. 'As well as giving you a hand here I have to divide up my free time between night school, going out with my mates and seeing Rita.'

'You're still seeing her?' Vera grinned.

'You know I am! I've already told you that once I've finished my apprenticeship we'll get engaged.'

'In that case, shouldn't you both be saving up? Rita needs to start a bottom drawer in readiness, you know.'

'What are you getting at?' Eddy frowned.

'Instead of the two of you spending money on going to the pictures and so on, why don't you stay in occasionally. Bring Rita round here, then you can keep an eye on Benny, and I will be able to have a night out,' she suggested.

Eddy pursed his lips in a silent whistle. 'Got it all worked out, haven't you? Have you spoken to Dad about it. I don't imagine he'll go a bundle on the idea. You know what he's like. He's never allowed us to bring any friends home.'

'Yes, I know,' Vera said, 'but we can't leave Benny here on his own with him.'

Eddy nodded glumly. 'Yes, if Dad decided he wanted to go out for a drink he'd go without a second thought about Benny.'

'Quite, and if Benny gets upset or does something he doesn't approve of he'll . . .'

'Thump his bloody skull,' Eddy said bitterly.

'That's right!'

They looked at each other and smiled. 'We can't risk it,' Eddy agreed. 'Tell you what, you talk to Dad about it, see if he raises any objections, and I'll ask Rita if she'll agree to do it.'

It was easier to persuade Rita than their father. Rita had always been curious about Vee's home, and wondered why it was that in all the time they'd known each other Vee had never invited her for tea.

Added to that she was quite taken by the idea of her and Eddy being able to spend an evening on their own. Her mam and dad made quite sure that whenever she took him back to her place they were never left alone for a second.

'I can't guarantee that my dad will go out, mind luv,' Eddy warned, when she mentioned this fact to him.

'Have to keep our fingers crossed then, won't we,' she giggled.

At first, Michael Quinn was stubbornly against Edmund bringing his girlfriend home.

'What the hell do you think this place is, a bloody brothel?' he asked Vera scornfully when she suggested it.

'Of course not, Dad. Don't say things like that. They just want the chance to be together, somewhere where they can sit and talk.'

'Well, let them do it some other place, not here. When I've finished work I want to sit down and read the *Echo*, not listen to the sort of twaddle those two will be nattering on about. Why can't they go and do it at her house, not here in this bloody tip.'

'It will give me a chance to have a night out if Rita and Eddy come here,' Vera persisted.

'Why the hell do they have to be here because you want to go gallivanting off somewhere?'

'To keep an eye on young Benny, of course.'

'What the bloody hell for when I'm here?'

'Well, you might want to go out for a drink . . .'

'So what's soddin' wrong with that?'

'It would mean Benny would be left in the house on his own.'

'Once the little beggar is in bed and asleep what does it matter whether I'm here or down the boozer?'

'He might wake up, and if he found himself all on his own, he'd probably be frightened to death.'

'At his age? What a load of bloody rubbish you come out with sometimes!' Michael Quinn sneered.

'No, it's a fact, Dad. He's only seven, remember, and he's still terribly upset over Mam and . . .'

'OK!' he interrupted, 'S'all right they can come here if you want them to, then. But tell that soddin' brother of yours that there's to be no hanky-panky or they'll be out on their bloody ears before you can blink.'

Vera was overjoyed. 'I'll make sure that Benny is in bed before I go out, and I'll leave some milk and biscuits ready in case he wakes up before I come home,' she promised Eddy, when she told him the good news.

Eddy tried to warn Rita what their dad was like. 'He's selfish, pompous, bad-tempered, bigoted, self-opinionated . . .'

'Give up, Eddy,' Rita laughed. 'I know he's no angel, but you're making him sound like an ogre.'

'He's a damn sight worse than that,' he told her gloomily.

Her grey eyes widened. 'You're trying to put me off coming round to your place, aren't you?' she said huffily.

'No, I'm not,' he assured her. 'I'm simply warning you so that you won't be shocked when you find out that most of the time he's like a bear with a sore head. You ask our Vee!'

Rita looked at him with raised eyebrows. 'I'm sure you're exaggerating. Anyway, if I come round tonight then I'll be able to judge for myself.'

Eddy was on tenterhooks waiting for Rita to arrive. He'd warned her not to put on too much lipstick and asked her to wear the dark green dress that she usually wore to church on Sundays.

'Are you trying to make me look plain and dowdy?'

'No! Of course not,' he said quickly. 'That frock looks good with the colour of your hair.'

'A compliment from you at last, Eddy Quinn,' she smiled, blushing.

'There's just one thing,' she teased, 'that green dress has quite a low neckline so do you want me to wear a modesty vest?'

He reddened. 'Come here!' Holding her plump cheeks between his hands he kissed her deeply.

To Eddy's astonishment, his dad was so nice to Rita that she was impressed.

'He's not a bit like what you said he was, Eddy,' Rita scolded after Michael Quinn had gone out to the pub.

Eddy shrugged, shaking his head in disbelief. 'He must have taken a fancy to you, kiddo. Believe me, he's not like that when he's talking to our Vee.'

'Well, he was quite charming to me and my mam says you should take people as you find them,' she told him firmly.

Although he was mystified by his father's behaviour Eddy was extremely relieved to find that he hadn't been rude, or offhand, with Rita and scared her away. Even her barbed comments that their home wasn't a bit like she'd imagined, and that she would hate to have to live at the back of the shop like they did, didn't upset him.

Vera thoroughly enjoyed her one night a week out, especially after Joan introduced her to her brother Steve.

Steve Frith was nineteen, which made him three years older than Vera. He was tall, with light brown hair, hazel eyes and a winning smile. Vera was bowled over the moment she met him.

Steve was equally enamoured by his sister's attractive dark-haired friend and wanted to see more of her. Whenever Joan mentioned that the two of them were going to the pictures, or off to a dance, he suggested that they should make up a foursome. He knew Joan was keen on his best friend, Liam Kelly, a green-eyed, redheaded Irishman who could charm the birds off the trees.

Vee found a whole new world was opening up for her as they happily paired off whenever they went out. She stopped feeling like a drudge and began to take more care over her appearance, vying with Joan to try out new shades of lipstick or other cosmetics.

At first it was pictures or dancing, but when they found how much they enjoyed each other's company they ventured into doing other things. In fact, it worked so well for all of them that it became a regular arrangement for Eddy and Rita to stay in one night a week and Vera found herself seeing more and more of Steve Frith.

'Are you and my big brother going steady?' Joan teased.

'You're the one who always brings him along when we go out,' Vera parried, her blue eyes glowing.

'He always wants to come and I think it's because he's sweet on you!'

'Or do you want him there so that you can be with Liam Kelly,' Vera laughed.

The two girls had become very good friends, both at work and in their leisure time.

Without consulting Miss Linacre they helped each other out, making sure that neither of them ever got behind with their work. Vera was now a reasonably proficient typist and it no longer worried her when she was interrupted to attend to the switchboard.

'Now that the weather is better and it is lighter at nights, why don't we go to the park with Steve and Liam,' Joan suggested.

'Do you think they would want to do that?'

'We won't know unless we ask them,' Joan smiled.

When she did ask, they were not too keen. 'Well, perhaps one Sunday we could all go to New Brighton for the day,' Joan suggested.

Vera sighed. 'That would be smashing, but I couldn't leave Benny, and I'm not sure if Rita and Eddy would look after him for a whole day,' she explained regretfully.

'Then we'll take him with us! They can come as well if they want to.'

The extended friendships were a new experience for Vera. She found that both Joan and Rita were full of bright ideas on how she could make life easier for herself.

'Instead of spending Sunday doing the washing, why don't you take it down to the public washhouse in Upper Frederick Street,' Rita suggested.

'It will be full of Slummies! Anyway, I couldn't afford to do that!' Vera told her.

'Yes you could. It wouldn't cost any more than the coal you use to boil up all the water at home. Anyway, you would only need to go every other week,' Joan told her. 'What's more, while the washing is in the machine you can sit and enjoy the magazines I bring in to work for you. You're always saying that you never have time to sit and read them.'

Vera laughed. 'It all sounds wonderful but I change the sheets each week so I'd have a mountain of things to wash if I left it longer than that.'

'Start changing them every two weeks instead,' Rita suggested.

'Mam always . . .'

'Your mother didn't have to do a full-time job as well as look after the home,' Joan told her quickly. 'Try changing them every two weeks and see if anyone notices.'

Vera nodded, but she still looked worried. 'There's Dad's shirts, too. He'd run out of clean shirts if I only washed them every two weeks.'

'Tell him to buy some more,' Rita prompted. 'Once he runs out he'll do it quick enough, you'll see.'

'It will only be something else for him to grumble about,' Vera said gloomily. 'Still,' she added with a weak smile, 'it might take his mind off constantly criticising my cooking.'

'What's the matter with your cooking. I've always enjoyed the meals I've had at your place,' Rita told her.

'You haven't had my lumpy custard or soggy pastry when I make an apple pie, yet, Rita.'

'Buy ready-made custard,' Joan said calmly. 'I think it is better than home-made anyway.'

'My dad would go mad if I served shop-bought stuff,' Vera sighed.

'Don't tell him! Anyway, it is home-made, the factory where they make it is in Liverpool!' Joan giggled.

'Yes, and buy an apple pie from Prestwood's in Great Homer Street. My mam does and she says they're better than anything she could make.'

Vera shook her head doubtfully, but their suggestions kept buzzing around in her mind. When she finally capitulated she found they were right on all points. The apple pie was delicious, and so was the custard. For the first time since she'd taken over the housekeeping there was a clean plate and no complaints from her father.

Full of confidence she began to sound out Rita and Joan for other labour-saving tips; in fact, anything to make her life easier.

'My mum hates housework so she's bound to know plenty of good shortcuts,' Joan told her. 'Perhaps you should come to tea one night and ask her yourself about them.'

'That would be wonderful, but . . .'

'You can bring Benny with you, he'd probably enjoy it, he doesn't have much fun for a little boy does he. Our Steve will love the chance to play with him!' she promised. 'Steve's still got a bedroom full of toys and games that he had when he was a nipper.'

Chapter Fourteen

Vera never failed to be amazed at the ways in which Rita seemed to become more and more a part of their lives. She regularly collected Benny from school, but, instead of taking him to the park, or back to her place when it was raining, she had started delivering the boots and shoes with him.

Both Eddy and Vera really appreciated this. Fitting it in had not been easy. Sometimes when she had been taking a load of washing to the public washhouse Vera had also taken along the boots and shoes that needed to be delivered. While the clothes were in the washing machine she'd dashed around doing her deliveries, praying she'd get back before the boiling cycle was completed. She knew that if she didn't, someone would empty her washing out so that they could use the machine and, in all probability, she'd return to find everything dumped on the floor.

'Use the time to sit there and read the stories in the magazines Joan gives you,' Rita told her. 'I quite enjoy delivering the boots with Benny. The customers all love him. I send him to the door on his own and they usually give him a biscuit or a sweet. He likes it best of all when they give him a penny, mind. He tells me he's saving up to buy a bicycle.'

Sometimes, Vera couldn't help feeling a little bit jealous. It seemed as though Rita was seeing more of Benny than she was, and that Rita was being taken into his confidence more than she was. When these thoughts flashed through her mind she shook herself and told herself she was lucky to have Rita to help out.

Having Rita around made life easier in other ways as well. When she was in their house Vera noticed that her father was all smiles. Rita never saw his dark moods, never heard his vituperate grumbles. She certainly never felt the impact of his clenched knuckles across the top of her head.

Rita was rarely there for a meal, so she never witnessed the way he grabbed the best of any food that was served. Even though he no longer had grounds for saying that 'they didn't need meat because they weren't working' he still couldn't resist leaning across the table and stabbing his fork into anything on their plates that looked tempting.

Vera and Eddy had long ago learned to eat the most succulent piece of meat first. Benny was not yet sharp enough to do this and more often than not he lost the best bits on his plate.

In some ways, they also had Rita to thank for many of the improvements in their home. Vera couldn't remember any of their rooms ever being redecorated. Rita talked so much about the decorating her father was doing that, not to be out-done, Vera asked at Elbrown's whether she could buy any finished lines of wallpaper or tins of paint that were going cheap.

'Will you help me redecorate, Eddy?' she begged. 'It won't half brighten the place up.'

Eddy hadn't any idea how to go about decorating, but with Steve Frith's help they managed to do a pretty good job on re-papering their living room.

Since the completion coincided with Eddy qualifying as a fully fledged marine engineer, he suggested that they should have a party.

'We could invite Rita and her parents, as well as Joan, Steve and Liam Kelly,' he told her.

'Do you think they would all come? I know Rita's mam, of course, from schooldays, but I don't know her father. What's he like?'

'Quite a bit older, but he's easy-going and friendly.'

Since they'd never had a party, or even entertained guests before, apart from Rita, Vera was unsure how to go about preparing for such a momentous event.

Rita's face creased with smiles. 'Don't go making a lot of work or fuss. Simply relax and enjoy yourself.'

'It's all very well you saying that, but I will have to provide them with food and drink.'

'That's easy enough. Send Eddy out for some beer and buy some sausage rolls and meat pies from Prestwood's.'

'Shh! My dad still thinks I make them.'

'Well let him think you make the pies and rolls for the party as well if that keeps him happy,' she advised.

'Do you think my dad will get on with your mam and dad?' Vera asked worriedly.

'They'd better.' Rita grinned. 'I think Eddy wants them all to be together when he announces some other special news . . .'

'You mean he's asked you to marry him?' Vera exclaimed excitedly.

'Not yet, but I'm pretty sure he will do so on the night of the party.'

'That makes it even more special,' Vera said delightedly. 'Now I really am looking forward to it.'

Michael Quinn scowled when the party was first mentioned. 'Waste of bloody money. Anyway, what do we want other people coming here for.'

'It's a celebration,' Vera told him. 'It will show how proud we are of Eddy because it will mark the end of his four-year apprenticeship.'

'Well, let's hope he's the one who is going to pay for it, and clean up the mess afterwards,' Michael grunted ungraciously.

At work, Vera and Joan Frith talked of nothing else. Two days before the party they even had the idea of dashing to Paddy's Market, in their lunch break, to buy something new to wear.

'Rita won't say what she will be wearing, but she always seems to be buying new clothes, so I suppose it will be something spectacular. I don't want to let our Eddy down by turning up in the blouse and skirt I wear for work every day.'

'I'll come with you,' Joan offered.

Miss Linacre scotched the idea the moment Joan mentioned it to her. 'Who do you think will attend to the switchboard if you two are both out to lunch at the same time?' she demanded.

'We have considered that,' Joan said smoothly, 'and we thought if we left the main line through here to the office, and put the other two through to the shop extensions, that would be all right for just half an hour. Not many people ring up in the lunch hour and it is just this once.'

Miss Linacre didn't approve, but she finally agreed. 'Half an hour, remember, not a moment longer.'

They abandoned all thought of eating their lunch and dashed out of the shop and up Great Homer Street to the market.

'We can eat our sarnies in the office when we get back,' Joan suggested.

There were so many pretty dresses to choose from that they found it difficult to make up their minds which ones to buy. In the end, common sense ruled for Vera and she chose a low-waisted, blue and white flowered cotton dress with a pleated skirt, something that she would be able to wear again and again during the summer.

Joan had no such qualms and bought a dusky red floral dress in a shiny, silky material. It was very short and the full top was gathered into a dropped waistband.

To Vera's surprise her dad dressed up for the occasion, too. Right up to the last minute, though, he grumbled about all the expense, and stressed the fact that he didn't like strangers invading his home.

Vera felt so nervous that she was sure she wouldn't enjoy herself. As the evening wore on and she saw how friendly and easy-going Rita's mam and dad were she relaxed and joined in the fun.

As well as a plentiful supply of beer, and some ginger pop for Benny and anyone else who preferred it, Eddy bought a bottle of sweet sherry for the girls. It was the first time Vera had tasted sherry and she was surprised by how much she liked it.

'You want to go easy on that, it will make your head spin,' Steve warned when she held out her glass for a refill.

Vera pulled a face. 'Oh dear, I'd better settle for ginger pop instead, then. I need to keep my wits about me to see everything goes well,' she giggled.

What she really meant was that she was worried about her dad. He seemed to be drinking twice as much as anyone else, and he was becoming more affable by the minute. She had never seen him in such a good mood. Far too friendly, she thought as she saw him slip an arm round Rita's waist after he'd opened another bottle of beer.

'We're nearly out of booze,' she told Eddy worriedly. 'Do you think you could nip out and get some more?'

He looked surprised. 'We shouldn't be! I bought enough for four pints each!'

'Yes, I know, but the way Dad is drinking he's downing two bottles to everybody else's one.'

Eddy frowned. 'That means he'll be pissed before the night's out.'

'Well, he's been more friendly than I've ever seen him in my life.' Vera grinned. 'Let's hope he stays that way. I'd hate it if he passed out or anything.'

Eddy snorted. 'He's not likely to do that, he's had years and years of practise. I bet he could drink everyone here under the table, no trouble at all.'

'Yes, you're probably right,' she agreed. 'So you'd better get in some more beer or he'll be complaining when his glass is empty and there's no more to fill it.'

'Right. Well you pass the food around and keep everyone occupied with that and I'll go and fetch some more supplies.'

Vera grabbed Joan by the arm and whispered into her ear that it was time to test out their 'home cooking' and see if anyone spotted the difference.

Vera was so caught up with dishing out food, and listening to the compliments everyone was paying her on how well everything had been organised, that she didn't realise that her dad was missing, or that Rita wasn't there, until Eddy returned with extra beer and the row erupted.

She heard Eddy's yell, blanched at the oath he let out, and then heard the sound of a scuffle out in the shop. The thuds and grunts as blows were exchanged alarmed Vera. Dropping the plates of food she was carrying she rushed through into the shop to see what was going on.

Her shocked scream brought everyone else crowding into the shop. Like Vera they were startled to see that Rita was already in there, cringing behind the counter. Her hand was over her mouth and she was shaking uncontrollably as she watched, eyes wide, as Eddy and his father traded blows with unbridled ferocity. Eddy was hurling abuse, Michael Quinn was cursing him and threatening to kill him.

'Stop it, stop it, stop it,' Vera's raised voice cut through the racket. As she sprang forward, hanging onto Eddy's arm, Rita's father, Steve and Liam all grabbed at Michael. He struggled maniacally, but they finally overpowered him, all of them ending up in a pile on the floor.

Eddy shook Vera off him as he went over to Rita. Stiffening against his embrace she covered her face with her hands. 'Get away, get away from me,' she begged in a hoarse whisper. 'Don't touch me! Ever!'

'Please Rita, tell me what happened . . .'

'You know what happened. Your father . . . he's an animal!' She moved across to where her own father was standing looking embarrassed and bemused. 'Take me home, Dad. Now!' she pleaded. 'I'll never come here again,' she sobbed as he put a protective arm around her shoulders and held her close.

'I think Liam and me had better go as well,' Joan told Vera. 'You coming Steve?'

Steve hesitated, looking from Joan to Vera in bewilderment. 'Do you want me to stay, Vee? Is there anything I can do to help?'

'I don't know,' Vera shivered. 'I don't know what's happening, it's like a bad dream.'

'I'll hang on for a bit,' Steve told his sister. 'There must be something I can do to help you, Vee,' he added anxiously.

'Well, if you could you take Benny up to his room,' she said hesitantly, 'this is no place for him and it is time he was in bed.'

'Yes . . . of course I will.' He reached out and took Benny by the hand.

'OK.' Joan slipped her hand through Liam's arm. 'See you at home later on then, Steve,' she called over her shoulder.

Vera waited until Joan had gone before she turned back to her father and Eddy.

'If you two have quite finished perhaps we can sort out what's wrong,' she said scathingly.

'Do you need an explanation of why I thumped him, the dirty old bugger!' Eddy snarled. 'He'd got his hand down the front of Rita's dress and she was fighting him off like a wild cat.'

'Rubbish,' their father slurred, 'she was all for it until you came barging in, and then she pretended she didn't know what was happening.'

'You foul-mouthed old bugger!' Eddy was about to lunge at his father again, but Vera stepped between them.

'You've disgraced yourselves in front of my friends quite enough for one night. You've ruined all my hard work.'

'He has, not me,' Eddy cried. 'You didn't think I was going to stand by and watch him maul my girlfriend, did you?'

'Eddy, why don't you go for a walk with Steve,' she suggested.

'And leave you here on your own with him?' He scowled, looking contemptuously at his father. 'Not after the way he's behaved tonight. And God knows what Rita's parents will have to say about this; or Rita, if I ever get to talk to her again,' he added gloomily.

Vera didn't know what to say to try and comfort Eddy. She felt so sorry that this had happened to mar what should have been a wonderful night for him. In addition she knew that Rita had been expecting him to announce their engagement. Now it all seemed to be in ruins. She could well understand if Rita never wanted to speak to him again.

She knew how desperately embarrassed she herself felt about what had happened, and yet it must be twenty times worse for Eddy. And she couldn't even start to think how Rita was feeling. It was horrendous that their father had done such a thing. Rita must be wondering how she will ever face him or Eddy again. Perhaps Eddy should go to her right away and try and comfort her. Vera felt sure that that is what she would want if she was in Rita's situation.

Could Eddy bring himself to do that, though, she wondered. He was in such a raging temper that it was probably asking too much of him. One part of him must want to kill his father, whilst the other part must be so deeply ashamed about what had happened that he'd have no words that would be adequate to put things right between himself and Rita.

Surely, though, Rita would see that it wasn't Eddy's fault. He hadn't even been in the house at the time! If I hadn't sent him out for more beer then it might never have happened, Vera thought despairingly. Blaming herself wouldn't help, though; that wouldn't put matters right. Only one person would be able to do that, as far as Rita was concerned, and that was Eddy.

'Rita will understand if you go and see her right away and comfort her,' Vera told him. 'She'll understand that it was all the beer Dad had been drinking that made him behave in such a way. After all, he's old enough to be her father!'

'Don't you think I know all that,' Eddy said wearily. 'But he's probably ruined my chances with Rita . . . for good! I'd like to hammer him! He does nothing but cause trouble. He makes all our lives hell.'

'Leave him to me, I'll talk to him,' Vera said quietly.

'No. After what happened I don't trust him to behave himself even with you,' Eddy protested.

'He will. You go and see Rita. She needs you to reassure her that everything is all right between the two of you. That's all that matters to her, not the drunken fumblings of a stupid old man.'

Chapter Fifteen

Despite all her brave talk, Vera was scared. She was afraid that Eddy would leave home after what had happened with Rita, and she was worried about her father's reaction when he sobered up and remembered what he'd done. He was bound to feel ashamed of his behaviour, but, knowing him and his terrible moods, she was on tenterhooks in case he might take it out on her and Benny.

Vera was also concerned about how Rita was going to react once she was over the initial shock. Common sense told her that Rita would be too scared ever to come to the house again, but what worried her more was that Rita might not want to collect Benny from school any more.

He was big enough to walk to and from school himself, of course. It was simply that remembering how her mother had always needed to protect her and Eddy from their father's moods she was afraid that Benny would have no one to look out for him once he arrived home. He'd once again be expected to help sort out the soles and he would be at the mercy of their dad's temper if he made any mistakes.

She could hardly tell Benny all this, or explain her worries to him. Even though he had witnessed the fight between his dad and Eddy, she doubted if he was old enough to understand the reason for it.

She should have put Benny to bed long before the fight had started, but they had all been enjoying themselves so much that she'd thought he would have hated to be made to go off upstairs on his own.

Her fears were justified. Rita refused point blank ever to go near the Quinns' home again. She even told Eddy that she felt they ought to stop seeing each other, for the present at any rate.

Eddy was heartbroken. He refused to speak to his father, or even to sit at the same table as him. The atmosphere was so fraught that Vera felt like she was stuck in the middle of it all. What worried her most, though, was Benny's future.

He seemed to accept the fact that Rita was gone from his life and stoically took himself to school and came home on his own when school ended. But Vera wondered what he did when he got home. Although she asked him time and time again, she never managed to get a satisfactory answer. He usually ignored her question or shrugged his shoulders and went on playing with one of his toys.

Whenever she pressed him further and asked, 'Do you stay in the shop with Dad sorting out the soles?' he always shook his head.

Another thing that mystified her was that often when she was out delivering the boots and shoes with Benny, men she'd never seen or spoken to in her life would speak to him or ruffle his thick curls as they walked by. Whenever this happened he would respond with a smile as though he knew them. Puzzled, she mentioned it to Eddy, but he wasn't able to throw any light on the matter.

'Can you try and find out,' she begged. 'I'm sure there's something going on.'

'Like what?'

'I don't know,' she said worriedly. 'I've got my suspicions, though.'

'Go on, tell me!'

'Don't laugh at me, then!'

'Of course I won't. I'm as worried as you are. It seems obvious that he's not being made to sort soles like I was,' Eddy muttered, 'so what is he doing?'

'He's not delivering boots and shoes either, yet often when I get home, if it's been raining, his hair is wet, so he's going out somewhere.'

'His hair would get wet walking home from school.'

'Yes, but it would be dry by the time I got home, that's well over an hour later.'

'He could be playing out with other kids. He must have friends who play out in the street or in the back jiggers after school's over.'

'I've asked him, but he says not.'

'So what do you think is going on?'

Vera looked uncomfortable. 'I think it has something to do with betting.'

For a moment Eddy didn't answer, he simply stared at her in disbelief. 'That's illegal!'

'Of course it is . . . that's why I'm so worried.'

'What makes you think that might be what it is, anyway?'

Vera shrugged. 'I found him crying when I came in the other night and when I asked what was wrong he said he'd lost a ticket. I didn't know what he was on about and then later on I found this piece of card that had become caught up in the lining of his trouser pocket. When I took it out I saw it was one of the tickets that dad uses when he labels the boots and shoes he's repaired, but it had some weird letters and numbers on it. It made me suspicious.'

'Have you still got it?'

'No!' She shook her head. 'Benny was so happy when we found it that I let him have it. It was only afterwards that I wondered if it was some sort of betting slip.'

'Christ! I hope not. It's just the sort of mad trick Dad would play, though. I told you ages ago that I thought Dad's started betting and no one would ever dream of suspecting a young kid of being a go-between. The police are always on the look out for men acting as runners. In fact, they go to all sorts of lengths to try and catch them.'

'You mean they wouldn't give a little kid like Benny a second thought!'

'Exactly! So, if the old man is using him to carry bets then the crafty old bugger is taking one hell of a risk. He could land himself inside.'

'Never mind about him, what happens if Benny is caught?' Vera said worriedly. 'They'd probably say he was in need of care and attention, and might even put him in a reform school. Have you thought about that?'

Eddy pulled a face. 'We've got to find out for

sure and stop him doing it. If I face Dad with it, pretend I have proof, then it might scare the old fool into stopping it.'

'The shock of you speaking to him again will scare him if nothing else does.' Vera grinned.

Eddy didn't respond to her quip. 'What, apart from that ticket with the letters and figures on it, makes you think that Dad might be using Benny as a runner?'

Vera shrugged. 'All the men who seem to know who he is when we are out.'

'Perhaps we should try and find out a bit more and be sure of our facts before we tackle Dad,' Eddy said uncomfortably. 'There'd be hell to pay if we were the ones in the wrong.'

The matter was decided for them a few nights later. Vera arrived home to find Benny almost hysterical and her father in a towering rage.

'What's happened? What's he done?' Vera asked worriedly

'Silly little sod has made a cock-up of an errand I sent him on.'

'What sort of errand? Was it delivering a pair of boots?'

'No, it wasn't delivering any bloody boots. I simply told him to take a note to some chap up the road. He's seven years old, for Christ's sake, he's old enough to go to school, so he should be able to deliver a simple message like that.'

'Depends what the message was and how far he had to go,' Vera prevaricated.

'As far as Great Homer Street and then hand a piece of paper to a chap.'

'So what went wrong.'

'He lost the bloody note, didn't he.'

'I didn't lose it,' Benny sobbed, his breath coming in great gulps. 'It was stolen from me.'

'Stolen?' Vera knelt down in front of the little boy and gathered him into her arms. 'Who stole it then, Benny? Was it a bigger boy?'

He rubbed his hand across his tear-stained face angrily. 'I keep telling Dad it was a man. He was waiting out in the jigger and as I ran past him he grabbed at me . . .' His tears choked the rest of the sentence.

Vera hugged him tighter. 'Was . . . was that all he did?' she asked hesitantly.

Benny nodded.

'He simply took the note from you, nothing else? He didn't hurt you?'

'Only my arm. He twisted my arm to make me give him the note I was holding.'

Vera stood up and faced her father. 'Was this a betting slip?' she demanded stonily.

Michael Quinn was so taken by surprise that guilt showed on his face.

'What the bloody hell does it matter what it was,' he barked.

Vera chewed on her lower lip thoughtfully. 'Then in that case, if it was some innocent message, it won't matter if we tell the police what has happened.'

'Tell the scuffers! Don't talk so bloody daft, girl. What do you think they are going to do about a trivial thing like this?'

'This man, whoever he was, attacked a little boy

147

who was doing nothing wrong. That's a crime. If they catch him, they'll punish him.'

Tight lipped, Michael Quinn turned away. 'Forget the whole bloody matter,' he ordered. He moved to the polishing machine, picked up a boot and began operating the foot pedal so that the noise made talking difficult.

'Take him away out of my sight and stop him snivelling before I thump his skull and give him something to really bleat about,' he rasped nodding towards Benny.

'Thump his skull! That's your solution to everything, isn't it!'

They all looked round in surprise as Eddy came through into the shop from the back room. 'Don't bother to try and explain,' he said quickly, cutting Vera short as she began to speak. 'I've heard all I want to hear. You don't want the police brought in, do you Dad, because you're using young Benny here as a runner.'

Michael's face darkened. 'What the hell are you going on about?'

'You know quite well what I'm going on about and that what I'm saying is the truth. I've got witnesses to prove it. That harmless little message that bloke took off Benny was a bunch of betting slips. You've got men coming in here regularly under the pretence of bringing their boots and shoes in for repair, but it's actually betting slips they are bringing in. You bundle them all up and send Benny along to Hillson's in Great Homer Street with them.'

'If they're other people's bets then why on earth

are you doing all this and taking such risks?' Vera exclaimed aghast.

'I'll tell you why he's doing it,' Eddy said before his father could reply. 'He gets a cut from the bookie and then another handout from the punters when they win! Isn't that right, Dad?'

'You mean you risk our Benny being caught and sent to a reform school so that you can make yourself a few bob on the side,' Vera accused him angrily. 'What sort of father are you?'

'One who struggles to keep a roof over your heads and food in your bellies.'

'Don't come that with us, we know different,' Vera told him, her blue eyes flashing. 'We pay our way, so it doesn't cost you anything to clothe and feed me and Eddy. What little housekeeping money you hand over barely covers what you eat, and certainly isn't enough to keep Benny,' she told him.

'All you're doing is putting more money in your own pocket so that you can go out and get drunk every night of the week,' Eddy said contemptuously.

'Don't you dare talk to me like that, not as long as you're living under my roof,' Michael Quinn blustered.

'I wouldn't stay under your roof another minute if I didn't feel I had to to make sure you don't mistreat my sister and little brother,' Eddy told him.

'The lot of you've always been well looked after, cared for and had a good home,' their dad thundered.

'We did most of the time when Mam was alive,' Vera conceded. 'And that was only because she went without to make sure that we had everything we needed.'

'That'll do! One more word from either of you and I'll give the pair of you a sound thrashing, one you won't forget in a hurry.'

'That's right, throw your weight around,' Eddy taunted him. 'I haven't forgotten the beatings you gave me when I was growing up, or the number of times you thumped my skull. Mam's better off out of it. You led her a dog's life right up to the day when you pushed her down the stairs,' he added heatedly.

Chapter Sixteen

Vera and Eddy were unsure what to do about the betting situation. Although he refused to admit to it, they were pretty sure that this was what their father was up to, and they were worried about what the consequences might be if the police found out.

Michael Quinn's temper and mood changes were erratic enough as it was, and knowing that when Benny came home from school he was there on his own with him every evening, until Vera got in from work, was worrying enough. If he was using him as a runner, then if he thought that Benny had been the one who'd told them he might retaliate in some way.

Vera knew that he was continuing to use his punishment of swiping his clenched knuckles across the top of Benny's head, the same as he'd done when Eddy was Benny's age. When she'd been combing Benny's hair she'd felt him flinch and draw his breath in sharply.

When she'd questioned Benny he'd denied that their dad was still thumping him, so she'd waited until he was asleep and then investigated further. As she'd gently parted the thick curls at the top of his head she'd felt enraged at the sight of the huge lumps she found there.

Eddy was equally concerned when she told him about the state of Benny's head. He was sure it was all linked to the betting slips in some way. Although he knew he was taking a risk, he had gone directly to the manager at Hillson's to ask if Benny Quinn was bringing in slips.

'What the hell has it got to do with you,' the bookie asked belligerently, wiping the back of his hand across his mouth and staring hostilely at Eddy.

'I'm worried about him, that's all,' Eddy said nonchalantly. 'He's my little brother and I wondered what he was getting up to running around the streets after school.'

'He won't come to much harm. He's a bright lad is your young Benny, and he knows all the streets and back jiggers off Scotland Road like the back of his hand.'

Eddy didn't know what to say. His mind was working overtime. The bookie obviously knew Benny, and his comments were confirming what he didn't want to hear. Benny was definitely being used to collect and deliver bets.

'In my opinion he should be playing with his mates and kicking a ball around,' he commented.

'You can't always make a youngster do what you want him to,' the man said cryptically.

Vera and Eddy brooded over what he had been told, but before they'd decided what action to take a policeman arrived at the shop just as Michael Quinn was about to close.

'A pile of betting slips have been handed in at the station,' he told Michael Quinn.

'So what's that got to do with me? If you don't mind I'm shutting up shop for the night, so will you push off.'

'Not until you've answered a few questions.'

'Can't you come back tomorrow when I'm open, my grub's on the table.'

From the room behind the shop, Vera and Eddy could hear what was going on. Quickly, Vera opened the door and slipped into the shop on the pretext of telling her dad that they were all waiting to start their meal.

'Evening, Miss. I'm PC Walters from Atholl Road Police Station. This won't take more than a minute, but there's some questions I need to ask.'

'She knows nothing about it,' Michael Quinn said abruptly. 'Go on, start without me,' he ordered, pushing Vera back towards the living room. 'I'll only be a minute.' Turning to the policeman, he again asked him if he'd come back in the morning.

'If it is only going to take a minute then why not get it over and done with right now, Dad,' Vera suggested.

'Thank you, Miss! It's about some betting slips. The cards they've been written out on originally came from here. The words 'Quinn's Boot and Shoe Repairer's' is on all of them.'

Michael Quinn frowned. 'I issue tickets on all the repairs I handle. Nothing to do with me if the ticket has been used again for some other purpose.'

'We've also been informed a short time ago that someone saw a man grab hold of a little boy, in the jowler that runs between the back of this shop and Great Homer Street. The lad was about seven or eight with fair, curly hair. Was that your little boy who was attacked, Mr Quinn?'

Before their father could answer, Eddy pushed Benny into the room. 'Go on Benny, tell the Bobby what happened in the jigger,' he ordered.

'Perhaps we should leave it for now,' Vera said worriedly as Benny wriggled away from Eddy and grabbed at her hand.

'I'm sorry, Miss, but it is my duty. The name of this shop is on all of these tickets. Since the information on them appears to indicate that they have been used as betting slips we are trying to find out how this came about.'

Michael Quinn seemed to suddenly have a change of heart. 'I think I may be able to help you officer. We had a bit of a celebration here recently, a party because my son Eddy finished his apprenticeship. Amongst the people here was a young chap called Steve Frith . . .'

Michael Quinn paused, raising his eyebrows knowingly, leaving the police officer to draw his own conclusions. He ignored Vera's sharp intake of breath and her quick denial that Steve could be implicated in any way.

'So you're saying that you think this chap Frith has something to do with these betting slips and that he was the one who grabbed your little boy?'

'It's possible . . . I've heard rumours. Perhaps you should cut along and have a word with him and leave me to shut up shop for the night,' Michael Quinn said dismissively.

'Hold on, Dad. Steve couldn't possibly have anything to do with this!' Vera protested heatedly.

PC Walters looked puzzled. 'Was the man who attacked you someone you knew son?' he asked, turning to Benny.

Benny nodded timidly.

'Was his name Steve Frith?'

'Speak up, son,' Michael Quinn said brusquely. 'Tell the policeman that's who it was.'

'This is absolutely ridiculous,' Vera stormed. 'It couldn't possibly have been Steve.'

'Why do you repeatedly say that?' PC Walters frowned. 'Is there something you should be telling me?'

Vera looked nervously at her father. 'I know it wasn't Steve Frith who grabbed hold of Benny because I know Steve too well. We . . . we're going out together.'

PC Walters closed his notebook and put it back into his pocket. 'Thank you for your help, Miss. We'll have to look into this,' he said ominously. 'The whole thing will have to be investigated further, Mr Quinn, and since your name is on the tickets we'll get back to you, you can be sure of that. Yes, we'll certainly need an explanation on how your shop's name was on all those betting slips,' he repeated as he rammed his helmet back on his head.

The moment he had locked the shop door behind PC Walters, Michael Quinn turned angrily on his family. 'What the hell are you lot playing at?' he hissed furiously. 'Do you want to see me in jail and you all out in the street without a roof over your head? If the law can pin a betting offence on me that is what will happen. And as for this silly little bugger,' he shook his first threateningly at Benny, 'if he opens his trap and lands me in it, I'll see he ends up in reform school and no two ways about it!'

'You're wicked,' Vera said contemptuously. 'Is that how little you care about your family? Save your own neck and damn the rest of us. And why mention Steve Frith's name? He has nothing to do with any of this.'

'Then he'll have no trouble proving that he's innocent, will he. It gets the cops off our backs while we sort our story out.'

'So we're right, then, are we?' Eddy interposed. 'You are involved in some sort of betting ring and you are using little Benny as a runner.'

'You want to watch your mouth, whacker!' Michael Quinn scowled. 'I can kick you out any time I like.'

'Don't worry, I'll be going soon enough. I've already told you I'd have gone before now if it wasn't for Vera and Benny. I have to make sure that they're safe.'

A dark flush spread over their father's face. 'What's that supposed to mean?' he snarled.

'You know perfectly well what I mean. After the way you behaved with Rita I wouldn't trust you as far as I could throw you. I also know that you thump young Benny across the head when you're in one of your foul moods, too. I know how much it hurts because it's exactly what you did to me when I was that age.'

'I'll thump your skull again right now if I have any more of your bloody lip!'

'No you won't,' Eddy told him confidently. 'You wouldn't dare. Take me on and I'll come out on top, whether you're sober or fighting drunk like you were at our party.'

'Beat me? A runt like you!' his father scoffed.

'I may not be as tall as you, but I'm a damned sight stronger, and I'll prove it any time you like,' Eddy told him calmly.

'Look, you two, instead of bickering like a couple of rough-necks, shouldn't we be discussing how to get out of this mess?' Vera asked quietly.

'You mean we should be dreaming up a pack of lies to save his skin,' Eddy muttered contemptuously.

'I was thinking more about protecting Benny. If they prove he has been a runner, no matter who it was for, they'll say he is in need of care and guidance, and you know what that means. When they look into his family background they're bound to feel they have to take him into care because he has no mother.'

'There's plenty of kids around here without mothers, though. Compared to most of them our Benny is well looked after. He's got boots on his feet, and even if his clothes are patched and darned they're always clean, and so is he. No, I don't think he will be taken away. Not quite so sure about Dad though. When I've finished having my say they may well think that it would be better for all of us if he was banged up.'

The officious hammering on the shop door

silenced them all. Squinting through the gap of the half-open door between the living room and the shop beyond, Vera could make out the burly figure of PC Walters outside. 'He's back!' she gasped in a frightened voice, 'and he's got someone with him.'

'You go and let them in and be careful what you say,' Michael Quinn said, nodding towards Eddy.

Vera was taken aback when they came through into the living room and she saw that it was Steve Frith who was with PC Walters. She tried to catch his eye, but he studiously avoided her stare.

'Is this the man who grabbed hold of you, sonny?' PC Walters asked in a kindly tone, speaking directly to Benny.

'No! That's Steve and he's Vera's friend.' Tears filled Benny's big blue eyes as he violently shook his head and held on tightly to Vera's hand. 'It wasn't him, it was another man.'

'You're not going to take a young kid's word for it, are you?' Michael Quinn laughed.

'Well, he has confirmed what Mr Frith told me.'

'Oh yes, what was that? Some cock and bull yarn I imagine.'

'Mr Frith has told me that he's a very close friend of your daughter and that they are going out together.'

'And you believed him?' Michael Quinn said scornfully. Then he spun round and faced Vera. 'Go on, tell him it's not true?'

Vera hesitated. She knew the predicament she was in and that unless she was careful she would antagonise her father. Yet Steve's good name, and perhaps even his freedom, was in jeopardy if she said what her dad wanted her to say.

'Well?' Her father's keen blue eyes glinted sharply.

Vera took a deep breath. 'Steve is a friend, a very special friend,' she pronounced, her voice shaking.

'So it seems highly unlikely that he was the one who grabbed young Benny, or that he dropped the betting slips that seem to incriminate you, Mr Quinn,' PC Walters commented as he walked towards the door.

He paused briefly. 'You'll be hearing more about this,' he called back over his shoulder.

Michael Quinn waited until the shop door slammed behind PC Walters before turning viciously on Vera, his face livid.

'Why tell trumped up lies to save that sod's neck?' he snarled, nodding towards Steve Frith. Without waiting for her to reply, he went on, 'You're to stop seeing him right now. Understand?'

'You know very well that Steve had nothing to do with what happened to Benny, so how could you be so wicked as to imply that it was him?' Vera railed. 'Do you know the trouble he could have been in?'

'A few months inside the Waldorf Astoria would have kept him out of our way,' her father muttered, glowering at Steve.

'Ruin his life, more likely!' Vera said bitterly.

'It would have kept him away from you, though,' her father retorted grimly. 'I don't want to see him around here again and I don't want to find out that you're meeting him on the sly either, so he can piss off, right now,' he added savagely.

'Why don't you want us seeing each other?' Steve questioned. 'I have a good job, and I've never been in any trouble in my life.'

'Don't give me any of your lip, I saw the way you were all over my daughter at the party,' Michael Quinn roared. 'You'll put her in the family way and then sod off before any of us know what's happening. That will be another mouth for me to slug my guts out trying to bring up,' he railed.

'Stop it, stop it!' Vera clamped her hands over her ears. 'Stop saying such dreadful things.' She reached out and took Steve's hand. 'I love him!'

'That's right and I love her. We're getting married as soon as Vee's old enough to do so without having to ask your permission.'

'Certainly no point in you asking because you wouldn't get it,' Michael told them scathingly.

'There's nothing to stop us eloping,' Steve declared. 'Isn't that right, Vera?'

As she opened her mouth to reply, her father's eyes narrowed.

'If she clears off with you then I'll stick Benny into some sort of home or orphanage the very next day,' he warned.

Caught up in a new dilemma, Vera looked from one to the other of them beseechingly.

Steve Frith shook his head in disbelief. 'He wouldn't do that, not with his own little kid.'

Vera shivered as she looked up at her father and saw the cold challenge in his eyes as they met hers.

'He would,' she said in a dull whisper. 'He'd do it all right. I can't condemn Benny to a fate like that.'

Steve stood his ground. 'He doesn't mean it, he's only bluffing,' he insisted.

'Steve, much as I want to be with you I could never let that happen to Benny,' she said dispiritedly.

Michael laughed cynically. 'My daughter knows that when I say something I damn well mean it. She knows I'm not bluffing.'

'Come on, Vera? You're not going to let him bully you like this are you?' There was deep anguish in Steve Frith's voice as he pleaded with her.

Vera shook her head in despair, tears making rivulets down her ashen cheeks. 'It's no good, Steve. I could never desert little Benny.'

'What about if we take him with us . . .'

'Take him! Take him with you? What do you think he is, a bag of potatoes or a sack of coal that you can pick up and take without so much as a by-your-leave. I'm the kid's bloody father . . .'

'And such a caring father that you'd stick him in a home rather than look after him yourself,' sneered Steve.

Michael laughed harshly. 'Our Vera's made her choice. She wants to stay put so the best thing you can do is sling your hook. Don't come round here ever again because you're not welcome,' he pronounced triumphantly. 'Now bugger off and leave me and mine to get on with our lives.'

Chapter Seventeen

Vera tried hard to hide her tears and despair over losing Steve Frith from her friends and family. She stubbornly refused to let her father see how upset she was, although she deeply resented his callous interference.

She missed Steve dreadfully. Surely he could see the predicament she was in! He loved her, so he must understand how important it was that she made sure Benny was safe. She didn't blame him for staying away, not after the way her father had treated him, and the things he'd said to him, but they could always have arranged to meet somewhere else, he didn't have to come to the house. They'd been so close that she was deeply hurt that he had simply walked away.

At work, Joan Frith wasn't exactly hostile, but she was certainly very cool. Vera wanted to talk to her about what had happened, why she and Steve had broken up, but she couldn't find the right words to do so. She couldn't explain without disclosing things about her father that she preferred to keep private.

She loved Steve and now that she knew he loved her too she felt devastated, but she simply couldn't abandon her little brother. Benny was so vulnerable. Although he'd grown up in Scotland Road he wasn't nearly as tough as most of the children of his own age.

That was her fault, she thought sadly. She had probably been too protective after her mother died, but she had felt it was necessary to show him all the love and affection she could. As a result, he was far more dependent on her than he should be.

Night after night Vera cried herself to sleep with tears of frustration and despair. She found she was missing her mother more than she would have believed possible. She longed to be able to confide in her about her love for Steve Frith. She needed her not only to console her, but to tell her how to face the future without him.

At work, an even deeper rift developed between her and Joan Frith when Joan told her brusquely that Steve had packed up his job in Liverpool and gone off to Australia.

'Mam cried buckets when he told her what he was going to do. She tried her best to get him to change his mind, but he wouldn't listen to a word she was saying,' Joan said bitterly.

Vera was heartbroken by the news. If Steve had truly loved her, as much as she loved him, she thought sadly, then surely he wouldn't have done such a thing. He would have stayed close and waited to see if her dad would change his mind, not only about them going out together, but about them getting married, too.

Australia was on the other side of the world. It would be years before Steve would have enough money to come home again. No matter how hard she saved, she'd never be able to afford to go and find him.

It was all so permanent. It meant that their relationship was completely over. She knew that the only thing she could do was dry her eyes and get on with her life, but it was easier said than done. Seeing Joan and Liam Kelly together constantly reminded her that it was all over between her and Steve and made her feel more desolate than ever.

She spent more and more time with Benny. She went somewhere with him every evening, whether there were boots to be delivered or not. She refused to let him out on his own in case he came to some harm.

'You're making a right nincompoop out of that kid,' her father told her scornfully. 'Let him stand on his own two feet! He's almost eight, old enough to do things on his own without you holding his hand.'

Vera ignored him. When her father grumbled about the dirty dishes in the sink, or that his shirt wasn't ironed properly, or anything else, she simply shrugged and took no notice.

His constant bickering, and his anger, washed over her. It was as if there was a wall between her and the rest of the world, one that only Benny could penetrate.

When Michael found that his repetitive grumbling and shouting at Vera had no effect, he craftily tried a different ruse to bring his daughter to heel.

In the weeks that followed, when she came home from work Vera found he was rarely on his own in the shop. A chap called Bill Martin, one of his drinking companions, was usually there with him.

Vera didn't like the man who had suddenly become so friendly with her father. He was thickset, of medium height, and had a pock-marked face and small dark eyes. His scant brown hair was receding, and he had a thin, pencil moustache, which she thought not only looked ridiculous, but drew attention to the cruel twist of his thin lips.

Vera hated the way he leered at her and the suggestive compliments he made about her appearance. Even more, she disliked the fact that he continually tried to curry favour with Benny, and win him over with gifts of sweets and toys.

Encouraged by Michael, he would even offer to accompany her and Benny when they went off to do the deliveries.

'Could you give them a hand, Bill,' her father would suggest. 'Rather a load for the two of them to manage.'

'There's no need, I'll take Benny's old pram,' Vera would say quickly, hoping to discourage him.

'You don't want to be seen out pushing that,' Bill would laugh. 'People might start getting the wrong idea,' he'd add as his eyes raked over her from top to toe.

She knew it brought the colour rushing to her face and she resented his smug laugh in response.

Vera found that the more she tried to snub Bill Martin, the more persistent he became. It worried her that her father encouraged him so much and seemed to find nothing wrong with his attitude towards her.

Soon it led to rows between the two of them.

Her father became angry when she constantly rejected Bill's help, and told her to mind her manners.

'Manners? My manners?' she questioned angrily. 'He's the one who needs to mind his manners. I don't like him, in fact I can't stand him, and the sooner he realises that and leaves me alone the better.'

'You'll have a long wait then you silly bint because Bill Martin wants to marry you. What's more to the point, I've told him he can.'

'You've done what?' The colour drained from her face and she felt herself shaking. 'Me, have Bill Martin as my husband! I'd sooner die.'

Her answer infuriated Michael. 'You'll do as you're bloody well told, so tell him "yes" when he asks you to marry him, and do it with a bloody smile on your face or I'll . . .'

'Thump my bloody skull?' she sneered. 'You can thump it all you like, but it won't make me change my mind.'

The thought of being made to marry Bill Martin haunted Vera. She had nightmares about the situation and woke in the middle of the night, sweat pouring from her as she imagined that she was already committed to him. It was as if she could feel his rough, unshaven face pressing against her own, and smell his beery breath. She could even feel those cruel thin lips pressing down on hers, taking possession of her mouth and stopping her breathing, preventing her from screaming out for help.

Even during the day, he played on her mind. She became nervous and jumpy. She kept seeing men she thought were him in the street, or reflected in shop windows.

As she waited in trepidation for Bill to ask her to marry him, as her father had said he would, she planned what she would say to him, rehearsing the words in her head over and over again. She wanted him to know she meant it when she said that her mind was made up, and that she would never even consider such a proposition.

Bill Martin was too astute to fall into that trap, though. He had the tenacity and patience of a wily old fox. He knew how tense Vera was and he intended biding his time. He resolved to pick his moment, and when he did ask her it would be at a time when it was the most difficult for her to turn him down.

He was waiting for the right opportunity. It would come, he told himself. It would result from some good turn he did for either young Benny or Michael Quinn, something that put Vera into his indebtedness. When that happened she wouldn't be able to refuse his proposal.

He knew Eddy was watching him like a hawk, but he considered him to be of no importance. Old man Quinn was on his side, and that was half the battle. He didn't mind waiting.

He took special delight in seeing Vera as often as possible and watching her every movement, knowing that one day she would be his. She was a prize so well worth waiting for, he gloated, since she was growing more attractive by the day.

One of the reasons he was so confident that she would soon be his was because he knew she wasn't seeing anyone else. Her old man was making sure of that. She was the prize Michael Quinn was bestowing on him for not squealing to the police about the betting slips. Instead he'd gone one better, he'd tipped them off with the name of another bookie's runner and the poor sod had ended up being arrested.

It gave Bill Martin a warped feeling of power to see how nervous Vera was whenever he was around. When she and Benny set out each evening to do the deliveries he would sometimes follow them. He kept at a distance and chuckled to himself as he saw how she looked back nervously every few hundred yards to check where he was.

He never approached her, or even spoke to her in the street, only tailed her. He liked to be near enough to watch the fear on her face when she looked over her shoulder. He made sure, though, that he was never close enough that she could call out to a passer-by, or a scuffer, and say that she was afraid of being molested.

His intention to scare Vera began to pay off. She became increasingly jittery, began to lose weight, and was short-tempered, even with Benny.

Michael Quinn noticed the changes in his daughter, but he put it down to disappointment that Bill hadn't popped the question. The delay worried him, he wondered if Bill Martin had gone off the idea, or whether he had hinted about marriage to Vera and she had turned him down.

Bill was a useful ally, and he could foresee a

great many lucrative deals they could do together once they were both certain that they could trust each other completely.

If Bill became a member of the family, Michael reasoned, there would be no possibility of him squealing if things ever went wrong again. Once he and Vera were safely hitched then he'd take him into his confidence. He was pretty sure that Bill also had some interesting sidelines he'd be willing to share with his new father-in-law, so the outcome could be beneficial all round.

Impatient to start developing some of the schemes he'd already hatched in his mind, Michael finally asked Bill if he'd broached the subject of marriage with Vera.

'Not yet! Don't rush things.'

'What're you playing at, you silly bugger. Ask her now while she's still missing that Steve Frith, that way you'll have no trouble getting her to agree.'

'I'm not so sure about that, she's a strong-minded little bitch. Leave me to my cat and mouse technique.'

'Cat and mouse technique? What the hell's that?'

'Tail her, frighten her, break her spirit, then strike when she's at her lowest ebb.'

'Christ! You sound as if you're game hunting, not courting.'

Bill Martin laughed sourly. 'I want her to be docile on our wedding night. I don't want a kick in the balls the moment I get her into bed.'

Michael Quinn frowned. For one brief moment he wondered if he was doing the right thing in telling Vera she was to marry this man. Vera was his daughter, after all. He thought back to the days before he'd gone in the army, when Vee had been a sweet little toddler, with a rosebud mouth that would suddenly expand into the sweetest of smiles. She'd been a little beauty with her dark hair and the biggest and brightest blue eyes he'd ever seen.

She was still a looker. Tall and slim, with a good shape to her. She was a grafter too. She doted on young Benny, and had been a real little mother to him since Annie died.

He knew he was hard on her sometimes, but his life had been full of frustration since he came back from the war so it was only natural that he took it out on her. Things would have been different if Annie was still alive, but since Vera was the only woman in his life it followed that she had to bear the brunt of his moods.

For all his criticism of her, he thought Vera was worth two of Eddy. She had guts, whereas Eddy had always been a wimp. She was taller and more spirited than her brother. He had to admit, though, that Eddy had broadened out a fair bit, as he'd found to his cost during their last tangle.

Vera waited on tenterhooks for Bill Martin to ask her to marry him, but when he didn't do so she began to think that it was all some kind of evil threat on her father's part.

Gradually she resumed her normal way of life. She continued to go on deliveries with Benny, but that was because she was concerned about his safety. It wasn't Bill she worried about, but the children of the man who'd finally been sent to prison for six months over the betting slips.

Things came unexpectedly to a head in September, on Benny's eighth birthday. Vera had put on a special tea for him, but it was only to be her, Eddy and her father there. She'd hoped that Rita would have come as well, but she still staunchly refused to set foot in their house since the evening their father had molested her.

As she laid out the spread – jelly, blancmange and a sponge cake with white icing that had chocolate grated over the top – she wondered if her dad had bought Benny a present like she'd begged him to do.

The moment Eddy arrived home from work, and had given Benny the football he'd been longing for, she made the tea. She knew her father wouldn't want to join them and she suspected that Eddy would want to get their party over as soon as possible since it was his night for seeing Rita.

She was quite taken aback when, within minutes of Eddy leaving, Bill Martin came through from the shop with a present for Benny. When he saw the clockwork train, complete with rails and a set of carriages to run on it, Benny was overawed. He'd never had a present like it. Excitedly, he thanked Bill and asked if he could play with it right away.

'Of course you can, whack,' Bill told him. 'Come on, let's clear a space on the floor and I'll fix the rails for you . . . that's if it is all right with Vera.'

Vera wanted to say no, to ask him to leave and

take his present with him, but she realised that her father had followed Bill into the room. She felt as if her privacy had been invaded. Seeing Bill Martin in the shop was bad enough, but she resented him coming uninvited into their living room. She bit back her refusal, though, as she saw the ecstatic look on Benny's face as he helped unpack his new present.

'Perhaps you should finish your tea first, Benny,' she suggested.

He shook his head. 'I've had enough,' he said dismissively, his entire attention focussed on the train set.

An hour later, Michael Quinn had finished reading through the *Liverpool Echo* and was impatient for his own meal.

'Come on, Vera, pack young Benny off to bed and do me and Bill a fry-up,' he ordered.

Benny objected. He wanted to go on playing with his new toy, but their father was tired of him being underfoot. Vera knew the signs, knew her dad's expansive mood was about to revert to a skull-thumping session.

'I'll take him upstairs while you see to the food,' Bill suggested.

Vera hesitated. Benny was used to her putting him to bed, she wasn't sure how he would react. She also wanted to avoid Bill invading their home any further, or getting even closer to Benny.

'It's all right,' she said quickly. 'Leave him to play, I'll cook something for you two and then I'll take him up.'

'What's wrong with you, girl, are you deaf?' her

father muttered irritably. 'It's his bedtime ...
NOW! Go on, you take him upstairs, Bill.'

'No!' Vera laid a hand on Benny's shoulder, pro-
pelling him towards the stairs. 'I said I would see
to him. If you want him in bed first then you can
wait for your fry-up.'

Bill leaned against the door and pursed his lips
in a silent whistle, then at a nod from Michael he
quietly followed Vera up the stairs.

Benny was overtired and sulky. He wanted to stay
and play with his new train set and he resented
being sent to bed. Vera did her best to calm him
down, but she knew she wasn't being as patient
as usual because her own nerves were on edge.
She blamed it all on Bill Martin gate-crashing the
party and buying Benny such an expensive
present.

'While you're getting undressed I'll go down
and fetch you a glass of milk, and another slice of
cake, and you can sit up in bed and have them,'
she cajoled.

'And can I look at the new book you bought
me?'

'Yes, I'll bring it back upstairs with me,' she
promised.

As she walked out onto the landing, Vera almost
jumped out of her skin when she found Bill had
followed her upstairs and was standing there
waiting for her.

Before she could cry out he'd clamped his hand
over her mouth and roughly pushed her into one
of the other bedrooms.

She struggled wildly as he tried to overpower her, his eyes gleaming. She screwed up her eyes, trying to shut out his hideous leering face, as he thrust her backwards onto the bed and pinned her there with the weight of his own body.

Her heart thundered and she could hear her own breath rasping as she tried to twist free. One of his hands remained clamped over her mouth, with the other one he tore at her clothes.

She felt bile rising, burning and bitter in her throat as his calloused hand explored the soft flesh of her inner thigh. She knew that something terrible and irrevocable was about to happen.

Although she managed to fight him off, Bill's brutal attack as he tried to rape her left Vera on the edge of hysteria. For a minute, after he released her and moved away, she remained lying prone, trying to calm the fearful churning in her head. Benny was in the next room, so for his sake she had to try and act calmly.

Trembling, she scrambled from the rumpled bed and straightened her clothes as best she could. With tears streaming down her face she headed for the stairs. Bill followed her, straightening his own clothes as he did so.

Her father guffawed loudly as she entered the living room and she felt sickened as she saw the smug look on his face.

Bill flopped down onto one of the chairs. 'So what about that fry-up?' He smirked. 'I hope when we're married you'll treat me a damn sight better than you seem to treat your old man,' he went on. 'If I ask you to see to my meal I'll expect you to do it right away, not keep me waiting half an hour.'

'Me marry you, after the way you've just treated me?' Vera exclaimed scornfully.

The sharp slap across her face from her father's open hand sent Vera reeling.

'Hey, steady on! I don't want her marked before I take delivery!' Bill laughed.

Cowering back against the table, Vera looked from one to the other. The loathing she felt for both men choked her. Defiantly she held her head up.

'I wouldn't marry you Bill Martin if you were the last man left in Liverpool,' she told him contemptuously. 'You're so uncouth it turns my stomach just to look at you!'

'Then we're quits!' Bill Martin snarled, his face livid. 'I don't want to marry a snooty bitch like you!'

In anger, he kicked his foot out and smashed up the train layout, then he ground his heel on the train and its carriages. As he left, he slammed the shop door behind him so hard that the glass in the upper half splintered into an unsightly crack.

Chapter Eighteen

The atmosphere between Vera and her father reached an all-time low after Bill Martin walked out of their lives.

'Do you know what you've done, you stupid bint,' he railed.

'Of course I do,' she told him with a show of bravado, struggling to hold her tears in check. 'He tried to rape me! He's the most hateful person I've ever known. I wouldn't marry him if he was the last man Liverpool. I don't know what gave you the idea that . . .'

The rest of her sentence ended in a scream of pain as Michael, his face mottled with fury, seized her by the hair.

The severe beating that followed left her bruised, breathless and terrified. He'd often threatened her, but a beating that left her in such pain that she was almost unable to move not only horrified her, but filled her with foreboding.

She knew that her dad had changed over the years, that he had been partly responsible for her mother's death, that he had no time for Eddy and generally ignored Benny. Right up until a few months ago, though, she had always thought that she held a special place in his heart. That belief had stood her in good stead when his bad moods made life difficult for all of them.

Although she would never forgive him for driving Steve Frith away, she understood his reason for doing so. She realised that he didn't want her to marry Steve because it would mean that he was left with no one to run the home and take care of Benny.

For the same reason she'd not taken him seriously when he talked about her marrying Bill Martin. Not only was he twice her age, but it was well known that he was a dubious character. She'd thought it was all talk, some jape they'd dreamed up when they'd been drunk, and that her father was using it as a threat. She'd thought his talk of money-making schemes involving Bill had also been figments of their imagination.

Now she knew better. Her father had made it quite clear that he had not only believed in these schemes, but had built his hopes on the two of them making a fortune.

She was to have been the bait! She was the reward, or prize, that he had promised to Bill in return for his cooperation.

For weeks afterwards, Vera and her father avoided each other. When he came into a room she left it. When Eddy realised what was going on he demanded to know what was wrong. When she eventually told him, and showed him some of her bruises, Eddy wanted to sort things out with him once and for all.

'I'll beat the living daylights out of him,' he threatened. 'I should have done it years ago, only I've always been too scared of him.'

'Don't do anything that either of us will regret, Eddy,' she begged. 'You can leave any time and clear off, but what about me and Benny? I don't earn enough to support him on my own.'

'I could look after you both!'

She shook her head ruefully. 'You are still planning to marry Rita . . .'

'Well? You could come and live with us.'

'Rita wouldn't like that, now would she,' Vera pointed out in a toneless voice.

Eddy shrugged. 'She'd understand. She knows what a pig the old man can be.'

Vera smiled uneasily. 'I don't think it would work. It wouldn't be fair on the two of you and I don't suppose for one minute that Dad would let Benny come with us. He'd rather see him in a home,' she added bitterly.

'You can't go on living here, Vee . . . it's not safe. Next time it mightn't simply be bruises. You could end up with a broken arm, or worse . . . just like Mam!'

'I don't think he'll hit me again . . . he seemed sorry after it happened.'

'Did he say so?' Eddy asked cynically.

'Of course not.' Vera gave a harsh little laugh. 'You've never heard him say sorry in his life, now have you?'

'No, you're right, about that! Take care, though, Vee. If you are worried about the way he's acting then tell me and let me deal with it.'

Gradually life returned to normal. Vera and her father stopped avoiding each other, but they were still uneasy in each other's company, and they spoke to each other only when they had to do so.

Michael spent more and more time out drinking with his cronies. Vera left a covered plate of sandwiches on the table for him each night and made sure that she was in bed when he came home.

It was quite by chance that Vera discovered that when Benny came home from school her father was sending him on messages to the manager of James Coombes's, a company-owned boot and shoe repairer's in Great Homer Street.

She didn't approve of Benny going there on his own, but at eight years old he was big enough to carry out such a simple task. When he assured her that there was no money involved she reasoned that it was unlikely he would be waylaid, even though he nipped through the jigger behind their shop.

However, she discovered the true nature of the messages Benny had been delivering when one evening, shortly before closing time, a drunken, brassy blonde, with a cigarette dangling from one corner of her vividly painted mouth, came into the shop.

When she started threatening to report what she declared she knew about Michael's apparently illegal dealings in front of his other customers, he hurriedly propelled the woman out of the shop and into their living room.

'Trying to shut my mouth are you, Michael Quinn?' she laughed garrulously, when he ordered Vera to make her a cup of tea. 'Well, you'll have to offer me more than a cuppa to make me do that.'

'The minute I close the shop I'll take you for a bevvy,' Michael promised. 'For the moment though, sit down by the fire and talk to my daughter, Vera.'

As the woman lurched across the room and flopped down in Michael's armchair by the fire, the smell of cheap California Poppy perfume mixed with fumes of alcohol almost choked Vera.

'I suppose you're wondering who the hell I am and what I want,' the woman stated. She took a long draw on her cigarette, letting the grey ash spill down the front of her low-necked bright red satin blouse and onto her short black skirt.

Vera watched, fascinated as the woman crossed one shapely leg over the other, her cheap silk stockings rasping against each other as she did so.

'Did you say you'd like a cup of tea?' Vera asked non-committally.

The woman shrugged. 'If that's all you have to offer me. What I really need is a drink . . . a real drink.'

'I'm afraid we haven't any beer in the house,' Vera told her stiffly.

'Beer! Who mentioned beer? I need a proper drink. Whisky, brandy, gin, or even a port if you've nothing else.'

Vera shook her head. 'You're out of luck. There's nothing like that in this house.'

'Bugger me! No wonder Mike is down at the pub every night. What sort of home is this?' She looked round the room disdainfully. 'Not much of a place by the look of it.'

Vera felt her anger rising. Their home might be

sparsely furnished, but she kept it spotlessly clean. As far as she was concerned her first priority was to use the limited money she had to put food on the table and clothes on their backs. And since most of the clothes she bought for herself and Benny were seconds from Paddy's Market she couldn't economise any more than she did.

It was with difficulty that she managed to hold her tongue as she made a pot of tea and poured out a cup for both of them. She watched in silence as the stranger spooned three helpings of sugar into hers.

She was relieved when her father came through from the shop. Quickly, she poured a cup of tea for him and then offered to refill their guest's cup.

The woman shook her head. 'No more cat's piss for me! I wonder you can drink it, Mike, when you're used to something a damn sight stronger,' she jibed.

'Not during the day! I never drink while I am working. I save my thirst for when I go for a bevvy in the evening.'

'You certainly put it away then!'

Vera waited for him to explode in anger at her comment, but he merely smiled. 'So now, Di, to what do we owe this unexpected pleasure?'

Her heavily rouged lips pressed together in a grimace and her sharp green eyes gleamed. She leaned forward, displaying her ample cleavage, and tapped the side of her nose with a nicotine-stained finger.

'I've just come from Coombes's shop in Great Homer Street,' she stated with a knowing grin.

'Patronising the opposition are you? So why come to tell me about it?'

'Not patronising them, Mike Quinn, but picking up nuggets of information!' She sat back with a gloating expression on her face. 'I know all about the little racket you and the manager there, Tom Gray, are running between you.'

Michael Quinn straightened up in his chair. 'I don't know what you're talking about. I hardly know the man.'

'Come off it! I'm not blind and I'm not green. I've seen the two of you in a huddle down the boozer, and then passing a wad between you!' She paused and took another long drag on her cigarette, letting the smoke out so that there was a blue haze in the air around her. 'I couldn't help wondering what might be going on, so I made it my business to find out.'

Vera tried to quell the thundering of her heart. James Coombes's was where her dad regularly sent Benny on messages, so what was going on? She didn't want to believe what she was thinking, but she was pretty sure from what the woman was saying that her dad was engaged in some sort of a fiddle again.

'Knowing that your cosy little arrangement with the bookie was at an end it didn't take much for me to work out that you had a new enterprise under way.' Di grinned. 'One that amounts to thieving, no less!'

'You're talking a load of rubbish, Di Deverill,' Michael blustered. 'Any transactions you've seen between me and Tom Gray are strictly business dealings. As fellow cobblers we help each other out. Sometimes I run short of soles and he loans me some until my next delivery comes through. I then repay him by sending the same number back.'

Di laughed coarsely. 'Of course that's what's going on! He pinches the bloody things, passes them on to you and you pay him half what they're worth.'

'Nothing of the sort! We simply loan them to each other.'

'Bloody rubbish! The soles you send back to him are only half the number he has loaned you. And, more to the point, they are cheap and inferior. You must be making a tidy sum out of this little racket, Mike!'

He opened his mouth to refute her claim, then held back. Giving her a cool smile, he asked calmly, 'So what are you going to do about it?'

Di Deverill again took a long pull on her cigarette. 'Depends!' she said cryptically.

'Depends on what?'

'Well, I did think of going to the police, but I don't like getting involved with scuffers, even when I am in the clear. Then I thought I would let the top boss man at Coombes's know what was going on. That would get Tom Gray the sack. It would also get you into trouble. That kid of yours, who shuttles the stuff between the two of you, would probably end up being sent to Borstal. Now what good would all that do me?'

'None at all!' Michael agreed heartily.

'So then I had another idea.' Di paused and stubbed out her cigarette in her saucer.

Vera and her father waited anxiously for her to go on, but it was obvious she was enjoying herself and in no hurry to do so.

Di looked across the room at Vera and then turned back to Michael with a knowing wink. 'I think it might be better if we went somewhere else, somewhere we can be on our own, before we discuss my idea any further,' she said with deliberate coyness.

He frowned. Inwardly he was shaking with fear knowing that if she did go to the police they would be more than happy to pursue the matter. He might have escaped from their suspicions over handling the betting slips, but he knew they didn't believe he was innocent. PC Walters would take a perverse delight in seeing him up in court on some other charge.

To be accused of conspiring to steal from a company the size of Coombes's would bring him real grief. He couldn't rely on Tom Gray to keep his name out of it. Even if Tom did there were far too many people who, like Di Deverill, had seen them huddled together.

Although he had closed the shop he didn't want to go to the boozer in his working clothes, but he didn't want to leave Di alone with Vera any longer either.

'Shouldn't you and Benny be out doing deliveries instead of hanging around here listening to other people's business?' he asked her brusquely.

Vera looked from him to Di and back again. There was something serious going on and it scared her. He obviously wanted her out of the way and she knew better than to defy him.

'I'll get our coats and we'll be off then,' she said quietly. She smiled at Di. 'It was very nice to meet you, perhaps I'll see you again someday.'

'You'll be seeing me again, you can count on it, luv,' Di told her with a grin.

Vera was surprised to find Di Deverill was still sitting in the armchair in their living room when she and Benny came back from doing the deliveries. She was looking smug, but her father was scowling.

'How about making another cuppa, luv?' Di said before Vera had even had a chance to take off her coat.

'Hurry up! You heard what Di said,' her father snapped, when she hesitated.

'You'd better get used to taking orders from me,' Di told her happily, 'because I'm moving in.'

Startled, Vera looked questioningly at her father. 'Is that right, Dad?'

'Get that tea made and pack young Benny off to bed, then we'll tell you all about it,' he muttered gruffly.

Vera was on the point of arguing, reminding him that Benny hadn't had his supper, but there was such a strange atmosphere in the room that she decided to do as he asked. She couldn't believe for one minute that this woman was telling the truth and she wanted to know exactly what she was doing.

'Go on, there's a good lad, I'll bring you up a jam butty and a glass of ginger beer and you can have them upstairs in bed,' she promised.

'Can I take my comic up to read?'

'Yes, of course you can,' she told him, giving him a little push towards the stairs.

'And will you come up and read to me?'

'Perhaps. Later on, when I've heard what Dad has to tell me,' she whispered.

By the time she'd taken the ginger beer and jam butty up to Benny her mind was in turmoil. In that short space of time she'd considered so many interpretations of what was going on and what her dad was going to say.

She felt very uneasy as she carried the tea through for her father and Di. She perched awkwardly on the edge of one of the straight-backed wooden chairs wondering what exactly her father had to tell her. Di's remark about moving in, and that she'd have to get used to taking orders from her, made her feel pretty sure that she wasn't going to like what she was about to hear.

Michael Quinn waited until she'd poured out the tea and Di had helped herself to her three heaped spoonfuls of sugar.

'Now, girl, listen carefully.' He paused and cleared his throat. 'We've got some news for you. Di's decided she wants to live here with us and I've agreed.'

'I don't understand,' Vera challenged. 'You can't mean she is going to be here all the time?'

'That's what I've just told you, isn't it?' he barked, his face set with anger.

Vera frowned. 'But there's no room. Where will she sleep?'

Di laughed raucously. 'Grow up girl, where do you think I will sleep?'

'I don't know. We haven't got a spare bedroom ...'

'I'll be sleeping with your old man, you silly bint,' Di told her mockingly.

Vera looked taken aback. The colour drained from her face. 'You mean in his bed ... where my mam used to sleep?' she gasped.

The shock and horror in Vera's voice brought a hoot of laughter from Di.

'Your girl's a right bloody caution, isn't she, Mike,' she cackled. 'Are you going to tell me you've never brought any women back here since your Annie died?'

'Of course he hasn't!' Vera told her emphatically, her eyes wide with shock.

'Well it's high time he did then, isn't it!'

'I can't believe that you mean to sleep in his bed with him ... my mam's bed,' Vera repeated incredulously.

'It's not her bloody bed now, it's his, so stop making such a fuss,' Di told her caustically.

'Yes, but ...'

'If he wants me in it then what sodding business is it of yours?' Di snapped.

Vera shook her head and looked at her dad for confirmation.

She felt her insides turn to water as Michael nodded his head. 'Yes, Di is moving in, so from now on I want you to do what she asks. Understand? And make sure that Eddy and Benny do whatever she tells them as well,' he added darkly.

'I can't make Eddy do anything he doesn't want to do,' Vera told him stubbornly.

'Well, you can explain to him what's happening and tell him what I've said,' her father insisted.

Vera shook her head. 'He'd never believe me. You'd better tell him yourself.'

'You'll do as you're bloody well told,' her father thundered. 'Di and I are off for a bevvy so when Eddy comes home you can break the news to him. Tell him to make sure he keeps a civil tongue in his head and treats Di as he should.'

'Treat her as I should,' Eddy muttered in disgust when Vera relayed the news to him. 'If I did that I'd kick her out into the street, and him with her.'

'Well, since you can't do that how are we going to handle things?'

'Do you think if we ignore her she might clear off?' he asked gloomily.

'I doubt it, she knows she's on to a good thing. She's got something on Dad and she's making him pay her to keep quiet.'

'Something on Dad? What're you on about?'

Eddy listened in amusement as Vera told him the details.

'It's nothing to laugh about,' Vera told him. 'If she goes to the police and Dad is arrested, heaven knows what might happen.'

'He'll probably get a good stretch at the Waldorf Astoria,' Eddy grinned.

'It's more than likely that he will,' Vera agreed worriedly.

'So what is the problem? If he's sent to prison we'll get him off our backs!'

'And what about Benny?'

'What has he got to do with it?' Eddy frowned.

'Well he's been involved hasn't he? Dad's been using him to deliver and collect the soles and heels from Coombes's shop.'

'Yes, but Benny doesn't realise what he's doing. He's only a kid who is being sent on messages by his old man. He hasn't had anything to do with the money side. Dad did all the graft down the boozer.'

'True, but the authorities are bound to think that Benny has been in danger. They'll take him away, probably send him to a reform school.'

'At eight years old?'

'If they don't do that they'll certainly take him into care and put him in a Home if Dad is sent down because they'll say I'm not old enough to look after him.'

'I could undertake to be responsible for him, with you to help me, of course,' Eddy told her.

Vera shook her head. 'I'm not sure they would agree to that. We can't risk it. No, I think we are going to have to accept that Di Deverill is moving in and make the best of it.'

Chapter Nineteen

The effects of Diverill living in their home were devastating for all of them. From the very first moment, Vera hated the arrangement since she found she was the one who had to bear the brunt of the newcomer's moods.

Di was quite affable to all of them when Michael was in the room. But when he was working in the shop, she was surly and treated Vera like a skivvy. Nothing Vera did was good enough. There was no way she could please Di, no matter how hard she tried. She had never felt so lonely in her life; she couldn't talk to Joan or Rita about it and Benny was too young to understand. Eddy hated Di so much that he wanted to walk out, but that was out of the question while Benny was so young.

They were all used to Michael demanding the first pick of everything they had to eat, but now they found that Di was equally selfish. As a result, the food left on their own plates became more and more meagre.

'I can't work on scraps in this cold weather, Vee,' Eddy protested. 'You'll have to buy more food, make allowances for the fact that there's an extra mouth to feed.'

'Great idea! And what do you suggest I use for money?' she asked sarcastically.

Eddy shrugged. 'You'll have to ask Dad for more housekeeping, I suppose. He's the one who invited her to live here, isn't he!'

'I've tried doing that, but he takes no notice. He says you and me ought to put more money in the pot.'

'Buggered if I'm going to do that,' Eddy exclaimed hotly, 'not when that old harridan takes the best of everything. I'd sooner stop putting anything in the pot and buy my meals down at Cammell Laird's canteen, or somewhere like that.'

'If you do that then Benny and me will starve,' Vera said desperately.

'I'm sorry, Vee. I know it's not your fault, but I can't live like this. These days, every time I go round to Rita's all I can think about is what sort of scoff she's going to offer me.'

'At least you can go there and get a snack,' she said with a humourless smile.

'I'm given a feed, not a snack! Her mam is a good cook and likes to see someone appreciate her handiwork. Rita gets a bit fed up with me always wanting a nosh before we go out, though.'

Vera sympathised with Eddy, but as far as she was concerned the matter of food was only one of many other irritations that she had to contend with each day.

Di's influence on Benny was worrying, too. He didn't like her, but he responded to her bribes when she wanted him to run messages for her. Most days when he came in from school she'd send him out for cigarettes. He never refused because there was always the lingering hope that he would be told he could spend a penny on toffee or gob-stoppers.

Vera didn't approve. She'd never been able to afford to buy him many sweets, but now he always seemed to be sucking or chewing them.

When she warned him that they weren't good for him he denied having any, but his pockets were always full of sticky papers and often there was a grubby ring around his mouth that told its own story.

Di complained about absolutely everything. She didn't lift a finger around the house, and she demanded that before she went to work Vera should bring her breakfast up to her in bed.

What irritated Vera even more was that when she came home at night there was always a pile of dirty cups and dishes in the sink waiting to be washed up.

Di wouldn't even do the shopping. 'You managed to do it before I came so you can go on doing it,' she would say vehemently.

When finally, in desperation because she had so much to do, Vera asked if she could lend a hand around the house and help with the day-to-day cleaning, Di simply laughed.

'I've never done any cleaning in my life and I don't intend to start now. You get on with it, girl, and make sure you do a good job, I can't stand dirty floors. I like the sheets on the bed to be changed every week, as well. You only seem to do it once a fortnight. That might do for you and the boys, but the bed your Dad and me sleeps in needs to be done every week. Understand?'

On top of all the extra cleaning there was always a pile of Di's clothes to be laundered, and most of them needed to be hand-washed.

'Surely you could do those yourself, you're here all day doing nothing and I have to go out to work,' Vera protested.

The slap across the face not only took Vera by surprise, but the sharp edge of one of Di's rings caused a deep weal that bled profusely.

'You wicked bitch!' The words were out before Vera could stop them.

Di grabbed her by the forearms, her fingers digging painfully into the soft flesh as she thrust her face close to Vera's. 'Let that be a lesson to you and don't go complaining to your Dad about me or there will be far worse to come,' she warned.

Vera could only feel comfortable at home when her father and Di set off for their nightly pub crawl. She would watch them go with a sense of relief. Di was always dressed up in her gaudy finery. Her dad would wear his best suit, freshly laundered shirt, and shoes that she had to polish until they reflected the lamplight.

But even once they'd gone there was a mountain of work to get through. Although Eddy helped with some of the heavy jobs, for the most part it was Vera who was left to cope with the cleaning, ironing, washing and preparing the lunch boxes and food for the next day.

It was an endless stream of drudgery. She wouldn't have minded quite so much if they were a happy, united family, but that was far from the case.

Her father's moods were worse than they'd ever been. It seemed that he saved all his smiles and patience for Di Deverill. When dealing with his own children he was brusque and critical. Benny was again the butt of his temper. He would thump his small son over the head with his clenched knuckles, bringing up lumps that were so tender that often Benny couldn't even put his head down on the pillow when he went to bed.

Eddy fumed about what was happening and time and again Vera had to restrain him from speaking his mind and telling their father that things had to change.

'It won't do any good, Eddy. It will only make things worse. He's besotted by Di Deverill, even though she's no better than a shawlie. A right Judy! One word against her to Dad and you'll be facing a thrashing.'

'He'll get as good as he gets if he tries anything like that with me,' Eddy vowed.

The row, when it finally came, was caused by Di. Afterwards, when she had calmed down and thought it through coolly, Vera was sure that she had instigated it deliberately.

It was a storm in a teacup, all because of the way Di had screwed up her nose at the meal Vera had dished up. It was a Thursday night and Vera had run out of housekeeping money, so the scouse she'd prepared had been thin because it even lacked the assortment of vegetables that normally disguised the poor quality of the meat.

'Christ, this is tasteless!' Di complained. 'Pass the salt, Mike, it tastes like dishwater.'

Michael Quinn stared across the table at his daughter, his face dark with anger. 'Is this the best you could do?' he demanded.

'There was no money left . . .'

'No money left! What the hell do you do with all the housekeeping I give you?'

'Spend it on food, of course. You don't give me enough,' she added nervously. 'You only give me the same amount as you did before Di came to live with us.'

'Blaming me for your bad management, are you?' Di said angrily. 'You're a mess, Vera Quinn. Look at yourself. You don't care how you look, the house is dirty and shabby, and the meals you serve aren't fit for a pig.'

'Hold on!' Eddy pushed back his chair from the table and glared at Di. 'Who the hell are you to criticise my sister. If you don't like it here then get out. We don't like you being here, anyway.'

Mike stood up without pushing his chair away from the table. It fell to the floor with a resounding crash as he leaned forward to grab hold of Eddy. But Eddy side-stepped and Michael lost his balance and stumbled forward onto the table. His hand smashed down onto Benny's plate and the hot scouse splashed all over the boy.

Benny was not hurt, but screamed with fright at what was happening around him.

Incensed, Michael slapped him hard across the side of his face. 'Now you have something to cry about,' he muttered.

Pushing Benny to one side he lunged towards Eddy. This time he managed to grab hold of him and pin him against the wall. As his fist came up, Eddy twisted and threw a jab that caught his father full on the nose. As blood spurted, Di rushed to Michael's side, pushing Vera away when she tried to help.

There was pandemonium. Michael was swearing, Benny was howling, and Eddy was intent on getting out of the house before his father recovered enough to retaliate. Vera, shaking with fright, was trying to calm and comfort Benny.

'Get a cold flannel to go on your dad's nose, Vee,' Di ordered. 'Quick, girl, he's bleeding all over the place.'

By the time they had stemmed the flow of blood from his nose and Vera had restored some sort of order in the room, she realised Eddy had gone.

Weary and unhappy, she cuddled Benny who was still sobbing, and tried to soothe him.

'Can't you shut him up?' Di complained. 'Send him up to his room, out of the way,' she ordered.

'Go on, do as you're told,' her father bellowed. 'The last thing I want is to hear him squalling. My head is aching enough as it is.'

His threats about what he intended to do once he laid his hands on Eddy went on all evening. His nose was so swollen that he couldn't face going for a bevvy, even though Di tried to nag him into doing so. In the end, she told Vera to go and get some beer in.

'Why can't you go?' Vera asked. 'I've still got housework to finish.'

'Do as you're bloody well told,' her father snarled.

'It's no good me going, I've no money,' she told him defiantly.

Reluctantly, he dug into his trouser pocket and brought out a handful of small change. 'Count that out and take enough for a couple of bottles of beer,' he told her.

'I'll do it!' Di snatched the money from him and spread it out on the corner of the table. She counted out two shillings, which she handed to Vera.

'I thought you meant you were going to fetch the beer,' Vera commented.

Di's eyes narrowed. 'One more crack like that and you'll have a nose to match your dad's,' she told her.

Vera was on her way back from the off-licence when she saw Eddy coming out of their house carrying a sack.

'What's going on now?' she asked in astonishment. 'What have you got in there?'

'All my clobber. I'm sorry, Vee, but I don't trust myself to stay another night under the same roof as those two.'

'Eddy, don't say that. Everything will have cooled down by morning. You know what he's like.'

'I thought I did, but since that woman's moved in he's been a bigger swine than ever. No, I'm not staying.'

'Are you going to Rita's place?'

'For tonight I am, but I can't stay there, things aren't too good between us at the moment. She's fed up with hearing about my problems. Tomorrow I'm going to look for a ship. I've been thinking about it for quite a while, but what's happened tonight has made my mind up.'

'Must you do that? If you go to sea I'll have no one to turn to . . .'

'I'm sorry, Vee, but my mind's made up. I'll keep in touch and I'll try and be back again in three or four months' time.'

Chapter Twenty

Vera found that living with Di Deverill was an ongoing nightmare. Not only was she slovenly and lazy, demanding and aggressive, but also a troublemaker. She was continually complaining to Michael Quinn about her and Benny.

'Benny,' she claimed, 'is a cheeky little devil and your Vera is that damn insolent that I want to knock her block off sometimes. The little cow doesn't do anything I ask her to do.'

Michael always believed Di, no matter what Vera said. He always took Di's side in an argument. In his eyes she could do no wrong and he had no interest in what Vera had to say.

To compensate Di for such constant bickering he spent lavishly on new clothes for her. The low-cut necklines, and short, alluring skirts on the dresses she chose, accentuated her plump, middle-aged figure. They attracted a mixture of amused and disgusted looks when she accompanied Michael to the pub.

When he found her new dresses thrown into a corner of their bedroom, all crumpled, creased and stained by spilled beer he berated Vera for the state they were in.

'Why should I pick up and wash her dirty

clothes,' Vera argued. 'She's quite capable of doing those things for herself.'

'You've scuppered enough of my plans, you little bitch. If you'd married Bill Martin you'd have had a home of your own by now. From now on you'll do as you're told, girl, or I'll thump your bloody skull,' he told her angrily.

With an effort, Vera suppressed the retort burning on her lips. She had no doubt that he meant it. She was well aware that lately she had become the prime target for his moods and temper. He blamed her for Eddy going to sea. He'd never been fond of his son, but it irked him that Eddy was no longer contributing to the family coffers.

Above all, he was resentful that Eddy had taken off without a word to him about his intentions.

'Are you sure that he's left Cammell Laird's? I've only got your word that he's gone to sea!'

He refused point blank to believe her when she said that Eddy had gone because he couldn't stand having Di Deverill in the house.

'I'd leave home as well if it wasn't for little Benny,' Vera told him. 'You had no right bringing her here and letting her take Mam's place in your bed.'

'That is none of your business, my girl, so keep your opinions to yourself,' he railed. 'This is my home and I'll do as I damned well like in it.'

Stung by his lack of concern for her and Benny, Vera retaliated.

'Is that so? Well let me tell you, she's only here because she's got something on you,' Vera said scornfully. 'She knows about the fiddle that's been going on between you and the manager at Coombes's. What she's doing is blackmail! I wouldn't trust her if I were you. If you upset her she'll drop you in it!'

'All the more bloody reason for you to keep her sweet then, isn't it! Don't you forget that, clever clogs!'

'I'll do my share if she does hers,' Vera told him sulkily. 'She never helps with the cleaning or cooking, she doesn't get up in the morning, and half the time she's awake she's drunk . . .'

The impact of Michael Quinn's hand across her cheek cut short her tirade.

'If only Mam hadn't died!' she exclaimed recklessly, her eyes blazing. It was a mantra she repeated to herself every night in bed as the hot tears trickled down her cheeks, soaking her pillow.

Life had changed so much since Di Deverill had come into their home that if it wasn't for Benny she'd do the same as Eddy, pack her bags and leave her dad to the mercy of his fancy woman. Without me here to clean and cook for them he'd soon see Di's true colours, she told herself.

If only her father hadn't sent Steve Frith packing. Life might have been bearable with him still around, she reasoned. As it was, even life at Elbrown's was no longer happy or fulfilling since Joan couldn't forgive her for what had happened to her brother. Work had become merely a means of earning some money, nothing more. The fun had gone.

Rita had no time for her either. Vera had hoped that while Eddy was away at sea their former close friendship would be restored, but this wasn't to be. When Rita wasn't working she now spent all of her time with the girls from the factory.

Even Benny had started making friends at school and wanted to go and play with them rather than keep his sister company. She knew it was only natural, but it left her feeling lonely and disillusioned.

She'd never felt in such low spirits. Because her father was so tight with housekeeping money she spent more and more of her own meagre wages on things for Benny. He seemed to outgrow his clothes so quickly and although any replacements she bought for him always came from Paddy's Market they still cost money.

Every time she had to spend money on Benny she had to go without. She had to dress reasonably smart for work, but she found it increasingly hard to do so. Not only were her clothes shabby, but she was down at heel as well. Her father had repaired her shoes so many times that the uppers were cracked. No matter how much she polished them her shoes always looked old and dull.

As soon as it was warm enough to do so she went barelegged, staining the whiteness of her skin with cold tea and using a black pencil to draw in a pretend seam. She was scared stiff of being caught in the rain because she knew that the colour would run down the back of her legs.

She tried to save money within the home, too, but renewing things there was almost impossible. She turned the sheets sides to middle to give them a new lease of life, and did the same with their towels. When these were too old even to do that she cut out the best pieces to make face flannels and used whatever was left for cleaning cloths.

Her father still spent money on himself. His tailored suits and smart topcoat brought admiring glances when he walked down the road, even when he had Di Deverill on his arm.

Her brassy blonde hair, heavy make-up and spindly high heels all added to her tarty look, but no one dared to say anything, not in Michael's presence.

To him she was the ideal woman. He was even proud of the fact that she could match him pint for pint and drink him under the table. She could even knock back as many whiskies as he did! It didn't seem to matter to either of them if she was as unsteady on her feet by the end of the evening as he was. Often Di would be singing her heart out as they stumbled up the stairs to bed, not caring in the slightest if they woke Benny, or disturbed Vera.

Christmas 1929 was the bleakest Vera had ever known. Her father and Di were out at the pub every night, and, as usual, they never rolled home until closing time. They generally shouted and screamed as they bickered with each other over some trivial incident that had happened during the evening. Vera would always wake up because of their noise, but she knew better than to say anything about it. It was no more than she expected now that the novelty of living with Di was beginning to wear off for her father, and he saw that the only thing they had in common was to go boozing together.

Both of them stayed in bed for most of Christmas Day sleeping off their hangovers. When they eventually came down in the evening they were both so befuddled that Vera wasn't even sure they knew it was Christmas.

Vera had expected to hear from Eddy, hoping he would send a card or perhaps even a present for Benny, but there was nothing. She did her best to make Christmas Day a special occasion for Benny, but with only the two of them to share the meal she'd cooked it was not very exciting.

Benny tucked into the mince pies and the trifle, played with the boxed game she'd bought him, and then read his *Chips* annual from cover to cover.

When Di finally came downstairs at five o'clock, her hair was hanging round her raddled face in rat's tails and her eyes were bloodshot.

'For Christ's sake get me something for this bloody head of mine, it feels as if my skull is splitting open,' she moaned.

'I'll make you a cup of tea.'

'I don't want bloody tea! Isn't there anything stronger?' she moaned, holding her head in her hands.

'You know there isn't!'

'Then go out and get something. Your dad feels the same. We need a slug of whisky or brandy, or if you can't get that then bring some gin.'

When Vera refused to go, telling her that it was Christmas Day and none of the off-licences would be open, Di started calling her every name she could think of and berating her for the way she ran the place.

Later, Di and her father went out to a club where, even though it was Christmas Day, they knew they could get some liquor to slake their craving. Vera went upstairs to tidy their room, as her father had ordered her to do. She felt bitter and resentful because he hadn't bought her a Christmas present or even anything for Benny, because he claimed he had no money to spare. Yet he'd bought Di the flashy fur stole she'd been hankering after and that must have cost more than he handed over in a month for housekeeping.

The state of their bedroom sent a shudder through her. The moment she opened the door the strong smell of California Poppy intermixed with stale cigarette smoke almost choked her. Dirty clothes lay in discarded piles. The rug by the side of the bed was stiff with vomit. Everywhere she looked there were dirty cups, the saucers full of stubbed out cigarettes. All the surfaces were covered in grey cigarette ash and spilled face powder. Brushes and combs thick with hair, soiled handkerchiefs and discarded chocolate wrappers littered the floor.

She shut the door on the scene, disgusted by the squalor, resolutely deciding she was not going to clean it up no matter how much Di, or even her father, might insist that she did.

As the day ended and so few of the things that Vera had promised came true, Benny became sullen and disappointed. 'You said our Eddy would be home for Christmas,' he said accusingly, when she told him it was time for bed.

'I thought he might be. I hoped he would be,' Vera told him.

'Bet he's gone to Rita's place and not bothered to come here,' Benny said glumly.

For a moment Vera's heart lifted. Could that possibly have happened, she asked herself. Was he spending Christmas with Rita and her family because he couldn't bring himself to come back home knowing that Di Deverill was still living here?

She was tempted to go round to Rita's house and find out if he was there, but then, she reasoned, Eddy wouldn't do that to her. Even if he intended to spend Christmas with Rita he would still have come to see them. He would know that Benny would be hoping for a present, and he'd know that she wouldn't be able to afford to buy him anything very worthwhile.

Boxing Day was on a Thursday and Vera wished that Elbrown's was open. At least it would put some purpose in her life, to be going to work. That would have meant leaving Benny at home on his own, of course, but if it was an ordinary weekday then his pals would be playing out in the road, or one of the side streets, and he'd be happy to spend his time with them.

It was mid-March 1930 before Eddy came home. His face was bronzed as though he'd spent much of the time in the sun. He'd also matured. He'd gone away as a boy and come home a man.

He stayed at Rita's place, but met Vera from work every evening. He gave her money to buy herself some new clothes. He bought some exciting presents for Benny, too. More important still, he took his young brother out; he took him once to a football match, and twice to the pictures.

On one of these occasions he insisted that Vera went with them, and afterwards they all went to Lyon's Corner House for what Benny described as the best nosh he'd ever had in his life.

They were all devastated when it was time for Eddy to return to his ship.

'Rita and me have talked things over,' he told Vera when he came to say goodbye. 'We are planning to get married the next time my ship's in dock. I've decided to get a shore job again and as soon as we have our own home you and Benny can come and live with us.'

Vera was afraid to believe what she was hearing, although her voice and face both showed the relief she felt.

'Are you both quite sure?' she asked dubiously. 'Does Rita agree to these plans? I never see her these days, she hasn't had anything to do with me since Dad made a pass at her. Does this mean she is ready to be friends again?'

Eddy shrugged. 'I suppose she is. Anyway, it will be another six months or so until it happens, so you've plenty of time to sort things out between you,' Eddy told her. 'Do you think you can stand living with Dad and that Di Deverill until then?'

'It will pass in no time now that I have something like that to look forward to, Eddy,' she said tremulously.

'If anything worse does happen then go to Rita's.

Her folks will let you stay there with them,' Eddy told her.

Vera shook her head. 'I wouldn't want to do that . . . I'd feel humiliated.'

'There's nothing to be ashamed about. I know you won't turn to Rita unless things become unbearable, but I want you to know that there is somewhere you can go if you have to.'

Chapter Twenty-one

Vera experienced a huge sense of loss when Eddy went back to sea. She felt there was no one she could confide in or rely on except Rita and she wasn't sure that Rita fully understood how worried she was about what the future held for her and Benny. Eddy was the only person who realised how difficult her father could be, how trying she found it was to be living with Di Deverill.

Now that Benny had turned ten he was very alert to what was going on around him. She hated him witnessing how drunk both their dad and Di Deverill were when they came home after their boozing sessions, or listening to their constant bickering.

He'd grown up living in fear of his dad's moods, fully aware of his temper, but things were growing worse all the time. The increased drinking was making Michael Quinn more malevolent than he had ever been.

Di's moods were equally volatile. Whenever my dad doesn't do what she asks then she sulks and takes her frustration out on me and Benny, Vera thought unhappily. One minute she's all smarmy and joking, the next sulky and demanding, or else finding fault with everyone and everything.

Lately, Di had taken to disappearing for half a

day or even longer whenever she was upset. Vera knew that this drove her dad to distraction. Each time she flounced out he was afraid that she had gone for good.

Secretly Vera wished she had, but she always came back. Often she was so drunk that the only thing to do was help her up to bed and leave her to sober up.

Vera wondered where she got the money for these binges since the rows between her father and Di were usually over money. Vera had her own theory, but she knew better than to let her father know what her suspicions were.

It was Joan Frith who confirmed what she was thinking.

'That woman who lives with you, your dad's fancy piece, do you know she's on the game, Vee?'

'On the game? What on earth do you mean?' she parried.

Joan sniggered and raised her eyebrows. 'You've heard the expression before, haven't you?'

'Yes, of course I have, but I mean she can't be. She's living at our place these days, and she's out boozing with my dad every night, so how can she be on the game as you put it. Anyway she's middle-aged.'

'Yes, and she's a brassy blonde that plies her trade down the Dock Road.'

'I . . . I don't believe you!'

This is what Vera had suspected, but she didn't want to accept it. She dreaded what her father's reaction would be if he ever found out. Yet how long could Di go on hiding such activities from him?

The next time Di disappeared Vera waited for her to come home, intending to find out if she really was leading a double life.

Di had been drinking and was in an expansive mood. She not only admitted to being 'on the game', but laughed raucously about it. Vera tried to persuade her to move out, promising, in return, that she would not reveal the truth to her dad about what she was doing.

'You must be out of your tiny mind if you think I'm going to go back to the hovel where I was living before I took up with your dad,' Di told her. 'This place is paradise compared with that dump. I know I haven't let you think that, but I've felt like a pig in clover since I've been living here.'

'You've certainly managed to keep pretty quiet about it,' Vera replied with some asperity. 'You do nothing but find fault with all I do for you.'

'Yeah! I've led you a dog's life, but that's just me! I think you're a brick the way you run this place and look after your dad and young Benny. Your old man's not easy to live with, I know that now, but it's better being here than shacked up on my own.'

'I do my best, but . . .'

'I know and I haven't made it easy for you, have I? Well, chook, things will be different in future.'

'There is no future,' Vera told her firmly. 'I want you to leave. I don't mind what excuse you make, I just want you out of our home and our lives.'

'Don't be like that!' Di exclaimed indignantly. 'I'm going to turn over a new leaf. I'll even give you a hand around the place! I might even do the cooking now and again. Anything except the cleaning . . .'

'Oh yes. You told me you never did cleaning.'

Di Deverill smirked. 'I know, I'm a lazy slut, but I can change. I promise you, Vee.'

Vera shook her head, determined to stand her ground now that she had the upper hand.

'Think what it will do to your dad if you tell him,' Di wheedled. 'I'll deny it, if you do. He thinks the sun shines out of my arse so he'll believe me, not you.'

'I've got a witness. Someone saw you down on the Dock Road trying to pick up a sailor.'

'Oh is that what you're on about!' Di Deverill looked at Vera in astonishment then she started to laugh again. A loud, hysterical laugh that set her double chins wobbling.

'All? What did you think I was talking about?'

Di shrugged. 'You may as well know the rest. I thought you were talking about my nicking things from C&A's, Frisby Dyke's and all the others.'

'Stealing? You've been stealing from all those shops?' Vera gasped.

'Stealing. Helping myself. Call it what you like. How else do you think I manage to have all the smart clothes I wear?'

'I thought my dad was buying them for you.'

'Huh! He stopped doing that a long time ago. He's as mean as sin these days, as you should know. He buys me booze when we're out, but other than that he never coughs up a penny piece. He says all his money's gone, but it doesn't stop him buying new shirts and stuff for himself.'

She laughed bitterly. 'You thought he was buying me clobber instead of giving you the money to put food on the table?'

Vera looked at her quizzically. 'Are you telling me the truth?'

'I most certainly am. In fact, it's a laugh and a half. Mean old bugger! These days he wouldn't part with a fart if he could sell it.'

'Then why do you stay here with him?'

Di shrugged. 'Because I like him, I suppose. He's a kindred spirit. He enjoys being involved in a good fiddle. Anyway, as I said, I like the place.'

'My dad's not a thief like you,' Vera defended hotly, her cheeks burning.

'Don't come that with me,' Di sneered. 'He's the biggest fiddler I've ever met. That's how I got involved with him in the first place! Remember? I found out about his fiddle with Tom Gray at Coombes's, didn't I . . .'

'I know all about that,' Vera told her dully.

'Clever bastard, using that kid brother of yours as a go-between. Everything seemed to be so above board that no one would suspect there was any pilfering going on. Got to admire his nerve, and Benny's, for that matter.'

'Benny didn't know,' Vera said quickly, 'he was only doing what he was told.'

'The same as when he used to carry betting slips? Did you know about that? Poor little bugger, he'll end up in an approved school if you're not careful, you see if I'm not right. He's been lucky up until now, but he'll get caught! Young lads like him always do. The scuffers aren't daft you know. They sniff out wrong-doers.'

'You've been very lucky then,' Vera told her scathingly. 'How come you've not been caught?'

'Because I'm a pro. Years of experience,' Di told her confidently.

'Pinching clothes, working as a prossy, what other tricks have you been up to then?'

Di tapped the side of her nose with her fore-finger. 'That would be telling. I'm not giving away all my secrets.'

'I think you should go,' Vera repeated. 'I don't want you living with us. We mightn't have much, but we've always managed to keep on the right side of the law. I don't want to be mixed up in any of your shady dealings.'

'You might be poor, but you're honest,' Di sneered. 'You're forgetting about your father, though, aren't you? If I told you about all the swindles he's been mixed up in then it would make your hair curl.'

'Go! Go now. I'll pack up your clothes, and the rest of your belongings, and bring them to you tomorrow, or you can come back for them. I want you out of here now, though. This very minute.'

Di Deverill shook her head. 'No, I don't think so. You've opened a can of worms this time, luv. I know I'm a bad 'un, but I like it here. As I've already told you, in my own way I'm fond of your old man and he's bloody besotted by me as you've probably noticed.'

'My mam must be turning in her grave. She was worth twenty of you,' Vera told her heatedly.

'Your mam might have been a lovely woman, but I don't reckon she gave poor old Mike anywhere near as good a time as I do,' Di told her, lighting up a cigarette.

Vera turned away in disgust. 'Please, I don't want to hear any more! I want you to leave.'

'I've already told you, I'm staying put whether you like it or not!' She took a long pull on her cigarette and laughed smugly.

'When I tell my dad what you've told me about you nicking clothes and going with other men he'll chuck you out, bag and baggage.'

'Tell your dad and I'll deny every word of it. Keep your trap shut and I'll give you a hand around the place, make your life easier.'

'Trying to blackmail me the same as you did him, are you?' Vera sneered.

'I'll even nick some decent clobber for you. Think about it. Smart skirts, snazzy blouses, silk stockings, a bit of flashy jewellery! All the things a girl of your age dreams of having, but can't afford to buy for herself.'

'Don't you dare! I wouldn't touch anything you gave me with a barge pole.'

'Please yourself, but you're not all that bad-looking, you know. Tarted up a bit, you might even find yourself another fella.'

'I'd sooner dress in rags than take anything from you,' Vera told her hotly.

Di shrugged resignedly. 'That's up to you!' Casually, she stubbed out her cigarette. 'Now, are we going to be friends? Are you going to keep your mouth shut? Or are you going to stir up a hornet's nest by telling your dad what you've found out about me? If he doesn't believe you, and I know he won't, then you might be the one who finds herself out bag and baggage as you put it.'

'He can't turn me out, this is my home.'

'He will if I ask him to,' Di told her softly, lighting a fresh cigarette. 'I have ways of persuading him, remember.'

'You wouldn't dare!'

'I most certainly would.' She breathed out a cloud of smoke. 'Say one word about any of this and I'll turn him against you. I'll make sure that he sends you packing. Think what life will be like then for young Benny without you to stand up for him when your dad is in one of his foul tempers.'

'I'll take Benny with me,' Vera declared hotly.

Di laughed. 'And where would you go? You can't afford to put a roof over your heads let alone feed him, not on the paltry wages you earn.'

'I'll find a way,' Vera vowed.

'There would only be one way, and that's by going on the game,' Di smirked. She drew hard on her cigarette before blowing out a long stream of blue smoke. 'You didn't seem to approve, though, when you heard about me doing that sort of thing!'

'Of course I don't approve, or of you stealing.'

'Quite right,' Di told her. 'Given time you might see things differently, though . . .'

Vera buried her face in her hands. She knew she was defeated. This woman twisted everything she said. Di also knew too much about her dad and

Vera didn't doubt that she would use it against him if it suited her purpose.

Vera wished Eddy was still at home so that she could talk to him, but she didn't even know where he was or when he would be in port again. He'd told her to go to Rita if she needed any help, but if she did that then she'd have to take Rita into her confidence. How could she tell her what had happened and why she wanted to move in with her. If she did that, it might even turn Rita against Eddy when she heard the whole story.

She was aware that Di had stubbed out her half-smoked cigarette and stood up. Di had won; she held all the trump cards. She was wicked and vindictive, but she had the power. Vera knew that for the moment, at any rate, all she could do was fall in with her plans.

'Come on, you'd better accept the situation and start getting a meal ready. Your dad will be closing up at any minute and he likes to find his food ready on the table for him when he comes through from the shop, now doesn't he,' Di told her smugly.

Chapter Twenty-two

Benny Quinn was bored. For the last three months he had been top of the class whenever they had tests in English, or arithmetic. He could reel off the names of all the kings and queens from William the Conqueror to their present king, George V. He knew the names of the ten most important cities and the six longest rivers in Britain. He liked school, he liked reading and he enjoyed lessons, but just lately he felt as if he knew everything there was to know.

When he'd taken the eleven-plus exam a few months back he'd found it so easy that he'd finished ages before the rest of the class. He'd even wondered if he'd missed some of the questions, but when he'd looked through the paper and checked again he found that he had done them all. He'd sat and daydreamed until the time was up, all the papers were gathered in and they were free to go out and play.

They hadn't had the results yet, but that didn't matter. Even if he passed his dad wouldn't want him to go to a grammar school, he thought gloomily. He'd already said that he expected him to work in the shop when he finished school.

Benny couldn't think of anything more boring. He hated the smell of leather, and the stink of the polish that his dad used to finish off the boots and shoes after he'd hammered on the new soles. Even worse was the stinky glue he used for the stick-on soles when people wanted a cheap job.

He'd been delivering boots and shoes ever since he could remember. Vera used to load them all into the pram beside him, or sometimes on top of him, when he was too small to walk. Now he delivered them on his own, as well as doing all sorts of other errands for his dad.

His dad always told him not to say anything about the messages he sent him on because he didn't want Vera knowing all his business.

For some reason his dad didn't seem to think he was capable of being able to work out how dodgy many of these errands were. First there'd been the betting slips. He'd only been about seven then and he'd been scared stiff when he knew he'd lost one and what could happen if it got into the wrong hands.

The trips to and from Coombes's shop with bags of soles and heels had been another risky one. Di Deverill had caught him out over that! She'd never told his dad how she'd got wind of it, thank goodness.

It had all happened because he'd left a bag full of them lying on the pavement whilst he played footie with a crowd of boys from school. She'd come round the corner and tripped over it and threatened to skin him alive.

He'd never be able to forget what happened next. It still went through his brain over and over again, especially when he was in bed at night. It was like watching a newsreel at the flicks!

'I nearly broke my bloody neck tripping over that bag,' the brassy blonde screeched at him, clinging onto a lamppost for support. 'Look at that!' She pointed with a painted fingernail to her leg. 'Laddered my sodding silk stockings. Have you any idea how much they cost a pair?'

'Sorry, missus,' he said quickly, crossing his fingers and hoping she'd go away.

She stood there glaring at him, a fag dangling from the corner of her mouth. 'What's in it, anyway. A pile of bricks?'

He grinned up at her. 'No, just some odd soles.'

'You taking the bloody mickey?' she snapped, blowing smoke into his face as she spoke.

He grinned again and muttered, 'Ace, King, Queen, Jack,' and flippantly crossed himself. 'Not those sort of souls, missus, but the sort that go on the bottoms of boots and shoes.'

She looked puzzled. 'What the hell are you doing with a bag full of those?' she asked.

'I've just collected them from Coombes's in Great Homer Street.'

'So where are you taking them?'

'Back to my dad. He's got a cobbler's shop in Scotland Road.'

She nodded as if she understood. 'You'd better get a bloody move on then, hadn't you, he's probably waiting for them.'

'Yes, missus!' His heart did a tap dance in his chest. She wasn't going to make an issue of it after all. 'I'm on my way,' he added with a cheery grin.

To his dismay she started walking along the road with him, keeping pace, but not saying anything.

'I know me way home, missus, I don't need an escort,' he piped up at last.

'I'm coming with you all the same,' she told him.

'What for?'

'None of your bleeding business.'

The nearer they got to his dad's shop the more worried he became, wondering what she had in mind. He'd said he was sorry about laddering her stockings so surely she wasn't going to tell his dad about what had happened. If she did he'd get his skull thumped and probably a good thrashing as well for playing around.

He kept looking at her sideways, wondering how he could explain all this to her. She wasn't like any other woman he knew. His sister Vera was young, dowdy and skinny. His mam had been short and cuddly and her hair had been fair, not a brassy yellow like this woman's.

Neither his mam nor Vera smoked, whereas this woman puffed away like a chimney. His brother's girlfriend, Rita, sometimes smoked, but she took little short puffs, like a bird pecking at a crumb. This woman smoked like his dad, taking big long draws on her fag, holding in the smoke and then blowing it out in a blue cloud.

Benny waited for his chance. As soon as they reached the corner of the next street, he decided, he would bunk off and make his way home through the back jiggers. She'd never catch him, not in those silly shoes with the spiked heels that she was teetering along in. He'd lose her easily enough.

As if reading his mind the woman's hand shot out and caught hold of his ear. 'It's not that I don't trust you, sunshine, but I ain't taking any chances. How far is it now?'

'Next block.' He wriggled uncomfortably. 'Ouch,' he muttered. 'You're hurting me.'

'Tough!'

'Look, missus, if I promise that I won't run off will you let go of me?' he asked hopefully.

'Give me that bag you're carrying first,' she ordered.

'What for? It's only got soles in it, and it's too heavy for you to carry.'

The sudden sharp twist to his ear brought a yelp from him.

'Hand it over!'

Sulkily he did as she asked. He'd still hoped he would be able to manage to give her the slip and nip down one of the back jiggers. He'd tell his dad that he'd been accosted and had his bag pinched, he decided, which meant that he'd probably get a hiding anyway.

Taking the bag in one hand the woman released her hold on his ear. Before he could dart away, though, she'd grabbed him by the shoulder, her fingers digging into him like talons.

'Right! Now, quick march. Straight to your dad's shop. OK?'

Benny knew when he was beaten. He gave in with as good a grace as possible.

When they reached the shop door he tried to make one last plea. 'My dad'll kill me if he sees you have that bag,' he said uneasily. 'Hand it back, missus. I've said I'm sorry that you fell over it and hurt yourself . . .'

'Come on, don't argue. You won't be in any kind of trouble.'

'You don't know my dad . . .'

It was too late. They were at the door and she was already pushing it open. She thrust him inside so hard that he almost fell in a heap at his dad's feet.

'What the bloody hell's going on here?' Michael Quinn asked, his face darkening.

'I had a bit of an accident, Dad . . .' Benny gabbled, hoping that if he got his story in first it wouldn't be so bad.

The woman laughed and pushed him to one side. 'I'll talk to your dad. You can bugger off.'

'Hey! Lay off my kid! If there's something wrong then let him tell me about it.'

The woman ignored him. 'Bugger off, kid,' she ordered.

He darted for the door that led into their living room, but made sure that he left it open just a crack when he came through it so that he could hear what was being said.

'I know all about you, Michael Quinn,' the woman said. 'We drink in the same boozers up and down Scottie Road, don't we.'

'Possibly, if you say so. I can't recall that we've

223

ever met,' he said cautiously. He picked up a boot, fitted it in position on the last and began stripping off the old sole.

'Well, we have now!' She shook the bag noisily. 'This is yours isn't it?'

'What makes you think that?'

'Your kid was carrying it, until I snatched it off him.'

His face remained stony. 'Go on.' He concentrated on the boot he was repairing.

'Nice little racket you and Tom Gray are running. I bet his bosses would be interested in hearing all about it.'

Michael Quinn removed the tacks he'd been holding between his lips and spat onto the floor. 'What the hell are you on about, missus?'

'Don't waste your breath, Mike Quinn. I've been watching what's been going on for weeks. As I said, nice little racket. I admire a fellow with a brain, someone who can think up an underhand plan and knows how to put it into action.'

'So what are you going to do about it? Shop poor Tom Gray, him with three small kids to feed and clothe,' he sneered.

She pursed her vivid red lips. 'Depends!'

'On what?'

'On how you treat me. Look after me and I'll keep my trap shut. Send me packing and I'll blow your game wide open.'

'What does treating you right involve?' he asked cautiously.

She shrugged. 'Got a fag? Helps me think when I've got a fag in me gob.'

Michael Quinn hesitated then took a half-full packet out of the pocket of his leather apron and held them out. He waited as she took one and then he lighted it for her.

'I'm Di Deverill,' she told him as she blew out a cloud of smoke.

'Yes, I know,' he told her. 'You've got quite a reputation.'

She grinned. 'I thought you said you didn't know me.' She placed a hand on his arm. 'Cards on the table. You've got a racket going, making a bit on the side, right?'

'And you want a cut?'

Di drew long and hard on her cigarette. 'Not really. I want more than a cut. I think we are birds of a feather and that we should team up.'

Michael Quinn looked perplexed. 'What does that mean?'

'Team up? It means that I move in here with you and your family. You look after me and I keep my mouth shut about your little money-making schemes. Now wouldn't you agree that's a good arrangement?'

As he listened to them, Benny grew more and more worried. He'd always been frightened of his dad, thought no one could stand up to him, because next to God he was the most powerful person in the universe. Now he knew he'd been wrong. This woman, this Di Deverill, was twisting his dad round her little finger.

She could talk the hind leg off a donkey, he thought gloomily, and she was getting the better of his dad. Any minute now he was pretty sure that his dad was going to give in and say that she could come and live with them and it would be all his fault.

That had been months ago, Benny thought gloomily and things had changed so much since then. Their Eddy couldn't stand her. He'd hated living with Di Deverill so much that he'd packed his things and gone to sea.

Di Deverill treated Vera like a skivvy, but there was nothing she could do about it because she couldn't afford to leave home.

He loved Vee so much. She'd taken the place of his mam; she looked after him and fought his corner with their dad. She made sure he had clothes to wear, food to eat and that he got to school on time. Now and again she even bought him sweets or a comic when she had a few coppers left over at the end of the week.

He wished he'd told her straight away about the errands he'd been sent on by his dad two or three times a week. But after what had happened over the betting slips his dad had threatened to thump his skull if he breathed a word to her about going to Coombes's.

She knew now, of course. Di Deverill had gloated about it to Vera. He'd felt so bad about it. He'd seen the hurt look in Vee's eyes because she hadn't known what was going on and he felt that he'd let her down.

He couldn't wait to tell her that he had passed his eleven-plus. He hoped she would be pleased and forgive him for the trouble he'd caused. He'd done his best because he'd wanted to prove himself to her.

Vera wasn't simply pleased, she was over the moon. She hugged him, kissed him and told him how proud their mam would have been because he was the only one in the family who'd ever managed to pass the exam. He was glad she was so happy, but he wondered if his dad would say anything.

When they sat down for their meal that night he found the whole lot of them were talking about nothing else. Di Deverill even gave him a shilling and told him he was a 'clever little bugger'.

'Well, Dad, does this mean that Benny will be off to grammar school in September?' Vera asked.

Benny looked at her in astonishment. He'd never dreamed that she would want him to do that.

'Christ no!' Mike Quinn took the wind out of his sails. 'Him, go to bloody grammar school? What the hell are you thinking of, girl?'

'He's worked hard and proved he's got brains, so why waste them?' Vera argued.

'Have you thought of what it costs to go to one of those bloody places?'

'Mam would have wanted him to go. She would have been so proud that he'd passed that exam.'

'Well he's not going and that's that. Now clear away the dishes and shut your trap.'

Vera refused to let the matter lie. She pleaded, she nagged, she threatened and she cajoled.

Di Deverill scoffed at the idea, Michael fought against it, but in the end Vera won. So, by the time September came Benny found that he had all the clothes, books and everything else he was going to need to start at the grammar school.

Chapter Twenty-three

It took Vera every penny she could squeeze out of the housekeeping, and what she managed to save from her own wages, to keep Benny at the grammar school.

She'd thought that once she'd bought his uniform – the grey trousers, the smart dark blue blazer with the school crest on the pocket, the blue and grey striped tie and the matching cap – that would be it.

But in next to no time she found out how wrong she was. There were so many other extras, things she'd known nothing about, but which were essential if he was to keep up with the other boys, most of whom came from families that were quite well-off.

There were special clothes for all the sports they played: football in the winter, cricket and swimming in the summer, as well as plimsoles and special vests and shorts needed for gym. There was also money for the school magazine each term, and for school dinners every week.

She hadn't taken any of these items into account because no one they knew had ever gone to grammar school.

She economised in every way possible to pay for these extras. In the home, she skimped on cleaning materials and, as far as possible, didn't replace anything that became worn out.

She even economised on food. She was afraid her father would notice, but she managed to placate him by making sure that he never went short. The only way she could do this was to give him food from her own plate, just as her mother had done when they'd been hard up.

She didn't mind this, she simply had to be sure that her father was happy and that Benny also had a good meal. He can't study properly if he isn't well fed, she told herself. Even though he had a midday meal at school, she also made sure that he never went to bed hungry.

Benny came home every night laden with homework, but their father still insisted he did the deliveries, even though Vera tried to intervene.

She knew Benny resented the fact when he had to set out with the basket on the second-hand carrier bike his dad had now bought piled high with boots and shoes, but he never openly rebelled.

When he had work to learn by heart he often took his textbook with him. He propped it up on the handlebars and repeated it to himself over and over again, as he rode from house to house, until he had memorised every word.

Vera was afraid he might have an accident because he wasn't watching the traffic. His father was afraid he might make a mistake in the deliveries. Benny's only worry was that he wouldn't have time to get through all the homework he'd been assigned.

* * *

Benny had been at the grammar school for almost two years, had settled in well and was loving every minute of it, when Vera had a stroke of good luck. Joan Frith had married Liam Kelly and that summer she fell pregnant.

When Joan left Elbrown's to have the baby, Vera found herself promoted. It meant extra work and much greater responsibility, but it also meant more money.

She told no one at home about this. She hoarded the extra money to pay for new items of uniform for Benny. It had been worrying her the way he grew out of his existing clothes so rapidly, even though she felt proud of the way he was developing. He was already head and shoulders taller than her and a great deal broader than their brother Eddy had ever been.

Extras at school had increased. He had to pay for field trips which he now went on at least once a term.

These jaunts, as her father termed them, had started so many rows that it seemed to be like one continuous battle. Vera found that pitting herself against her father and Di Deverill, in order to find the extra money to let him go on them, completely drained her. She never had any money for new clothes for herself or to pay to go out anywhere, even though her dad and Di seemed to find the money to enjoy themselves, she thought bitterly.

Sometimes she felt she wanted to throw in the sponge and do as they asked: take Benny out of grammar school and send him to work. They constantly argued about this, saying that if he wanted to better himself he should do it by going to night school.

Then, as she saw him poring over his books late into the evening, lost in a world that she couldn't begin to understand, learning subjects that were completely beyond her comprehension, she knew she couldn't do that.

She'd been bursting with pride when he'd passed his eleven-plus and she was still amazed by his ability and how he applied so much energy to learning.

Di Deverill took a special delight in needling Vera. Her caustic remarks about Benny and the fact that a boy who was as tall as his dad should still be going off to school every day, were her favourite ways of doing so.

'Benny should leave school as soon as he's fourteen and get a job. All this education stuff is a waste of time, in my opinion,' she commented time and time again.

'Then it's a good thing we don't have to take any notice of your opinion, isn't it,' Vera would tell her.

'If you have a decent brain then you can always find a way of making a living,' Di would argue, puffing out clouds of blue smoke.

Vera usually held her tongue when Di said this. She longed to ask her why she didn't go out and get a job, instead of sitting there smoking like a chimney and scrounging off everyone else. Or ask if the reason she didn't work was because she didn't have a brain.

Whatever she said, Vera knew it would only start up a row between herself and her dad. Michael seemed to be on Di's side no matter how much she criticised either of them, or what barbed remarks she made about their home or anything else.

She knew Di wanted to see Benny working in the shop alongside his father; that way, the shop could do more repairs and make more money. This would mean that Mike Quinn would have more time to take her out and about as well as more money to spend on her.

There had been a time when Vera had hoped that her father would tire of Di Deverill, or she of him. However, Di had become such a permanent fixture in their home over the past years that she'd given up even thinking about it.

Di and her father had established a routine that they both seemed to enjoy. They couldn't get to the pub quick enough each evening. The minute they'd finished their meal they were off upstairs to get ready to go out. Her father would put on one of his expensive, well-tailored suits. Di would change into one of her flashy dresses and apply lashings of lipstick and powder to her face.

The fact that they were leaving her to clear the table and wash up, even though she'd been the one who'd had to cook the meal, never seemed to bother them at all, Vera thought bitterly. All Di's promises to help were nothing more than hot air.

It was always chucking-out time before the pair of them arrived back home and, more often than not, they were completely drunk. Vera often wondered how her dad managed to work, he was so hung-over every morning.

Di always stayed in bed until mid-morning, but her father had to be up and get the shop open by eight o'clock so that people on their way to work could call in with their repairs.

Vera was concerned in case he had an accident of some kind when working with a hangover. It would be so easy for him to hammer his own fingers instead of the sole he was repairing, or swallow some of the tacks he held between his lips when he was working.

The regular bouts of drinking also made both her dad and Di more bad-tempered than ever. Because Vera was the one most likely to be around in the morning, and again in the evenings, she was the one who took the brunt of their carping, and she resented the constant disgruntled bullying she had to put up with all the time.

Benny spent his time either out doing deliveries or upstairs in his room doing homework. He had long ago given up trying to do any studying in the living room. Vera had bought a cheap little wooden desk and put it in his bedroom so that he could work up there in peace.

Sundays were the worst day of all, Vera reflected. The shop was closed, Di and her father usually had even worse hangovers than usual from their Saturday-night super binge. They either stayed in bed or sat in the living room nursing their heads and drinking copious cups of strong black coffee, which they expected her to make for them.

They found the noise and disturbance as Vera tried to catch up with the cleaning excruciating. As a result, the rows between the three of them became more and more intense.

Because she was tired, and frustrated by the direction her own life was taking, Vera no longer tried to keep the peace or even control her temper when the rows started.

Whenever her father began complaining about the noise or disruption she let fly.

'If Di helped by doing her share of the housework throughout the week, or even tried to tidy up after herself, there would be no need for me to spend all day on Sunday scrubbing and polishing and cleaning,' she pointed out forcibly.

When this happened, her dad would rise to Di's defence. 'We don't want any lip from you, so keep your bloody opinions to yourself,' he'd shout angrily.

'Then tell Di to pull her weight. She doesn't do much else, she doesn't even help get the meals ready. You two turn this place into a pigsty.'

Usually the rows petered out before they could develop into anything more than an exchange of a few angry words. Vera knew they took very little notice of what she said, but she felt better for airing her grievances.

Over the years she'd accepted that their bedroom was a jumble of dirty clothes, discarded wherever they took them off. Sometimes she refused to clean their room, but in the end she usually capitulated knowing that Di wouldn't do it, and she couldn't bear to think of it being in such a state.

What infuriated her the most was coming home each evening and finding that the kitchen was piled up with all the dishes they'd used during the day whilst she was out at work.

It was on Benny's fourteenth birthday that a violent dispute broke out. It was unseasonably warm for September, as if a thunderstorm was brewing, and all of them were feeling irritable.

Benny was piqued that his dad hadn't even wished him Happy Birthday. His only present had been a Brownie Box camera from Vera.

'Put that bloody thing away,' his father told him. 'You've done nothing but point it and click that bloody shutter all day.'

'It's a camera, that's what you do with them . . .'

'Don't you come that sarky stuff with me,' Michael Quinn shouted. His head ached and the air was oppressive, even indoors.

Benny grinned and made for the stairs, intending to go to his room and get on with his homework. He paused on the third step, and, leaning on the balustrade, lifted the camera and pretended to take a snap of his dad who had followed him out into the passageway.

Michael's arm shot out, catching Benny across the side of the head and knocking him off his feet. Benny slipped, lost his balance and came crashing back down the stairs; he ended up sprawled awkwardly on the ground.

Full of concern for his safety, Vera rushed to help him to his feet. She was tired and resented the way her father had ignored Benny's birthday.

Angrily, she turned on her father, her blue eyes

steely. 'What are you playing at, trying to kill him, are you?' she accused sardonically.

'Shut your soddin' gob and watch your bloody tongue!' Michael Quinn exploded. He lunged at her, but she was too quick for him. She had dodged away before he could reach her.

The fact that he had turned on her enraged Vera. Years of anger and frustration suddenly boiled up and erupted.

'You want to be on your guard, Di,' she warned spitefully. 'He killed our mam, you know! He pushed her down the stairs when he was in one of his rages. You want to watch out he doesn't do the same to you.'

'How dare you!' Michael slapped Vera hard across the side of her face, leaving a vivid red mark.

'You don't like the truth, do you,' Vera taunted, her eyes glistening with tears. 'If you ever strike me again I'll make you pay for it. It might be eight years since she died, but I could still go to the police and tell them what happened that day, you know!'

'And do you think that for one moment they would bother to listen to your trumped-up lies,' he sneered.

'Oh they'd listen all right. I'd make sure of that. I can remember every detail of what took place that day and I have Eddy as a witness. If we told them about the way our mam died they'd arrest you and put you inside . . . or hang you for what you did!'

Michael Quinn laughed cruelly. 'I wouldn't

count on that runt Eddy backing you up, he's frightened of his own bloody shadow.'

'Yes, and who made him like that?' Vera retaliated. 'Who taunted and bullied him when he was a little kid because he was small and puny? Whose fault is it that he's left home because he can't stand living here any longer? You'd treat Benny the same way as you did Eddy only he's bigger than you!'

Vera looked at her father with contempt. She could see how upset he was by her outburst. A nervous tic was pulling at the corner of his mouth as he tried to control his rage.

Vera felt so drained of energy as she waited for him to attack her that she faced him without flinching. She knew it would be her own fault for goading him, but something inside her had snapped and she'd been unable to suppress the fury that she had bottled up for so long.

She was aware that Di was watching them both, her painted mouth open in shock as she heard the accusations and revelations.

Gritting her teeth, forcing herself not to say anything further that could make things worse, Vera waited for her father's reaction. She felt angry, bitter and ashamed over the scene as she met his ferocious stare.

Clenching and unclenching his fists, he gave a growl that seemed to erupt from somewhere deep inside him, then turned on his heel and slammed out of the house.

It was as if time was standing still as the three of them – Benny, Vera and Di – stood staring after him in shocked silence.

Di was the first to speak. 'What the hell was all that about?' she demanded hoarsely, grabbing hold of Vera's arm. 'What did you mean about him killing your mother?'

Chapter Twenty-four

Di Deverill's mind was made up the moment the door slammed behind Michael Quinn. She didn't like what she'd just heard; she planned to be out of there before he returned. Di knew he had a violent temper, she'd seen the way he could turn on his kids, but hitting out at a grown woman, especially his wife, was something else, and she had no intention of finding out the hard way whether or not it was true.

She'd thought she was onto a good thing, but like most things in her life it had all fallen apart when she least expected it.

She'd had a good run for her money, she'd been shacked up with Mike Quinn longer than she'd been with any other man since her marriage had ended when she was twenty-six.

That hadn't been her fault. Danny Deverill had been killed in action right at the end of the war. She'd been more annoyed than upset by the news. Then she felt relieved that they'd had no kids, so to all effects she was free again.

She'd looked round for another husband, but so many of the men of her generation had been killed in battle that she found herself competing with dozens of other women all looking for a man they could call their own. In the end she'd resigned herself to staying single and having as good a time as she could.

Throughout the war she'd been working in a munitions factory, but once the war ended so did her job. Many of the men coming home again were prepared to take on any kind of work they could get, no matter how measly the pay. Woman were left on the scrap heap, unless they were prepared to skivvy, and she'd never taken to housework of any kind.

Immediately after the war ended she'd done a stint in the biscuit factory in Scotland Road, but that was shift work and got in the way of her enjoying herself. She tried shop work, but she didn't like that, because the customers were uppity bitches who spoke to her as if she was dirt. Then she worked as a cleaner at offices near the docks, but that was too much like housework. What was more, it meant turning out very early in the morning or working late in the evening, so she soon packed that in.

The best jobs she'd had, and the ones she liked best, were in pubs. The trouble was she never lasted very long as a barmaid because she was too fond of a tipple herself, and most of the landlords objected to seeing their profits going down her throat.

It was through working as a barmaid that she'd got to know about Michael Quinn. At first she'd thought he was following her from one pub to the next each time she changed jobs. Then she realised that he was a man who liked to drink in four or five different pubs each night.

Once she'd established that fact, and realised he had the money to indulge his hobby, she'd taken a special interest in finding out all about him.

The fact that he had a home and a business of his own, and no wife to keep tabs on him, made her even more inquisitive.

She'd been discreet and taken it slowly, determined to worm her way into his confidence and not rush at things, like a bull at a gate, as she so often did. She wanted more than a few drinks or ciggies out of their relationship. She was no chicken, either, she was looking for a comfortable nest. She wanted her feet under his table so that he was not only paying for her booze, but feeding and clothing her as well.

Finding a way to make him notice her was the problem. For a man in his mid-forties he was in good fettle. He was tall, broad-shouldered and good-looking in a craggy sort of way. There was only a sprinkle of grey in his jet-black curly hair, and even though he was a steady boozer his blue eyes were bright and clear. He dressed smartly, so when she'd first spotted him she'd thought he was probably a manager of some sort. His cronies were all hard-drinking men like himself. She never saw him in the company of a woman.

By keeping her ears open she'd managed to pick up a good many nuggets of gossip about him and his family. She'd stored them away in her mind in the hope that sooner or later she'd be able to use them in some way.

She'd been surprised to learn that he was a cobbler, even though it was his own business. She was also taken aback to discover that he had three kids, all of them still living at home.

Although this factor was off-putting it didn't in any way dampen her determination to get to know him better; much better. By devious methods she had learned about a number of his shady dealings and was impressed by his cunning.

If she handled her approach right, she told herself, she'd be onto a winner. Mess it up and she wouldn't get a second chance, he'd avoid her like the plague.

Falling over the bag of soles had been a sign from the heavens. She couldn't believe her luck. What was more, the outcome had been better than her wildest dreams. He hadn't put up any fight at all. Moving in with him had been a complete walkover.

She planned to go on living there, being treated as the lady of the house, for as long as she could. It meant putting up with his kids, of course, but even that had some advantages. Vera had a job, but she was used to doing all the cooking and cleaning. Eddy was also working and soon learned to keep out of her way. Benny had no choice but to accept her, because he knew he'd get skinned alive if she ever told his dad the truth about tripping over the bag of soles.

Michael Quinn had a vile temper at times, but he was pretty free with his money where booze was concerned. He was as mean as muck, though, when it came to handing over any housekeeping or money for clothes for the youngest kid. Still, she told herself, that wasn't her problem. She didn't have to try and manage on it.

Mike Quinn was also a bit free with his fists and thought nothing of lashing out at his kids when they annoyed him.

The day he lashed out at her, she told herself, she'd pack her bags and leave. One thing she wouldn't stand for was being a punch bag. She'd had enough of that with one of the blokes she'd shacked up with briefly in the past.

Paddy Murphy had been a raw-boned Irishman. Most of the time he could charm the birds off the trees, and when he had money he'd throw it around like confetti. When he was in his cups, though, he was a different man altogether. Those times he was ready to fight anyone, even her, and she'd ended up with three broken ribs to prove it.

A few weeks later he'd turned on her again and given her two black eyes. Right there and then she'd decided to leave. First thing the next morning she'd packed her bags and walked out on him. He'd come running after her, begged her on bended knee to go back to him, but she knew better than to do that.

'Leopards don't change their bloody spots,' she told him. 'Find yourself another punch bag.'

For a while afterwards she thought she'd cut off her nose to spite her face; she was so hard up that she'd had to go charring. It was then that she'd managed to get taken on as a barmaid and worked her way through most of the boozers in Scotland Road and Great Homer Street.

Now it looked as though she was going to have to do the same again, or find someone else to keep her. She certainly wasn't going to risk staying at

Quinn's place, not if what his daughter Vera had said was true.

'Did you mean all that drivel you were spouting about your dad killing your mam?' she asked Vera.

Vera shrugged. 'What's it to you?'

'Interested, that's all. I never heard anybody else ever say anything like that about him before.'

'It's true all right.'

Di tried to keep her voice non-committal. 'So what happened? How did he do it?'

'Like I said, he pushed her down the stairs.'

Di's eyes widened. 'Here, in this place? Down these stairs?'

'That's right. From top to bottom.'

'Oh my God!'

'If you must know, my mam broke her neck,' Vera said in a hushed voice.

Di's hand crept up to her own throat and held on to it, her face registering sheer terror.

'Anything else you want to know, or can I get on and clear the dishes?' Vera asked coldly.

Di didn't answer. Walking unsteadily, holding tight to the balustrade, she went upstairs to her bedroom.

Twenty minutes later she came out onto the landing and called out to Benny to come and give her a hand.

'He's busy doing his homework, what do you want?' Vera asked, coming into the passageway and looking up the stairs.

'What on earth are you doing?' she asked as she saw the battered suitcases on the landing and Di struggling with two loaded shopping bags.

'What does it look like? I'm leaving!' Di puffed.

Vera looked bewildered. 'What do you mean, leaving? Where are you going?'

'As far from this house as I can get! You don't think I'm going to stay here after what you told me about your mother, do you?' she babbled hysterically. 'I want to be away before your dad comes back.'

'Why?' Vera looked bemused. 'I thought you knew, you seemed to know everything else about us,' she said with sour amusement.

'Of course I'd heard the rumours, but I wouldn't have moved in here if I'd had even an inkling that there was any truth to them.'

'Now you want to get out in case the same thing happens to you!'

'Too right I do.'

'Well, what a pity I didn't tell you sooner,' Vera smirked. 'I had no idea you were so sensitive.'

'Don't be so smart. If you've got any sense you'll get out of here yourself. You never know with a man like that. If he's killed once and got away with it then he won't think twice about doing it again. He can be violent, you know that to your cost.'

'Taken you long enough to find that out,' Vera said with a humourless smile.

'I've known ever since I first moved in here that he's free with his fists. Look at the way he was always thumping your brothers.'

'That never seemed to bother you. I don't remember you ever sticking up for Eddy,' Vera challenged.

'None of my business how he brought his kids up, now was it.' Di hedged.

'You thought you were safe because you had something on him,' Vera sneered. 'You blackmailed your way into our lives.'

'I haven't time to bandy words with you, Vera Quinn. I want to be well away from this place before your old man comes home again. I've lived with violence and I don't intend to get involved in anything like that ever again.'

'Don't worry, I'll gladly help you get your bags down. And so will Benny,' she confirmed. Her voice rose as she called out his name.

'I thought you said he was studying and couldn't be disturbed?'

'He wouldn't want to miss out on this treat,' Vera told her. 'Getting rid of you and getting our life back to how it was before you came here is something to celebrate, I can tell you.'

'You've never liked me, not from the first day I came here, have you?' Di spat at her.

Vera looked at her balefully. 'Do you blame me, the way you've treated me and the way you've expected me to clean up after you?'

They were all breathless by the time they'd brought Di's cases downstairs and put them out on the pavement.

'Can the two of you help me get them to the tram stop?' Di asked.

'You've not told us where you're going?' Benny said as he picked up the suitcases.

'You must think I'm bloody daft if you think I'm going to tell you that,' Di said. 'Your dad'd be after me like a dose of salts if I told you.'

'Oh no, we wouldn't dream of telling him where to find you,' Vera promised. 'We're only too glad to see the back of you.'

Vera and Benny were both in bed when Michael Quinn came home. They heard him lumber up to his bedroom and knew from the way he crashed into furniture and slammed his bedroom door that he was extremely drunk.

His roar of annoyance when he discovered that Di Deverill was not there waiting for him had them both shaking with fright.

He stormed back downstairs, calling out her name, then came back up again thumping on their bedroom doors, demanding to know where she was.

When neither of them answered he barged into Benny's room, dragged him out of bed and began shaking him.

Benny wasted no time arguing. Struggling free, his fist shot out and landed square on his father's chin knocking him into a quivering heap just as Vera came running to see what was happening.

The sight of her father looking completely dazed and nursing a bruised jaw as he retreated back into his own bedroom made her gasp.

'Benny!' She stared at her brother, suddenly aware of how big and brawny he'd become. 'Whatever have you done!'

'Something I've been waiting to do for years! I've taught him a lesson that he'll remember.'

'Oh, Benny! You shouldn't have hit him,' Vera

protested weakly. 'It's only natural that he's upset about Di clearing off.'

'Huh! If you take up with a slag then you should expect her to scarper when the mood takes her.'

'Benny! Where did you hear expressions like that?' she gasped.

'I've heard them since the first day I started at grammar school,' he told her derisively. 'Everyone knows about Di Deverill. They didn't waste any time in putting me wise to what sort of person she was and teasing the life out of me once they knew she was shacked up with my dad.'

'Benny, I'm sorry . . . I had no idea.' Vera's eyes brimmed with tears and she stretched out a hand to touch Benny's arm. 'Why didn't you tell me?'

He shrugged. 'What good would that have done? Anyway,' he grinned, 'I thought you had enough on your plate as it was keeping house, cooking and cleaning and waiting on her without rubbing your nose in it, or bleating to you about it.'

Vera shook her head sadly. 'You should have told me, Benny, I really am sorry.'

'Oh don't be. In some ways it was a good thing. I knew I couldn't fight them all, there were too many. Instead I vowed I'd show them that I was better than them. That's why I've been working so hard. I was determined to come top in class and beat them all. I did, too, in most subjects.'

'Benny . . . I had no idea . . .'

There was so much confusion and regret on Vera's face that Benny laughed wryly.

'I was only being teased, it was far worse for

you,' he told her. 'When she and Dad got pissed out of their minds, and then spewed up everywhere when they came home, you were the one who had to clear up after them the next day, now, weren't you!'

Chapter Twenty-five

Michael Quinn seemed to take Di Deverill's desertion very much to heart. He wouldn't talk to Vera the next morning. When he came through from the shop the next evening, his eyes glittered angrily whenever they met hers. He seemed to blame her for what had happened.

He ate his evening meal in silence, shoved his empty plate to one side, drank the cup of tea she put in front of him then pushed back his chair and walked out of the room without a word.

Vera and Benny exchanged glances as they heard him stumping around upstairs as if getting ready to go out for the evening.

When he left the house he was wearing a dark grey suit, watch chain gleaming across the front of his waistcoat, dark trilby settled full and square on his brushed-back hair.

'Pub crawl?' Benny asked, looking at Vera, his eyebrows lifting speculatively.

'I imagine so,' she agreed as she drained the teapot into her cup and added a dash of milk and a spoonful of sugar.

'He's probably gone looking for her,' she added as she stirred her tea thoughtfully.

'Do you think he will find her?'

'With any luck, no! She was so scared when she

heard about what had happened to Mam that she couldn't get away fast enough.'

'She might have had second thoughts by now,' Benny said. 'She had an easy time whilst she was living here, what with you doing all the housework and Dad spending every penny he earned on booze and fags for her.'

'No, she was too scared. From something she said I think it brought back unpleasant memories for her about someone she'd been living with before she came here.'

'Well, as long as we are free of her, that's all that matters,' Benny said unfeelingly.

'Provided it doesn't upset Dad too much. He was in a black mood when he went out tonight, but in a different way from usual. He was so cold and distant that he frightened me, Benny.'

'He'll have a skinful, come rolling home and sleep it off, and in a couple of days' time he'll be over it,' Benny told her optimistically.

It wasn't anywhere near as simple as that, though. Michael Quinn certainly had a skinful that night. He got so drunk that he couldn't stand up, and two men, who were complete strangers to Vera and Benny, brought him home and helped him into the living room.

He sat slumped in his armchair, his eyes glazed and his breathing laboured. He looked so odd that Vera thought he might be going to have a heart attack.

A few minutes later he was violently sick.

She thought he would feel better after that, but

far from it. The physical symptoms improved, but he seemed to be so distracted and strange that Vera felt very alarmed.

'Benny, do you think we ought to get a doctor to come and see him?' she said worriedly.

Benny pulled a face. 'What would we tell him? He's not ill. He's had too much to drink and been sick, but he's over that . . .'

'I know, but he's so depressed and distant. It's as if he's not with us.' She lowered her voice, 'I'm not sure that he knows where he is or who we are.'

'He's still drunk, though,' Benny said diffidently. 'Do you think we should try and get him up to bed?'

The moment they tried to move him, he fought them like a trapped tiger.

'Perhaps we should give up and leave him where he is in his chair,' Benny suggested.

'You're probably right. I'll get some blankets,' Vera agreed. 'Will you loosen his tie and see if you can take off his jacket?'

Between them they made him comfortable. Eventually he drifted off to sleep, emitting a deep guttural snore with every breath he took. Vera put the fireguard in place and they quietly made their way upstairs to their own beds.

Vera wasn't sure how long she had been asleep before the disturbance roused her. Benny heard it at about the same time and called out to her.

Concerned, they both went downstairs, wondering what they were going to find.

Benny led the way. When he pushed open the

door to the living room he let out a long, low whistle. The place was in utter disarray.

The armchair by the fire was empty and for a moment neither of them could see any sign of their dad.

Benny was the first to spot him. He grabbed hold of Vera's arm, nodding urgently in the direction of the table. The tablecloth had been pulled towards one end and draped like a curtain. Michael Quinn was under the table, hiding behind it.

'Dad?' Tentatively, Vera pulled the tablecloth to one side and bent down. 'What are you doing under there?'

Michael didn't answer. Instead he pushed himself as far away from her as possible. Cowering up against the back legs of the table he held a chair he'd taken under there in front of him, as though defending himself against an intruder.

Vera felt a shiver run down her spine. 'Whatever are you doing?' she asked, trying to keep the alarm she felt out of her voice. 'Why don't you come back out and sit in your chair by the fire where it's warm,' she suggested.

He stared at her as if he didn't recognise who she was and jabbed at her with the chair.

'Shall I try?' Benny asked, as he gently pushed her to one side and went down on his knees. But before he could talk to him, his father let out an angry roar and thrust the chair at Benny, catching him across the face with one of the legs.

Benny sprang back and pulled Vera to safety. 'I don't know what's the matter with him, but I think we'd better leave him where he is,' he muttered.

As soon as Vera lifted the corner of the tablecloth, Michael Quinn knew he was in danger. Fear gripped him like a cold hand. The enemy had discovered his hideout and were intent on taking him prisoner, but he wasn't going to let them succeed. He'd fight for his life every inch of the way.

It had been bad luck getting separated from the rest of his platoon. If he hadn't stopped in the last village they'd come through to filch a couple of eggs from the hen house then it wouldn't have happened. He'd be on jankers because of that, so, although he didn't want to be captured, he was in no rush to get back to his unit either.

Trapped between the devil and the deep blue sea, he thought ruefully. He wasn't cut out to be a soldier. When he'd joined up he'd looked forward to a taste of freedom, to not having to work from eight in the morning until seven at night hammering soles and heels onto other people's boots and shoes.

He'd never bargained on being trapped on such a treadmill when he'd married Annie. She'd been so pretty, so full of fun, he thought it would go on being like that. The minute she had a ring on her finger she became all prissy and dull.

The moment Charlie was born all she could think about was looking after the kid. At first that had been fun and he'd accepted the role of being a dad. Then, after Eddy and Vera had been born, Annie became even more of a mum and less and less like the girl he'd married. She'd been so caught up in feeds and teething, and the kids' bellyaches, that she'd had no time for him. It seemed that his whole life was centred on work, mending other people's broken down boots and shoes.

He didn't fancy spending the rest of his life in the same old routine, day in, day out. He wanted fun. He didn't want to have to turn up every penny he earned to keep his family, and he was fed up with being constantly told what to do. If it wasn't Annie lecturing him then it was his father-in-law, or his mother-in-law, giving him good advice.

There were times when he longed to drop every-thing and take Annie out dancing or to the pic-tures, but that was no longer possible. Everything had to be done to the routine that Annie imposed.

Annie was a good mam, he'd give her that. Her own mam and dad tried to help out as well, but he didn't like the way they were always bringing them food, or inviting them to their place for meals. It felt like charity and he'd had enough of the milk of human kindness when he'd been a kid to last him a lifetime.

He hated the way such benevolent people expected you to be grateful to them when they did something for you. Half the time, they only did it because it made them feel good. Yet they made you feel they owned you, body and soul. They were like leeches, sucking your lifeblood out of you.

His biggest gripe was having to act as if he was one of them. He hated that. He wasn't used to the way they were always polite and considerate to each other. They seemed to forget that he'd been bunged into an orphanage as a tiny tot and that he'd had to learn how to be tough.

His first meeting with Annie had sealed his fate. He'd fallen for her there and then. He'd tried to change, just to please her. He'd succeeded, too. He was proud of the way he'd done that, and of the guff he'd told her about his past. Most of it had been lies, but she'd swallowed every word, hook, line and sinker.

He'd never meant to marry her, or anyone else. He simply wanted to enjoy her company, take her dancing, or to the pictures and make love to her. It had taken the wind out of his sails when she'd told him she was preggers and that they'd have to do something about it pretty quick.

Getting spliced was her answer to the dilemma and like a fool he'd gone along with it, a lamb to the slaughter.

At first his new lifestyle had seemed cushy enough, but he soon tired of it. He'd always hated routine, it was like being back in the orphanage. Annie and her parents had plenty of ideas about what he should be doing, but they never listened when he opened his mouth and asked them to do something.

That's why he'd rushed to volunteer the minute the war had started.

The army sounded exciting. He looked forward to being in the company of men his own age, the stimulation of never knowing where you'd be, or what you'd be doing, from one day to the next. It was what he needed, the sort of excitement he craved for, in fact.

It had been like that for the first few weeks while they were in training. It was when they were sent overseas that he realised what a stupid mistake he'd made, being so quick to volunteer. They'd exchanged barrack rooms for tents, drill yards for mud and slush, regular meals in the mess for makeshift grub that they had to take turns in preparing. Most of the time, the results would put any self-respecting boy scouts outfit to shame.

The men he'd trained with were nothing more than cannon fodder. Two of his mates were picked off by snipers the very first week they were in France.

Living in dugouts, clambering up the slippery sides of water-logged trenches and risking your neck every time you did so, left him so scared that if he'd known how to get back to England he'd have deserted straight away.

He'd always known how to look after himself, and once he'd been called a 'Wallasey boy' he'd realised what the score was and mentally resolved to do just that. After he was made a corporal he never shared anything, not even water or a crust of bread, unless he had to.

As they advanced through the French villages he took anything he could find, whether it was food or something he could barter with.

Now he couldn't understand how he'd managed to get separated from the rest of his unit, or how he came to be wearing civvies, but he certainly wasn't going to put his hands up to the enemy. There must be some way of lying low and making his escape.

He was hungry and thirsty and his head ached

as if he had suffered a blow of some kind, but he couldn't remember being in any battle. He didn't know what had happened to his uniform. He'd obviously managed to get inside one of the houses so perhaps he'd killed some Frenchie and was wearing his clothes. Making a den for himself and defending it against all comers was second nature.

The couple who'd found him seemed to have retreated. He strained his ears, listening to try and find out what their movements were. Although he could hear their voices he couldn't make out what they were saying. If they were Frenchies he only knew a few words of their lingo, the rest was gibberish to him, so he stopped listening.

He didn't intend to give himself up. He was safe for the moment. He was in the dry and reasonably warm. They might go away if he waited, even if it was only to fetch help. The trouble was, he didn't know if they were friends or enemies.

He wished they'd make their minds up and do something. He felt so tired that he was having trouble trying to keep awake. As the minutes ticked by he wondered if that was their strategy and that they were waiting for him to nod off to sleep.

He could smell food somewhere, and he was immediately alerted to the growing hunger pains inside him. Was this a trick? Were they going to lure him out by offering him something to eat? If he let them do that, would they shoot him, take him prisoner, or hand him over to his own side?

He felt tears beginning to trickle down his cheeks and he dashed them away with the back of his hand. What a bloody mess!

He wished he was back on Merseyside, in his own bed, listening to Annie clatter around in the kitchen getting his breakfast ready, and the sound of Charlie and Eddy prattling away to her as she did so, and little Vera chortling away in her cot.

The dull routine that he had scorned suddenly seemed like heaven.

Overcome by fatigue and despair, his eyelids drooped. As he let sleep claim him he wondered if he would ever see any of them again.

Chapter Twenty-six

As the weeks passed, Vera was so concerned about her father's mental state that she found it difficult to keep her mind on her work and she knew that Miss Linacre was becoming very annoyed about this. Vera's greatest fear was that she might report her to Leonard Brown himself and that he might sack her.

She kept wondering exactly what the future held not only for her, but for all of them. She found herself starting each day tense and anxious, pondering on what fresh problems she was going to have to face. It was often mid-morning before her nerves settled down and she could concentrate on the work she was being paid to do rather than try and sort out her own personal troubles.

Benny still had two more years to complete at grammar school, but would she be able to afford for him to go on attending there for all that length of time?

So much depended on how much longer her father could cope with his day-to-day work. Unless business improved she wasn't sure they could even go on living at the shop. The overheads, the rent and rates, had to be met.

When her father was reliving his wartime experiences, his mind was usually far too disturbed for him to do any work. He was in another world, back in the mud, blood and horrors that he had known in France during the war.

She found it so confusing because the rest of the time he seemed to work as hard and efficiently as he ever did. It was the day-to-day uncertainty of the situation that worried her the most. She never knew if he was going to be fit to work or not and it meant she couldn't make any definite plans at all.

Money, or rather the lack of it, was one of her main concerns. But at least with Di Deverill out of their lives their expenses were considerably reduced. Di's smoking habit had been a drain on the housekeeping, and so, too, had the bottles of sherry and vodka that she had bought for herself whenever she undertook to do any of the shopping.

Now Vera was as frugal as she could possibly be and hoarded as much spare cash as she could. Sometime in the future she was sure she was going to need every penny she had if they were going to survive.

Benny accepted the situation far more pragmatically than she did. When she tried to talk to him about their future he simply shrugged his shoulders.

'We'll manage; things will work out,' he told her confidently. 'Take each day as it comes. We know Dad is deranged, but he may snap out of it as quickly as he went into it.'

Vera could only nod in agreement. She felt taken aback to hear him describe it as he did. To her ears that made it sound as though their dad was suffering from a mental problem.

She was sure it wasn't anything quite so serious, but she wished there was someone she could talk to about it. She didn't want to enter into a lengthy discussion with Benny in case it distracted him from his studies and his forthcoming exams.

'It's all to do with things that happened long ago,' she said lamely. 'Something has triggered off memories to do with his past.'

'I understand all that,' Benny told her. 'I think you should keep a note of the dates when he has these transgressions into wartime scenarios and see if they are becoming more frequent. It might be a good idea to get him to talk to you about the war. That way you might find out exactly what is worrying him.'

She knew Benny was right, but somehow trying to do as he suggested made it all seem even more frightening. As she listened to her dad's ramblings, some of the horrors that he had endured on the battlefield impressed themselves upon her.

She began to understand his distress and sympathise with his fears. She had no idea, though, what to say, or do, to bring him any comfort.

When he began looking over his shoulder, hiding in corners, crouching with his hands over his ears as if to shut out the sound of gunfire or bombs exploding, her heart went out to him.

She knew better than to try and console him physically. Once, when she had gone towards him, her arms outstretched to try and soothe him, he had lashed out at her viciously. It was only because of the fact that when he was in the throes of such an attack his vision seemed to be impaired, and he lacked coordination, that she had managed to avoid his flailing fists.

Since then she'd kept her distance when he was having one of his attacks. If he spoke to her she responded in a quiet voice, answering his questions no matter how weird they might sound.

Usually she was able to persuade him to 'hide' for his own safety. In the early days of these attacks he had always taken refuge in the living room, either under the table or crouched in his armchair. After a while he began to suspect that the enemy knew where he was and would rout him out.

'Perhaps you would be safer upstairs in your bedroom,' Vera suggested.

His eyes narrowed and he stared at her speculatively, but said nothing. She wasn't sure if he had understood, but the next time he had one of his attacks he made straight for his bedroom.

'I've got a new hideout where they won't find me,' he told her triumphantly as he raced for the stairs.

She didn't know whether to follow him or not. When she did, at a discreet distance, she found him cowering in a far corner of the room, his eyes wide with fear, his entire body shaking.

For safety's sake she asked Benny to help her to fix a bolt on the outside of the door. After that, once her father was inside, she would slip the bolt into place to make sure that she knew where he was whilst he was so disorientated.

No matter how much he ranted or raved she

would leave him there until she was quite sure he had calmed down.

She always knew when this happened. He would hammer on the door, calling out. 'Vera, when are you going to bring me up a cup of tea?'

For a couple of days after one of his attacks he would be quiet and subdued. Then something would remind him of Di and the fact that she had gone. For days he would sink into a dark depression, cursing Vera and blaming her for the slightest thing that went wrong.

This would start the cycle all over again. A drinking binge would follow and he would arrive home so drunk he could hardly stand up. Then his fearful illusions, his trips back into the past would come to haunt him and disrupt their lives.

At first his regular customers accepted that Mike Quinn was 'under the weather' and made allowances if their boots and shoes were not ready on time.

Gradually, though, their patience became strained and a great many of them began to take their repairs elsewhere.

The fact that their trade was rapidly diminishing worried Vera a great deal. She tried to conceal this new worry from Benny and did all she could to make sure that her father carried out any work the moment it was booked in. She also ensured that deliveries were done promptly, even if it meant her taking them herself in her lunch break.

Benny soon realised what was going on. 'Why don't I try my hand at putting on a sole or two. It can't be all that hard,' he offered.

Vera looked doubtful. 'I'm sure there is a right and wrong way of doing it, some sort of technique that you have to be taught, or which only comes with years of practice,' she warned.

'It's not all that scientific,' Benny told her scornfully. 'The soles are precut, it's only a case of selecting the right size and hammering it into place on the shoe.'

Benny found it was not as easy as he'd thought. After hitting a tack through one of his fingers and hammering his thumb rather badly, he was ready to admit this. He also had to agree that his work was so amateurish that it wouldn't be acceptable to any of their customers.

They both decided it was probably better to apologise and say that the repairs weren't ready due to unforeseen circumstances, than to offer shoddy workmanship.

'You could do the finishing off, of course,' Vera told him. 'The polishing machine is easy enough to use.'

'I'll give it a go. I certainly won't end up with smashed fingers,' Benny agreed.

'If you can operate that then I'll make a point of persuading Dad to do the basic work and leave the finishing off for you to do.'

'Won't he object to that?'

'He might, but he knows he's not keeping up with the orders so he'll hopefully see that it will be one thing less for him to worry about.'

Between them they managed to keep the business afloat. Vera frequently had nightmares about the future, though, knowing they couldn't continue for ever in such a haphazard manner.

She was also aware that the 'attacks', as she and Benny called them, were becoming ever more frequent and that they were lasting longer.

Benny was changing, too, Vera noticed. The worry and responsibility were gradually getting through to him. He was losing weight and growing more serious. These days, she thought sadly, she rarely heard him whistle or try to make her laugh with any of his light-hearted jests.

She knew he was working desperately hard at school and she sometimes wondered whether this desire to achieve academic supremacy was a sign of ambition or necessity.

She hadn't forgotten what Benny had told her about his early days at the grammar school, when he had been the butt of the other boys' jibes because Di Deverill was living with them. Had they somehow found out about his father's derangement? If they had, then were they teasing him about it? Was he again trying to prove himself by beating them all in class, she wondered.

Sometimes at night, when she lay listening in the darkness for the slightest sound from her father's room in case it might be the start of another attack, she wondered if things would have been better for all of them if Di Deverill was still living with them.

She was sure her father needed professional advice, but she wasn't sure how to go about getting it since he refused to go and see a doctor.

'I'm not ill, you stupid bitch,' he had said angrily, the last time she'd suggested it. 'I suffer from nightmares, that's all. It's probably the grub you dish up that is to blame,' he had told her sourly. 'They'll go away in time.'

Vera didn't think that they would and she wondered if one of the organisations like the British Legion, who claimed to help ex-soldiers, could offer her any advice.

The trouble was, they would want to see him and talk to him, but she wasn't sure if he would cooperate.

She'd tried to keep her concern from Benny, but it was impossible to do that. Benny was as worried as she was about their dad's condition and their own future.

'I don't want to leave school until I've sat for my School Certificate,' he confided in Vera. 'It would be such a waste of all the work I've been doing. The moment the exams are over then I'll look for a job.'

'Shouldn't you wait until the results are out so that you have something to show a prospective employer?'

'Probably, but I can always tell them what subjects I have taken and the sort of marks I expect to get.'

'You can't be sure of the results . . .'

'You mean you think I might fail,' he interrupted. 'Thanks for the vote of confidence!'

'I didn't mean it like that!'

'Well, that's certainly what it sounded like,' he scowled.

'Please, Benny,' Vera squeezed his hand. 'Don't let's quarrel. The only way we'll get through this is by sticking together and helping each other. It's not going to be easy.'

'I know. I'm sorry, Vee. I didn't mean to snap. You know what they say,' he grinned, 'once you reach rock bottom, things can only get better.'

His words cheered her. After a fairly peaceful weekend she went into work on the Monday feeling happier than she'd done for ages. But her confidence was soon sapped.

'Mr Brown wants a word with you in his office at ten o'clock,' Miss Linacre told her stiffly.

Feeling very apprehensive, Vera went to his office. The moment she went in she sensed from his attitude that something was wrong.

'Miss Quinn, it is not easy for me to say this,' he told her awkwardly, 'but I am afraid I am going to have to replace you.'

For a moment Vera was struck dumb. Then, her colour rising, she demanded, 'Why is that, Mr Brown? What have I done wrong?'

Leonard Brown cleared his throat uneasily. Ever since Thelma Linacre had complained about Vera's timekeeping he'd wondered if they weren't being a little bit harsh in dismissing her. He'd heard rumours that her father was ill and surmised that the root cause of the trouble was that she was having a rather difficult time at home.

'We're only a small company and everyone has to pull their weight,' he explained awkwardly, wishing he could soften the blow.

'I know that! My work is always up to par and I . . . I don't make many mistakes,' she said defensively.

'You do take rather a lot of time off . . . especially at lunch times, I understand.'

She bit her lower lip and looked away. 'I . . . I have things to do then, family things.'

'Like shopping?'

She stiffened. 'Occasionally. Usually I do things to help my dad.'

She knew he was waiting for a fuller explanation than that, but she couldn't think of anything other than the truth. Suddenly the story of her father's 'attacks' came rushing out.

Leonard Brown listened in silence, his admiration for Vera increasing with every word he heard. He had liked her, with her bright smile and vivid blue eyes, from the moment she had applied for the job three years ago. She'd been a good worker and he'd been secretly amused at the way she had stood up to Thelma Linacre.

He would be happy enough to turn a blind eye to her poor timekeeping, but he knew if he did that then there were other members of staff who would take advantage of such leniency. He'd always been a stickler on these matters so he could hardly relax the rules now.

'I can see you have a considerable burden on your shoulders, Miss Quinn, I only wish there was some way in which I could help you.'

'Could I work part time?' she asked timorously.

He pondered the matter for a few minutes then shook his head. 'I'm afraid that wouldn't be very convenient for us. You know how the office is run, and you know we need someone here all the time to attend to the switchboard.'

'What about if I did some of the invoice typing at home?' she persisted.

Again Leonard Brown shook his head. 'I don't think Miss Linacre would agree to such an arrangement,' he said firmly.

'I understand.'

'Isn't it possible for you to help your father in his business?'

'Repairing boots and shoes? I don't have the right skills. Anyway, the state things are in he won't be doing that much longer because we won't be able to afford the rent on the shop,' she added bitterly.

'Mmm!' He looked thoughtful. 'Have you ever thought about employing someone to do the repairs for you? If you did that,' he hurried on, 'then I'm sure if you took care of all the paper work and deliveries then you would be able to build up the business again.'

Vera smiled wanly. 'It sounds like a sensible idea, except that I wouldn't be able to afford to pay the sort of wages that a skilled repairer would expect. It would only be possible if we managed to get all our old customers back and trade was as brisk as it used to be.'

He nodded understandingly. 'I happen to know of a boot repairer who's recently retired. Now, he might be exactly the sort of person you are looking for. If business was slow at first then it would give him a chance to get back into the swing of things.'

'It sounds like a good idea, but we'd still have to find his wages each week,' Vera said doubtfully.

'You'd only pay him for the work he did so if

you priced things carefully you'd find you could afford to hire him and still make a living for yourselves,' Leonard Brown pointed out.

Vera nodded thoughtfully as she mulled the idea over.

'He has retired, so he might be prepared to work fairly cheaply,' Leonard Brown reminded her. 'Would you like me to ask him to come along and have a chat with you?'

Chapter Twenty-seven

Vera felt sure she was going to like Sam Dowty from the moment he walked into the shop. With his thatch of thick white hair, white whiskers, twinkling blue eyes and ready smile he reminded her of a jovial Father Christmas.

The morning he turned up her father was in bed recovering from one of his attacks. It had lasted for two days and it had been one of the worst Vera had witnessed. She had been pondering all morning about what she ought to do for the best.

She knew there was no way she and Benny could repair the pile of boots and shoes they had taken in over the past few days and she was wondering if she should return them to their owners. Perhaps she also ought to put a notice on the shop door saying that they were unable to take in any more work for the present, she thought disconsolately.

When the bell jangled, and she saw the elderly man standing there, instinct told her that this was Sam Dowty, the retired shoe repairer that Mr Brown had told her about. She felt so relieved that she could have hugged him.

'Mr Brown from Elbrown's said something about you needing someone to give you a hand, missy,' he greeted her. He nodded towards the mound of shoes waiting to be repaired. 'It looks as though I haven't arrived a moment too soon,' he added, his eyes twinkling.

'Does that mean you can commence work right away, Mr Dowty?' Vera asked in disbelief.

'As long as you don't want to check out my references or any damn silly thing like that.' He unrolled a bundle from under his arm and took out a long leather apron. 'I came prepared,' he told her with a chuckle.

'I think that apron's proof enough that you know what you're about.' Vera grinned.

'Then I might as well get started. Now if you'd like to sort out the ones that are most urgent I'll do those first.' He looked round the shop. 'Nice little set-up you've got here, all very ship-shape.'

He set to work so quickly, as if he knew where everything was and what had to be done, that it was almost as if he had worked there for years.

At first he said very little, humming tunelessly to himself as he worked. At mid-morning when Vera made them both a cup of tea he paused and sat back on the stool and looked at her questioningly.

'So what has happened to the man who usually sits here at this bench?' he asked gravely.

'My dad? Well, he's not been very well lately,' she said ruefully.

He nodded understandingly. 'I had heard something of the sort.'

He didn't press the point, but waited expectantly as if he knew she was going to tell him more. Sam Dowty would have to know the whole story sometime, Vera reasoned, and this seemed to be as good a time as any to explain things to him.

In as few words as possible she told him about the attacks her dad was having. 'I think you ought to be clear about the situation because he doesn't know you are working here,' she confessed. 'I'm not at all sure how he will react when he finds out,' she ended lamely.

'Don't you worry, my dear. Now that you have taken me into your confidence I know what to expect.'

'I'm not sure that you do, Mr Dowty,' Vera said almost apologetically. 'You see, he can be very violent.'

Sam Dowty nodded benignly. 'Oh, but I do, my dear! My son was the same. He died about a year ago. Shell shock. That's what it is, you see. That's what your dad's suffering from, too, I'm afraid.'

Vera looked puzzled. 'He's been out of the army for years and years, though, and he's only recently started having these attacks.'

'That's the way it is, luv. They push all the terrible sights they saw and all the horrible things they experienced to the back of their minds to try and forget about them. Then suddenly it all comes back to them. Has he had any sort of bad shock lately that could have triggered it?'

Vera nodded thoughtfully, hoping he wouldn't ask her for details.

He looked at her shrewdly, then drained his cup and passed it back to her. 'Better get on. We don't want your dad coming in here and finding a pile of work waiting to be done. It would only worry him, now, wouldn't it.'

It was late afternoon before Vera heard her father stirring. A wave of panic swept over her as he blundered down the stairs. She glanced at him anxiously, trying to gauge what sort of mood he was in. She was nervous about what his reaction would be when he saw a stranger working at his bench.

'Afternoon, guv. Feeling a bit better?'

Michael Quinn stared at Sam Dowty in a dazed way, then rubbed his hand over his unshaven chin and shook his head from side to side as if trying to clear his mind.

'Who the hell are you? I don't know you!'

'Of course you do, guv. Sam Dowty. You asked me to come along and give you a hand.'

Vera held her breath, waiting for her father to explode. Instead, he ran his hand over his chin again and slowly nodded as if in agreement.

'I'll go and make you both a cup of tea,' Vera said quickly.

As she waited for the kettle to boil Vera watched through a crack in the door to see what was going on. Sam Dowty went on with his work as if there was no one else there. Her father sat with his head in his hands, looking up from time to time to watch what the older man was doing.

When Vera took the tea through, Sam Dowty signalled for her to leave them alone. Back in the living room she could hear the rise and fall of their voices and to her surprise she heard her father going into detail about his attacks.

'My son had the same problem,' she heard Sam Dowty tell her father. 'Some of the things he told me about the sights he'd seen would turn your guts. He wasn't a bloke who was squeamish, either, but he couldn't get them out of his mind. Haunted him they did. Made his life hell.'

Vera could hardly wait for Benny to come home so that she could tell him all about Sam Dowty and how well everything had gone.

'To hear him and Dad talking things over and exchanging confidences, you'd think they'd been buddies for years,' she enthused.

'Does this mean I won't have to do any more work in the shop?' Benny asked as he lowered his heavy satchel with all his homework in it from his shoulder onto the floor.

'No, you needn't do anything at all to help,' Vera told him happily.

'What about all the deliveries?'

'No, I'll do those. Now that I'm not working at Elbrown's I'll have plenty of time during the day,' she pointed out.

'Couldn't you get your job back at Elbrown's now that this old chap is here to help Dad out? If the two of them are as friendly as you said then he probably wouldn't mind keeping an eye on him.'

'I don't think that's possible, even if I could get reinstated. Mr Dowty is quite old and it wouldn't be fair to impose on him. I'm grateful enough that he's agreed to put in a full day until the backlog of work is cleared. Mind, I doubt if he will be able to work at that pace all the time. Once we've got things running properly again I should think he will only be working part time.'

'Yeah, well, that's better than nothing, I suppose.'

'It certainly is because it will give you time to study for your exams!'

'True! And once I've passed them, and managed to find a job, perhaps we could sell up and you could find another position. If Dad didn't need to work then . . .'

'Hey! Steady on!' Vera laughed. 'You can't plan that far ahead, who knows what is going to happen over the next few months.'

As it happened, Vera was right to be cautious. Although Sam Dowty and their father got on far better than she had ever dared to hope it wasn't the answer to their problems by any means.

Their father's attacks became more and more frequent and left him in such a dazed state that it became impossible for him to do any work at all.

Sam Dowty did his best, but his eyesight was not too good and with the approach of winter, and the need to use gas lighting most of the time to see what he was doing, the standard of his work began to suffer.

Vera was at her wits' end. She liked Sam Dowty so much, and she was so grateful for the way he was helping them out, that she didn't like to say anything about it to him.

The matter was brought to a head when an irate customer returned a pair of recently repaired boots.

He started making a fuss at the top of his voice in front of Sam Dowty.

'Look at the mess someone's made of these,' he shouted, waving the boots menacingly at Vera. 'They were black, but they've been finished off with brown polish! What's more, the polish has been splashed all over the upper of one of them. I can't wear them in this condition so what are you going to do about it?'

Vera had no idea, but she tried to placate him. 'If you leave them with me I'll make sure it is put right,' she promised.

'Put right? They're ruined! Any fool can see that,' he ranted.

'The young lady has already said we will rectify the matter,' Sam Dowty intervened. He took the offending boots from the customer, examined them critically, then put them down on the counter.

'You'd better, and make sure you do a good job. I don't expect to be charged for it, either. Daylight robbery! You've ruined a good pair of boots . . .'

The rest of his sentence was lost as he slammed out of the shop.

Vera sighed as she picked up the boots from the counter. She could see that his complaint was fully justified. He wasn't the only customer who had complained about the standard of their work recently and she wondered how many more there were going to be.

'It was my fault,' Sam Dowty said quietly. 'Don't worry, I'll see what I can do to put matters right.'

'It's a mistake anyone could have made,' Vera told him, squeezing his arm reassuringly.

He shook his head. 'No, only a half-blind old fool like me could have messed things up so much. What you need is a younger man working here. There's too much for an old codger like me to do and your father is no help at all these days, now is he.'

Vera knew he was right, but she still didn't have an answer to the problem.

'I could recommend a bright young chap if you would consider taking him on permanently.' Sam Dowty told her. 'Nice fellow, good workman. I can vouch for him.'

'It's certainly the sort of person we need, but I wouldn't be able to afford to employ anyone else,' she murmured regretfully.

'I'm talking about a young chap to replace me.'

'You don't want to give up work, surely!' Vera said in surprise. 'I thought you were enjoying being back in the harness.'

'I did at first,' he admitted, 'but I'm beginning to realise why you have to retire. I'm knocking seventy and I can't put in the hours like I used to do. I can't do the work the same, either,' he said sadly.

'You seem to be doing all right to me,' Vera told him loyally.

'You know that's not true. I've heard the complaints being fired at you over the past weeks. You've never said anything to me, but it's not good for your business. Your father has worked hard to build up a reputation for good service, now you don't want me to go and ruin all that, do you?'

'I'm sure you won't . . .'

'No!' Sam Dowty took off his leather apron and rolled it up into a ball. 'This needs to go back into the cupboard under the stairs. My wife said I was a silly old fool when I told her I was going back to work. I don't like having to admit she was right, but there you are, she seems to have been. You women!' He shook his head in mock dismay. 'You're always right, aren't you?'

Vera knew he was trying to break the news to her gently that he was leaving, but even though his work wasn't as good as she would have liked it was better having him here than no one.

She had to keep the business going until Benny was through with his schooling. She'd promised him she would and she didn't intend to let him down.

'Stay on for just a few more weeks, until I can find someone,' she begged.

'I've already told you that I know of a young chap,' he reminded her. 'I can recommend him because I trained him. That was in the days when my eyesight was as good as yours is, young lady, and I was able to take pride in my work,' he added with a wry smile.

Chapter Twenty-eight

It wasn't until after Sam Dowty had gone home that Vera realised he hadn't told her the name of the young man he'd suggested might come and work for her.

She wondered if he would remember and come back in the morning with the details. Or, because of her lack of enthusiasm, would he assume that she wasn't interested?

As she locked the shop door and went through into the living room, she decided she was too tired to worry about it any more. She wasn't too sure if it was the right thing to do, so it might be better if she slept on it anyway and made up her mind in the morning.

She prepared their evening meal, took her father's upstairs on a tray and then called Benny down from his bedroom where he'd gone to study the moment he got home from school.

As they ate their meal she talked to Benny about the day's happenings and the problem over the ruined boots. She also told him about Sam Dowty's decision to pack in work and his advice that they should hire a full-time younger cobbler.

'If you know where this Sam Dowty lives then I'll nip round and ask him the name of the chap,' Benny offered.

'I don't know where he lives, though,' Vera confessed. 'Mr Brown sent him along.'

'Then you'll have to wait and see if he comes back tomorrow.'

Vera sighed. 'I'm not too sure he will. I wasn't very keen on the idea when he mentioned it so he may think I'm not interested. I did tell him later on that I thought it was a good idea,' she added quickly as Benny raised his eyebrows questioningly.

A noise from upstairs distracted them. Vera rushed up to her father's bedroom to find that he was once again in the throes of an attack.

As she walked in through the door he hurled the plate of food she had brought up for him at her, then cowered down under the bedclothes, screaming at her to go away.

Wearily she picked up the broken plate and went to fetch a cloth to clean up the mess.

'We'll have to call in a doctor to take a look at him,' Benny told her. 'He needs something to quieten him down when he has one of these attacks. We can't go on like this any longer.'

'Perhaps we can persuade him to go and see the doctor at his surgery.'

'Don't talk daft, Vee! You know he won't do that. You'll have to get in touch with the doctor, explain what is happening, and ask him to call here.'

Benny sounded so determined that this was the right course of action to take that Vera accepted his decision. She felt too drained to argue.

In bed that night, her brain spinning like a top,

she thought back over the things that had happened lately.

Sometimes she felt as if other people were taking over her life. There always seemed to be someone deciding what she should do. Leonard Brown had told her she couldn't work for his company any more; a man she didn't even know had told her that the standard of work she was providing at the shop was not good enough; Sam Dowty had told her she needed a younger man to work in the business; and now Benny was telling her that she must call in a doctor to see her father.

Did they all know better than her? Or was she so tired out with looking after her father, and trying to keep their home and business together, that she could no longer think for herself?

As she opened up the shop next morning she toyed with the idea of not taking in any more work until she'd had a chance to talk to Sam Dowty. Perhaps he was right and the only way forward was to take on the young chap he had recommended.

She was still mulling over the problem when the shop door opened and a youngish man came in. He was tall and thin and his mid-brown hair flopped down over his hazel eyes. As he raised a hand and pushed it back there was something familiar about the gesture. Vera stared at him in disbelief. It was as though she was seeing a ghost from the past.

An older version; the same, yet not the same. There was a big difference between the physique of a very young schoolboy and a man in his twenties. Yet, though the face was more mature, the expression on it was one she would never forget.

'Jack . . . Jack Winter?'

'Vera Quinn?'

They spoke in unison and both of them answered 'Yes' at the same time.

He reached out and grabbed her hand. 'It must be twelve years?'

'No, it's much longer than that!'

'Yes, you're quite right! It was at the end of the war!'

'It was in 1919!'

He shook his head in disbelief. 'What happened? You suddenly vanished!'

'We moved here,' she explained, freeing her hand from his grasp.

'Yeah! Without even saying goodbye.'

'I didn't know you cared,' she quipped.

'Of course I did!' He pushed back his hair. 'You were my first and only heartthrob. Black hair, big blue eyes and such a special smile . . . In fact, that's why I recognised you the moment I walked through the door.'

Vera laughed and shook her head. 'You don't change, do you!'

Jack Winter's hazel eyes twinkled. 'Didn't you have a couple of big brothers?' he asked.

'Yes,' Vera nodded. 'There was Charlie. He was six years older than me, but he died from flu . . .'

'At the same time as your grandparents, Mr and Mrs Simmonds. I was only about nine, but I can remember what a dreadful time it was. People were dying within days of being taken ill.'

'Yes, it was dreadful.' Her face clouded for a moment. 'It happened at the same time as my dad came home from the army.'

Jack nodded understandingly. 'And what about Eddy?'

'He's at sea now. I have a younger brother, too, called Benny. He was born after we left Wallasey.'

'So he must be about thirteen ...'

'Fifteen, actually.'

'Fifteen years and I've never forgotten you.' He smiled. 'In fact, I've thought about you a lot. You took my heart with you when you disappeared.'

'You always could tell whoppers, Jack Winter,' Vera laughed. 'It's great to see you again, though.'

It certainly was, she thought. It brought back so many memories of happier days. Of her dear grandparents and of Charlie. Her recollections of those long-ago times in Wallasey had a magical golden glow to them. In those days they had been such a happy family.

She'd loved her dad so much, then. He had seemed such a kindly, loving giant who had treated her like a princess. She could remember riding high on his shoulders as he chased after Charlie and Eddy. He would play all sorts of games with her and read her a story after she was tucked up in bed at night.

Most of all, she remembered her mother. In those days she'd been plump, cuddly and so very kind and cheerful. She'd been so brave and dependable all the time her dad had been away in the army. She'd carried on as though nothing was the matter, yet she must have been dreadfully lonely without him, as well as worried about all the danger he might be in.

It was true that they'd had Gran and Grand-dad Simmonds popping in every day to see how they were, but her mother must still have been scared that something bad might happen to their father.

Vera had been too young at the time to under-stand why he had been so different when he'd come back from the war. Looking back, though, she now realised how much the change in him must have distressed her mother, especially when so many other things had gone wrong at the same time.

Almost overnight, or so it seemed, her grand-parents and Charlie were gone and absolutely everything had altered. Within a matter of weeks they'd moved away from Wallasey to Liverpool. They'd exchanged their comfortable home in Exeter Road to the barrack-like rooms behind the shop in Scotland Road.

Her mam had done her best to make it into a home, but it had always remained bare. So much of their furniture had been sold that it was never as comfortable or cosy as the home they'd grown up in.

School hadn't been as friendly, either, Vera thought with a shiver. When she'd attended Manor Road with Jack Winter and all the other friends she and her brothers had then, it had been like one big, happy family. They'd all walked to and from school with each other and played together afterwards.

'Yes, they were great days when we were both at Manor Road School, weren't they,' Jack commented as if reading her mind.

'It was a long time ago. Another life, almost,' she agreed sadly.

'And now we're both grown up.' He looked at her speculatively. 'Are you married, Vera?'

She shook her head emphatically. Colour drained from her face as she remembered Bill Martin.

'I seemed to have touched a raw nerve,' Jack said hastily.

'No, it's all right.' She bit down on her bottom lip and held her head high. 'How about you?' she asked quickly.

'Me, married! I could never find a girl who came anywhere near the one with black shining hair and big blue eyes who'd stolen my heart when I was so young,' he quipped.

Vera laughed. 'Still the same old Jack, you always could talk your way out of anything! Anyway, what are you doing in Liverpool?'

The smile went and was replaced by a puzzled look. 'An old chap called Sam Dowty came to see me last night and told me there was possibly an opening for a manager at a snob shop in Scotland Road.' He looked at a crumpled scrap of paper he took from his pocket. 'This was the number he gave me . . .'

Vera nodded. 'That's right, but I had no idea who Mr Dowty was thinking of as he forgot to tell me your name. I was hoping that he would come by this morning and let me know who it was.'

'Instead of which, I turn up! Well,' he looked round the shop and work area, 'all very business-like. Plenty of customers?'

Vera shrugged. 'We did have, but since my dad's been ill trade has dropped off a bit. It picked up again when Mr Dowty began helping out, but I'm afraid . . .'

'His eyesight isn't what it should be and his work wasn't up to standard. Don't worry, he explained it all to me. And about the owner's illness, so there's no need for us to talk about that either. The only thing Sam Dowty didn't tell me was the name over the shop!'

'So does this mean you are interested in coming to work here?'

'Well, I'm anxious to change my job. I want to be a manager and I'll never get the chance where I am now. There's two blokes older than me already waiting for the boss to retire. When old Sam told me about this place I was in two minds as to whether I wanted to work in Liverpool or not. Now I know I'm going to see you every day then I'm quite sure that I do.'

Vera smiled. 'I remember you were always one for cheeky answers.'

'It's my smile that charms everybody,' he laughed. 'Well, do you want me to get started so that you can check out the standard of my work before we do a deal?'

'I suppose that is the right way to do things, but somehow I don't think it will be necessary. I know all about you and by the sound of it you haven't changed very much. If Sam Dowty recommends you and says you're a good worker then I'm sure he's right.'

'What about your dad? Won't he want to have a say in all this?'

Vera frowned. 'To tell you the truth, I'm rather hoping that he might not remember that it was Sam and not you who was working here.'

'Whew!' Jack puffed out his cheeks. 'I know I'm a lot older than I was when we last met, but I didn't think I'd aged that much! I could wear a white wig and a false beard, I suppose!'

Vera shook her head. 'Oh, come on, Jack. You know what I mean.'

'Of course I do. I was only trying to lighten what looks to be a very serious situation. I haven't seen your dad since you lived in Wallasey . . .'

Vera held up a hand to silence him as the door between the living room and the shop opened and Michael Quinn was suddenly standing there.

He looked tired and dishevelled, but his blood-shot blue eyes were alert and wary.

'So who is this, then?' he rasped.

'Jack Winter. We knew him when we lived in Wallasey. I . . . I went to school the same time as he did.'

'Hello, Mr Quinn.' Jack held out a hand, which Michael ignored.

'Sam Dowty sent Jack along to take his place,' Vera said quickly. 'He's only this minute arrived. He was just going to start work.'

'That's right!' Jack took down her father's leather apron from its hook and began to put it on.

'That's my bloody apron you've got there,' Michael Quinn roared. 'Haven't you got one of your own?'

'I most certainly have, but I didn't bring it with me this morning. You don't mind if I wear yours for today, do you?'

Michael didn't answer. He turned and shuffled back into the living room and slammed the door behind him.

Jack raised his eyebrows as his gaze locked with Vera's. 'What does that mean? Have I said or done the wrong thing?'

She shook her head. 'I'm not too sure, Jack,' she said uneasily. 'I'll try and explain the situation to him while I make a cup of tea for us all. Perhaps I can get him to talk things over with you while we're drinking it.'

Chapter Twenty-nine

The next few months were some of the busiest, as well as the happiest, that Vera had ever known. Sometimes she had to pinch herself to make sure she wasn't dreaming.

Jack Winter had achieved wonders in the shop. His work was impeccable, and in next to no time word had spread and most of their old customers came back. Not only that, but they were so delighted with the results of his handiwork, and so fulsome in their praise, that they were recommending Quinn's as the best cobbler's in Liverpool.

'The last pair of boots I brought in here were well past it, but you've given them a new lease of life,' were remarks Vera heard over and over again.

Jack had also found time to give the shop a complete overhaul. He'd even given the walls a new coat of paint so that everything looked fresh and clean.

'The spring sunshine shows up dingy corners,' he laughed, when Vera tried to thank him.

'I know that, but it isn't really part of your job to do the decorating.'

'I did it for my own benefit, really. I like to work in bright, clean surroundings,' he added as an afterthought.

Vera nodded understandingly. She'd noticed how meticulous he was in the way he arranged everything. Soles were all segregated in their correct sizes and stacked 'left' and 'right' the way her father had always insisted they should be.

She smiled to herself as she remembered the terrible rows there had been over this when her brothers had been told to sort them out.

'My dad used to get into a right rage with Eddy and Benny because they could never tell a right sole from a left one,' she told Jack. 'It used to scare me so much that I would creep in and sort the soles out for them when Dad wasn't looking.'

'Keeping things in order is the easy part,' Jack grinned. 'It's keeping tabs on the pricing of each job and making sure that all the money tallies that I find hard work.'

Vera looked at him in surprise. 'Really? You've not made any mistakes as far as I am aware since you've been working here.'

'Only because I've checked everything half a dozen times. I even wake up in the middle of the night wondering if I've made any mistakes. It bugs me like hell. Figures were never my strong point, not even when we were at school.'

'So that was why you were always leaning over my shoulder,' Vera mocked. 'I thought you were being friendly, but what you were really doing was copying my work.'

'Now you know the truth,' Jack groaned. 'So what are you going to do about it? Send me packing?'

'No, you're too good a workman for that,' she

told him. Her tone became serious. 'I tell you what, Jack, why don't I write out all the tags, do the pricing up, and then check that when the work is paid for the money is totalled up correctly?'

'You mean as well as ordering all the materials we need and checking all the invoices, and paying the bills as they come in?'

She nodded. 'That will give you more time to concentrate on doing the repairs.'

'Do you think your dad will settle for that? I don't want him to think that I'm only doing half a job.'

'Do we need to tell him the details of how we work?' Her blue eyes sparkled. 'He seems to be more than happy to have you here and he's coming into the shop less and less. Days go by and he doesn't even ask what's going on.'

It took them a few weeks to work out a satisfactory system that suited them both. Vera was finding that she had to spend more and more time caring for her father, especially when he was in the throes of one of his attacks, so it was nowhere near as straightforward as they'd intended.

Jack decided that it was important that he knew exactly what needed to be done when the repairs were handed in. Accordingly, he said that he would be accountable for attaching a label listing the details of the work that he would be carrying out. After that it would be Vera's responsibility to do the pricing up.

There was still the question of the deliveries, though. Vera often found it difficult to fit this chore in during her busy day because of the problems with her father.

'Perhaps we should make a small charge for deliveries and then more of our customers would come and pick their repairs up from the shop,' Jack suggested.

'That would mean we'd have to stay open later at night. Most people don't finish work until after we close at six o'clock.'

'How about Benny doing them before he starts on his homework at night? It wouldn't take him anywhere near as long as it does you because he could use the bike instead of walking.'

'No! Please don't mention it to him, not at the moment,' Vera said quickly.

Jack held up his hands and took a step back. 'I wouldn't dream of interfering. You know best!'

'It's only a few weeks before he has to sit his School Certificate exams and he's studying as hard as he can. It means such a lot to him, and to me as well, that he gets good marks,' Vera explained.

'Of course it does, I quite understand that,' Jack assured her. 'What sort of work does Benny intend to do once he's passed?'

'I've no idea. One thing's for sure, though, he doesn't want to come and work in the shop.'

'You mean that being a snob isn't good enough for him?'

'I don't think it's so much that as the fact that he knows he couldn't work with Dad. They both like doing things their own way.'

'So do I and your dad seems to have accepted that with no argument.'

'That's probably because you do things in the same way as he used to do them. He was always a stickler for order. Even the tacks had to be in their right boxes, graded according to their size, and if he found them muddled up he would get really mad.'

Jack nodded, then frowned. 'He hasn't challenged any of the changes, I've made, has he?'

'You haven't made all that many, Jack. His workbench is still in the same place, and you've left the buffing machine and the sewing machine exactly where he likes to have them. Even though you've cleaned everything up, and varnished the counter, he can still find everything. I'm sure that's why he's accepted you working here so readily.'

'What about you? Are you still happy about me working here?' Jack probed.

'Absolutely!'

His lean face beamed. 'It's good to hear you say that! It's the best thing that's ever happened to me. I'll always be grateful to Sam Dowty for putting us in touch.'

'And so will I. I'm very thankful indeed,' she agreed enthusiastically.

As she spoke she saw a flicker in Jack's hazel eyes that made her colour rise, and she quickly looked away in confusion.

Jack sighed. He'd been wondering whether perhaps he should be looking around for another job, but now that Vera had said Benny had no interest in taking over the business he felt that his own position was safe.

He liked working there. It was not only because

he was more or less his own boss, but because he was back in touch with Vera Quinn.

He'd never forgotten about her in all the years that they'd been apart. Now, being able to work alongside her, day in, day out, made him unbelievably happy. He was extremely anxious, though, to know exactly how she felt about him.

'Do you really mean that, Vera? That you are pleased we've met up again?' The inflexion in his voice as well as the eager look on his face warned her to be careful.

She knew they'd been the best of friends when they'd been at school in Wallasey, but that was a whole lifetime ago. They had both grown up in such very different circumstances. Any feelings he may have had for her then had been childish ones.

She'd enjoyed his company in those days, too. She'd preferred playing with him than with her own brothers, but perhaps that had been because he was nearer her age than they were. He had been a friend of Eddy's, of course, and in those days anything that Eddy had she'd always wanted to share.

If her family had stayed in Wallasey, and she had grown up seeing Jack Winter every day of her life, then she would probably have tired of his company long before now, she told herself.

But would she? Discreetly she studied his profile as he concentrated on the boot he was resoling. His brown hair flopped forward over his brow in such an appealing way that she felt her heart beat faster. The determined set of his chin and the tilt of his head endeared him to her.

When he looked up and she saw the warmth in his hazel eyes, and the ready smile on his face, her heart pounded. She knew that instance that what she felt for him was more than mere gratitude because he was working so hard on their behalf. Her feelings went deeper than that. An inner glow seemed to fill her whenever she was with him.

Resolutely, she pulled herself together, knowing that under no circumstances must she allow herself to become involved in anything more than a good working relationship. She must never for a moment forget how important Jack Winter was to her family as a manager of their business. Falling in love with him was too great a risk.

She'd given her heart away once, to Steve Frith, and look where that had got her. She'd been so upset when he'd walked out on her that she'd felt there was nothing left to live for.

The horrendous memory of the incident that had followed that – the attempted rape by her father's crony, Bill Martin – came flooding back to her.

She'd tried desperately hard to blot the scene from her mind. By concentrating on her day-to-day problems she had practically succeeded. At night, though, lying there in the dark, too tired to sleep, there were times when she remembered the shameful details all too vividly. How could she ever become romantically involved ever again?

Although Rita and Eddy were still planning to get married, Rita was no longer a close friend to Vera. When they did meet up, Rita was so full of all the things happening in her own life that she rarely talked of anything else. And she still refused to come to the house, no matter how often she invited her to do so.

'Not on your life!' Rita told her. 'Not after what your father did to me. I don't want to be groped by him ever again, thank you very much!'

Vera didn't blame her for not wanting to see her father, but she did think that Rita was making more of the matter than she needed to do. She was sure it had only been a bit of silliness on her dad's part because he'd had too much to drink, and that really he'd meant no harm.

Unfortunately, Rita saw it in a different light. But remembering the horror she'd felt herself over what had happened when Bill Martin had attacked her, Vera could understand why Rita was determined to keep her distance. It meant, though, that there was no one she could share her worries with.

Even though she had strong feelings for Jack Winter, and was aware that he liked her a great deal, Vera felt she couldn't allow him to get any closer. She knew she was letting the fact that she'd been let down by Steve Frith and the horrible incident with Bill Martin scar her mind, but Jack's friendship meant so much to her that she couldn't bear the thought of losing it.

Chapter Thirty

Jack Winter had always spent a great deal of his time thinking about Vera Quinn. She had never really been out of his thoughts since they'd been at school together as small kids. He'd been very upset when she had simply vanished from his life. Even so, he was still shocked that when they met up again after so many years he felt more interested in her than ever.

She'd changed, but that wasn't surprising as it had been fifteen years. Then she'd been a bit of a madcap, but with her shiny black hair cut into a bob that framed her face, her bright blue eyes and rosy cheeks, he'd always thought she looked like Snow White. She still did, too, only a much more grown-up, serious version.

Now she had a calm, reserved air about her, and her eyes, although still a startling blue, were thoughtful rather than mischievous.

Her mind was razor-sharp when it came to dealing with business matters. She might not be physically capable of repairing boots and shoes, but she understood all that was involved and dealt with any problems that arose in an efficient manner that impressed him.

He'd changed, too, from a kid dressed in short grey flannel pants and a knitted jersey, who had scabby-knees and scuffed boots, to a respectable hard-working snob who wanted to make something of his life. That was why he'd been so eager to get a manager's job. The next step was to have a business of his own.

He'd learned to stand on his own two feet when he'd been sixteen and his mother had remarried. He didn't like or dislike her new husband, but he knew he couldn't live under the same roof as him, so he'd moved out. He'd found digs in New Brighton and quite enjoyed the freedom. His landlady was middle-aged, a fairly good cook and kept the place spotless.

There was plenty to do in New Brighton, even in the winter when the holidaymakers and day-trippers weren't there, so he was quite content with his lot. At least, he had been until he'd met up with Vera again and realised that he wanted more from life than he already had. He needed a home and family of his own and Vera figured prominently in his scheme of things.

Vera's problems troubled him and he tried to think of some way of making life easier for her, knowing full well the strain she must be under.

He kept wondering where he stood with her. She had been overjoyed to see him and happy to reminisce about their childhood escapades.

Friendship based on schoolday memories was not what he wanted, though. His feelings for Vera ran much deeper than that. He'd gone out with quite a few girls, but none of them had ever meant anything to him. He'd had fun, but it was merely a passing phase. None of them had dislodged the memories of a dark-haired, blue-eyed girl who'd captured his heart when he'd been too young to know that he was in love.

Jack cared a lot about Vera and wished he could reduce her worries. It irked him the way young Benny managed to keep well out of it all. He'd been out working at fifteen, not still at school like Benny.

He gathered from what Vera had said that Benny had no interest at all in the shop, which was a great pity for the family business because it was unlikely that Michael Quinn would ever put in a full day's work ever again. His attacks were not only becoming more frequent, but were increasing in severity and lasting longer.

It worried Jack to think of Vera being in the same house as her father when he was in one of his attacks. If you spoke to him he looked right through you. It was as if he didn't know anyone, or was even aware of where he was. He seemed to be holding conversations with imaginary people, waving his hands in the air and threatening everyone around him.

Jack had felt quite astonished by the way Michael would pull himself up to his fullest height, square his shoulders and become transformed into a man of incredible strength. He would lift pieces of furniture around as if they were made of cardboard, piling them one on top of the other to form a barricade.

His own father had suffered from shell shock when he'd come home from the war, but he had never been violent. Nor could he ever remember him going to the lengths that Michael Quinn did to protect himself from the enemy.

In his father's case the bouts of fear had caused him to shiver and tremble so much that he couldn't hold a cup or even sit still. If an attack came on while he was in bed his trembling was so severe that the entire bed would shake.

His father's spasms had lasted for anything up to a couple of hours and by the end of it he was so drained that he was as weak as a kitten. He would lie there limp and helpless, either with his eyes closed or staring blindly into the distance, saying nothing and taking no notice of anyone.

At first it had distressed his mother a great deal. But once she realised there was nothing she could do to help him she had hardened her heart and waited for him to recover from each episode in his own good time.

When the attacks became so frequent that he had barely recovered from one before another started he had been admitted to hospital. There they kept him sedated for most of the time.

Jack had no idea what sort of medication they'd given him, but gradually he had drifted into a twilight world of his own. He barely recognised any of them and sometimes it seemed pointless visiting him. Whenever he'd done so, he found that sitting by the side of the bed, holding his father's hand, not knowing what to say, had left him feeling wretched for days afterwards.

The end, when it came, left the entire family feeling more relieved than sorrowing. This was especially so for his mother, who had foreseen what the outcome would be long before anyone else.

Jack still found it distressing to think about his father. He had gone off to war so fit and healthy and returned a complete wreck. He knew he was only one of millions in the same boat, but it seemed such a terrible waste.

His mother had been a great deal stronger, refusing to give way and become a grieving widow. She had got on with her life, and, to the surprise of family and friends, she had even got married again.

Jack felt desperately sorry for Vera because he suspected that the worst was still to come and he wished he could do more to help her. It still brought a lump to his throat to think about his own dad lying in a hospital bed, unsure of where he was and unable to recognise the faces of the people who loved him the most.

There were times when Jack wondered if he ought to warn Vera about what could happen, but decided against doing so since every case was different. There was no point in adding to her worries, he told himself.

All he could do was try and be there for her when she needed him. To stand by her and give her all the support he could when the time came.

For all that, Jack's conscience worried him every time he saw Michael Quinn in one of his tearing rages. He could harm himself, but, even more important as far as he was concerned, he could do Vera a serious injury.

Several times he tried to talk to Benny about it,

but he sensed that the subject of his father's illness frightened him. His way of avoiding what was going on was to concentrate solely on his schoolwork.

'I don't know much about it. You should talk to our Vera,' he would prevaricate. 'She understands about Dad's problems. She always tells me to leave her to see to him whenever he has one of his attacks.'

'I know all about that,' Jack admitted, 'but I don't think it is safe for her to be left to cope with him on her own.'

'Why not? She manages all right.'

Jack shook his head. 'Not always. Your dad is terribly strong when he is in the throes of an attack. Sometimes he gets quite violent and I'm worried about what might happen to Vera one day when he loses control and lashes out at her.'

Benny looked uncomfortable. 'I know that does happen sometimes, but she's always ready for him. Up until now she's always been able to dodge out of the way whenever he's hit out.'

'Or that's what she's told you!'

'What do you mean?' Benny asked uneasily.

'How do you think she gets all those bruises on her arms? And sometimes there are cuts as well as bruises on her face!'

'Are you saying that those are caused when my Dad's flailing his arms around?' Benny exclaimed in alarm.

'That's right! One of these days he'll hit her so hard that he'll knock her unconscious.'

Benny ran a hand through his thick hair and looked overwhelmed. 'Are you certain about this?'

'Quite sure! She tries to cover up the marks and bruises on her face with cream and powder, but they're there all right.'

'Well, I didn't know. She's never said anything to me,' Benny said defensively. 'What do you want me to do about it? I can tell you now that Vee won't take any notice of anything I say.'

'What about Eddy? Does he know how ill he is?'

'I don't know,' Benny shrugged. 'He's away at sea, isn't he.'

'Perhaps you should tell him exactly what is going on, then.'

Benny shrugged again. 'He knows about what happens when Dad's in one of his moods. That's why he gave up his job at Cammell Laird's and went to sea. Dad used to thump him. He never had much time for Eddy, they were always rowing.'

'Why was that?'

'Dad was always calling him a runt because he's a short-arse. Dad thinks he should be at least as tall and broad shouldered as he is.'

'Like you are . . . like Charlie was.'

Benny frowned. 'I never knew Charlie. He died the year before I was born. How well did you know him? He was at the same school as you and Eddy and our Vee, wasn't he?'

'Yes, we were all at Manor Road School. He was in a higher class than me, though. I was in the same year as Vera.'

'Vee never told me about that!' Benny exclaimed.

'We were all at the same school. We all used to play together; Vee, Eddy and the rest of the gang.'

'Eddy is going to be very surprised next time he comes ashore to find you working in Dad's shop.'

'Yes, he probably will be. When is he due home again?'

'Any day now, I should think. He's been away for almost six months.'

Jack gave a silent whistle. 'As long as that? Then he won't have any idea that your dad is now a great deal worse than when he left.'

'Not unless his girlfriend, Rita Farthing, has written and told him. I don't suppose she has mentioned it, though, because she probably doesn't know either. She never comes near here and Vee doesn't seem to see much of her these days. They used to be the best of friends, but they fell out over something or the other and stopped seeing each other.'

'Would you let me know when Eddy's home on leave in case he decides not to come round. I'd like to see him again and catch up on what's been happening with him since he left Wallasey.'

'You're sure to see him because he always calls in to have a chat with our Vee.'

'Well, I'd like you to let me know all the same. He might come after the shop is closed and I'd hate to miss him.'

If Eddy was going back to sea again there would not be a lot he would be able to do to help, but he thought Vera had told him that Eddy was going to make this his last trip because he was planning on getting married.

He knew that it was really none of his business,

but he hated to see Vera looking so tired and worried. He felt it was time that someone else in the family took some of the responsibility for looking after Michael Quinn off her shoulders.

Since Eddy was now the eldest son then he felt that it was up to him to show a lot more consideration. He didn't approve of him simply leaving Vera to get on with things the best she could.

Perhaps if he had a quiet chat with Eddy he could make him understand how extremely ill his father was. He would also try and tactfully explain how dangerous it was for Vera to be the one looking after him.

In his opinion, Michael Quinn needed professional care. He was well aware, though, that unless they were able to afford to put him in a private nursing home, it probably meant he would have to go into a mental institution.

He suspected that Vera knew this only too well and that this was the reason why she refused to call in a doctor to see her father.

Chapter Thirty-one

Edmund Quinn leaned his elbows on the rails of the top deck, and watched as the fussy little tug boats guided the *SS Victoria* up the River Mersey. As usual when he returned from a long trip he didn't feel that he was home until he caught a glimpse of the magnificent birds perched high above the Liver Building, like sentinels guarding Liverpool.

He'd been standing on deck since the first moment they'd entered the estuary, completely oblivious to the sharp early morning nip in the air.

As the misty outlines of the Welsh mountains gave way to the coastlines of the Wirral peninsular on one side, and Lancashire on the other, he looked from one to the other, intent on taking in every detail.

As they sailed past Hoylake and Leasowe, Eddy felt a sudden pang of nostalgia. When New Brighton came into view, memories of his childhood days in Wallasey flashed through his mind. The memories of those happy times, full of sunshine and laughter, quickly slipped away, though, as he compared them with life after they moved to Scotland Road in Liverpool.

There had been such a change in his father when

he'd come home from the army. All the love and kindness had gone and it was as if he was still a sergeant in command of his troops. His attitude towards all of them had changed for good.

Remembering his father's behaviour before he left home, Eddy considered how the same changes had taken place in hundreds of other families since the war. He hadn't realised before he left that others were suffering in the same way. He knew that now, though, because he'd met so many other chaps in the navy who'd talked openly to him about such matters.

Many of them also had to face seeing their fathers suffering from the effects of shell shock, or severe physical injuries that left them bad tempered and irritable. Many had been so incapacitated that they'd been unable to hold down proper jobs since they'd returned to Civvy Street.

He learned that many of his shipmates found the differences in their fathers' personalities quite unbearable. For some it had been a turning point in their own lives.

Like him, when they'd been young they'd looked up to their dads, wanted to be like them when they grew up and to follow in their footsteps when they left school and were old enough to work.

For Eddy that would have meant learning to repair boots and shoes, but when his dad had been demobbed he'd altered so much that the thought of working alongside him was out of the question. He knew he couldn't, they simply didn't get on.

There was no chance of them ever becoming

reconciled. He'd been so scared when his dad flew into a temper. He could hear his voice even now. His standard threat, 'I'll thump your bloody skull' followed by the impact of the knuckles of his dad's screwed up fist on the top of his head and the excruciating pain that followed, had stayed with him ever since.

The night his dad had pushed their mum down the stairs still haunted him and was something he could never forget or forgive.

Vera had done her best, tried to take their mam's place, but she hadn't been able to keep his dad off his back, or make his dad like him any better.

No matter what he did his old man found fault with him. Right old bastard he'd turned into. Boozed up to the eyebrows most of the time. He'd never forget the night they had a party to celebrate the completion of his apprenticeship and his old man had tried to force himself on Rita. Nor had she, he thought wryly. It wasn't surprising really that she'd never let him forget about it for one moment.

Looking back he sometimes wished he'd finished with Rita right there and then. He should have known that she'd never be able to put his dad's attack out of her mind. It was something she brought up whenever they had the slightest difference of opinion.

Even so, he hadn't expected Rita to take up with someone else while he was away at sea. That ranked with the 'Dear John' letters that so many badly injured soldiers had received from their wives and girlfriends during the war.

He'd been away a lot, he knew that, but he'd done long trips so that he could earn enough money for them to get a place of their own once they were married. He wasn't a great letter writer so she'd probably been lonely and fed up, he told himself.

He hadn't told Vee yet that he and Rita were no longer together. He didn't know if they saw each other at all these days, but thought probably not or she would have mentioned it when she wrote to him. If Vera knew nothing about it then she would be incensed when she heard that Rita had got tired of waiting and had thrown him over for someone else.

Vee thought that this really was to be his last trip. In fact, he'd promised her that it would be. He kept telling her that he intended coming home to take a shore job and that as soon as he and Rita were married she and Benny could come and live with them.

He also had to face up to breaking the news to her that far from coming back to Liverpool he was intending to marry a Maltese girl and settle down in her home town. He knew it would be hard for Vee to take all this in, but he hoped she would understand.

As the Liver Building came into view he wondered why he had bothered to come back. He certainly didn't want to see Rita, or his dad or Di. It would have been so much easier to simply write and tell them what he was planning to do. He wanted to see Vera though, and to see for himself how Benny was doing.

A new day was dawning, the rising sun casting golden stripes on the murky waters of the Mersey as they came alongside the landing stage. He saw the tugs being detached from the *SS Victoria* and watched as they chugged away towards Birkenhead. He stayed where he was on deck as they tied up and the gangplank was lowered. Only then did he go down into the bowels of the ship to collect his kitbag.

As he walked up the floating roadway to the Pier Head where half a dozen trams were waiting, he considered which one he should take. He couldn't decide whether to travel direct to Scotland Road and walk in through the shop, or to take one that went along Great Homer Street so that he could sneak home down the jigger. He favoured the latter route; it was still early morning so he could surprise Vera at home before she had time to leave for work at Elbrown's.

Once aboard the *Green Goddess* he began rehearsing in his head how he was going to break all his news to Vera. It was going to be one of the hardest things he'd ever had to do.

He felt guilty about leaving her to continue holding the fort, shouldering all the responsibility for bringing up Benny and looking after their unstable father, but what else could he do?

Benny would be leaving school any day now, finding work and making a life of his own. There was still plenty of time for Vera to make a life for herself, too. She was only in her twenties, after all.

As he nipped through the jigger and headed for the back door, Eddy felt like a kid again. He realised that this would probably be the last time he visited the place. He'd only stay for a few days, just long enough to explain to Vera about what was happening. He'd tell his dad, of course, but he didn't suppose that he would care one way or the other.

As he turned the door handle and stepped into the kitchen he paused to listen. He could hear movement in the living room and judged it would be Vera either tidying up or getting ready for work.

Very quietly, he put his kitbag down on the floor and crept over to the living-room door. He paused, took a deep breath, then flung it open, at the same time as he called out, 'You'll never guess who this is!'

The room was in complete darkness. Eddy didn't see where the blow came from, but something hit him hard on the side of his head, sending him crashing to the ground. The next minute someone was on him, pinning him down, breathing heavily and hissing obscene threats into his ear.

He struggled wildly, trying to push his opponent away, and fight off the blows from the flailing arms. He had no idea who his attacker was, but reasoned that it must be a burglar, someone who had broken in and had been taken unawares by his surprise entry.

A fear that Vera might have been attacked and might be lying hurt flashed through his head and gave him added strength as he twisted and turned and grappled with his assailant.

Before he managed to overcome him, the connecting door between the shop and the living room opened. A figure stepped into the room, whether he was someone who was going to help him, or an accomplice of the man he was fighting with, Eddy had no idea.

Light flooded into the room through the open door and Eddy gasped as he saw the state of his surroundings. It resembled a battlefield. Upturned chairs were everywhere, some of them piled up as though to form a barricade around the table. Underneath the table was a stash of food as though someone was camping there.

Eddy had now quelled his attacker and was sitting astride him. Slowly, feeling unutterably stupid when he saw that it was his father he was pinning to the ground, he released him.

'What the hell is going on?'

Eddy looked up at the figure standing in the doorway, but because the light was behind him he couldn't see the man's face. Before he could answer, he heard Vera coming in through the back door and heard her give a sharp cry as she caught her leg against the kitbag he'd left just inside the doorway.

Eddy felt completely nonplussed. Who was this stranger, and why was the whole place in a shambles? What on earth was going on?

'Hello, Vee!' He pulled himself to his feet, leaving his father still lying on the ground trying to get his breath back.

'Eddy! What are you doing here? Oh it's so wonderful to see you!' She flung her arms around him, kissing his cheek, almost crying with sheer happiness because he was there.

Hugging her, he said, 'I came in through the back way, meaning to surprise you, but I think I was the one who got the surprise.' He waved an arm around indicating the state of the room and his father lying on the floor. 'What on earth is going on here? Dad almost knocked me out!'

'Ssh!' She put a finger to her lips. 'He's having one of his attacks,' she told him quietly. 'He thinks he is back in the war and he builds himself a hideout so that the enemy won't find him. He obviously thought you were coming to attack him.'

'How long has this been going on?'

She frowned. 'Quite some time. They're an extension of the rages he used to go into before you went away to sea.'

'So he's worse? How often does he have these persecution attacks then?'

She looked across at the figure still standing in the doorway. 'A couple of times a week, I would say, wouldn't you, Jack?'

Jack Winter shrugged. 'At least! Sometimes it is even more often than that.' He smiled at Eddy. 'You've forgotten me, haven't you, Eddy! Mind, it's a long time since we last saw each other.'

Eddy looked at him, frowning as if trying to remember his face. 'Jack Winter!' he exclaimed. 'What the hell are you doing here?'

'I work here, whacker. Your Vera hired me!' He grinned. 'I do the repairs for your dad.'

'You mean you're a snob?' Eddy shook his head in disbelief. 'And to be working here of all places! I can't credit it.'

'I've been working here for quite a while. It was

315

all getting to be too much for your dad. You mean that Vera didn't tell you?'

Eddy shook his head. 'Not that it was you! In her last letter she did say that an old chap was helping out. I think she said his name was Sam Dowty. What happened to him?'

'Poor old Sam's eyesight wasn't too good and he kept making mistakes. He used to be my boss. In fact, he trained me and we've always kept in touch. He was the one who recommended me to Vera. It was a surprise to her, too, when I turned up.'

'Can you two stop gabbing and help me get Dad up to bed?' Vera asked worriedly. 'He looks absolutely all in.' She looked up at Eddy and smiled. 'I think this is the first time he's actually had to face the enemy since he came back from the war.'

Between them, Eddy and Jack helped Michael Quinn upstairs and onto his bed. He made no resistance, the fight had gone out of him. Instead, he lay there unmoving, ignoring all of them.

'Leave him as he is, don't bother about undressing him,' Vera told them quietly. 'I'll take his boots off and then cover him over with a quilt and let him have a sleep.'

'I'll leave you two to see to him, then, I'd better get back to the shop,' Jack stated.

'Come on, we'll go downstairs, Eddy, and I'll make a pot of tea. Whilst we're drinking it you can tell me all your news,' Vera murmured, taking her brother's arm after they'd made their dad comfortable.

'Now,' she asked as soon as they were in the living room, 'have you and Rita fixed a date for your wedding and decided where you are going to live?'

Chapter Thirty-two

Vera insisted that Jack and Eddy went out to the pub for a drink at midday.

'Go on,' she urged. 'It will give you both a chance to catch up on all that has happened since you were at school together in Wallasey.'

'Do you want me to close the shop?' Jack asked as he took off his leather apron and hung it on its nail.

'No, there's no need to do that. You don't need to hurry back, either. I'll keep an eye on things here,' she told him.

'Are you sure you can manage on your own, Vee?' Eddy asked worriedly. 'I don't mean the shop, I know you can cope with that, but what if Dad starts getting difficult again?'

'He won't. The events of this morning have worn him out. He's fast asleep and probably won't wake up again until this evening.'

'Is that what usually happens?'

'Yes, he often sleeps for several hours after one of his attacks,' Jack assured him.

As soon as they were settled into a quiet corner of the Brewer's Arms, Eddy began to question Jack about the deterioration in his father's condition.

'I had no idea he was so bad,' he confessed. 'Vee didn't say much about it in her letters so I never

318

gave it a great deal of thought. He has always been moody and sometimes he can get a bit free with his fists, but what happened this morning was frightening.'

'It's been happening more and more,' Jack told him. 'It worries me, I can tell you. I hate having to go home at night, leaving Vee on her own with him.'

'Benny is there to give her a hand if necessary, isn't he?'

Jack shrugged. 'He seems to ignore what goes on. As soon as he comes home from school he goes off up to his bedroom to do his homework. I suppose he would help if Vera really needed him to.'

Eddy took a drink of his beer. 'He's only a kid, though! I don't suppose he'd be much good if the old man became violent.'

Jack raised his eyebrows. 'It must be some time since you've seen him! He's a big lad! He takes after your Charlie. Built like a shithouse on a Welsh hillside as some of his mates used to describe your brother.'

The reference to Charlie started them reminiscing about the days when they had all been at Manor Road School in Wallasey. Helped by a second beer, one anecdote sparked off another. The problems concerning Michael Quinn were temporarily forgotten.

'So if you're not married, does that mean you are still living at home?' Eddy asked as they once more refilled their glasses.

'No!' Jack pulled a face. 'At the moment I'm in digs in New Brighton. As I told you, my mam married again; I decided to get out from under their feet.'

'Are you happy living in digs?'

'I get by. I've got a decent room and the landlady cooks, cleans and does my washing. Some day I'll find a proper flat, but there's no rush.'

'Yeah, not easy finding a place of your own that you can afford, is it. I think in a way that was one of the main problems Rita and I had. She used to want us to get married, settle down and have kids. Before we could do that, though, I had to get enough money together for us to set up a home together.'

'Couldn't you have moved in with her folks?'

'And have her mother breathing down our necks and running our lives for us? No thanks!'

'No room at your own place? Or didn't Vera fancy the idea of having you as lodgers?'

'Actually there was room: there's a couple of attic rooms we could have done up and turned into a proper self-contained home.' He sighed. 'The trouble was that Rita wouldn't agree to it and I didn't get on with dad, as you know.'

'So you've been at sea making enough money to come back and get your own place?'

'Yeah,' Eddy snorted, 'and whilst I've been doing that she's found someone else!'

Jack gave a long low whistle. 'That's tough treatment, whacker!'

'You're telling me!'

Jack took a swig of his beer. 'What happened?'

'Right after my last shore leave I received a letter from her telling me the news. She must have felt this way when I came home, but she never breathed a word. She took all the clobber I brought back for her, as well as a load of stuff I'd bought for our new home, and seemed to be as pleased as punch with them. A couple of weeks later she wrote and told me it was all off.'

'Broke your heart, eh!' Jack commented.

'Yeah, you could say that!' Eddy paused and took a long drink of his beer. 'Then I did a bloody silly thing,' he admitted reluctantly. 'When we put into Valetta I started going out every night and getting pissed. I got a bit too friendly with a Judy who worked in one of the taverns I went to. One night, when I'd had a real skinful, and was too drunk to stand on my own two feet, she took pity on me and took me back to her place.'

'To sober you up?'

Eddy nodded. 'Her name's Maria. Lovely looking, olive skin, big brown eyes, thick dark hair. Well, the next time we docked in Malta she was there at the quayside to meet me. She told me she was expecting and she wanted us to get married right away.

'She was in quite a state because she's a Catholic and her folks are really strict. They said that she'd brought disgrace on the family, so they wanted her out of their home right away. We've got our own place and we've everything ready for the baby. We're getting married as soon as I get back to Malta.'

'You sure it is your kid? She could have been pulling a fast one?' Jack murmured cautiously.

'I'm sure she was telling the truth. She's crazy about me. Anyway,' he said with a grin, 'I'll know for certain in a few months' time when it's born.' He drained his beer and picked up Jack's empty glass. 'Another one before we go back to the shop?'

'I don't know,' Jack hesitated. 'I've got work to do. Anyway, it's not fair leaving Vera to cope on her own.'

'She told us to take all the time we wanted. She knows that we have a lot of catching up to do.'

'You haven't told her you've finished with her friend Rita or about your plans for the future,' Jack murmured.

'No, not yet. That's why I need another beer to give me the courage to do so.'

'Well, make it a half then,' Jack told him.

When Eddy returned with their beer, Jack said, 'Vera's going to be a bit shocked when you tell her that you're going to make your home in Malta, isn't she?'

'Yes, I suppose she is, but what can I do? I am in love with Maria. It's not simply about her having this baby, I really want to marry her.'

'Have you got a job fixed up in Malta then?'

'Not yet, but I do have engineering qualifications so I'll be able to find work in one of the shipyards easily enough.'

'So where will you live?'

'Like I said, we got our own place after Maria's family threw her out.'

'Her family will probably accept her back into

the fold once the baby arrives,' Jack commented wryly.

'Probably!'

'So why didn't you get spliced before anyone knew that she was preggers and save all the bother?'

'I'm not a Catholic, am I! I had to convert and undergo some religious training and we agreed to wait until I've finished all that before we got married.'

'I thought Catholics were allowed to marry non-Catholics as long as they promised to bring up any kids they have in the true faith?'

'Well, I'm doing it for Maria. It's what she wants.' Eddy hid his embarrassment by taking a long drink of his beer.

'I had no idea the old man was as bad as he is,' Eddy said, changing the subject abruptly as he put his beer glass down. 'Is he getting any sort of treatment?'

Jack shook his head. 'No, Vera's reluctant to call in the doctor. I think it's in case he decides that your father ought to be in some sort of hospital or home. She knows he would hate that.'

'Maybe he would, but if he needs someone to be there all the time to watch out for him then that's exactly where he ought to be.'

'Are you going to be the one to tell Vera that's what she ought to do?'

'She wouldn't take any notice if I did,' Eddy said glumly.

They sat there drinking and musing over the problem in silence for several minutes, until Eddy banged down his beer glass. 'I've got it,' he said jubilantly. 'I've got the perfect solution.'

'Oh yes, and what's that? Don't tell me, you're planning to take your dad back to Malta with you?'

'You must be bloody joking! Either that or you're not used to drinking beer at midday and it's addling your brain!'

'Go on then, tell me your idea.' Jack grinned.

Eddy looked thoughtful. 'Well, you were saying a while back that your mam had remarried and that you'd moved out into digs.'

'Yes, that's right.' Jack looked bemused. 'I don't see what that has got to do with it, though.'

'Earlier on, when we were talking about me and Rita getting married, remember I mentioned the attics up over the shop? Well, why don't you move in there? You'd kill two birds with one stone, as they say. You'd have a place of your own and you'd be there to give Vera a hand whenever she needed it.'

'Are you mad, Eddy? Vera would never stand for me living under the same roof as her.'

'Why not? You get on well, you always have.'

'But that was different altogether.'

'You work well enough together running the shop,' Eddy persisted.

'Again, that's different. I admit we have a business arrangement that works, but it's only for so many hours a day. When we shut the shop at six I go off home and she doesn't see me again until the morning.'

'She needn't see you until the next morning if you live up in the attics. Not unless she calls you down because Dad is acting up and she can't cope with him on her own,' Eddy pointed out.

'It's a good plan, I'll admit that. It would let you off the hook, too,' Jack laughed. 'But I'm not at all sure it would work, even if Vera did agree to such an arrangement.'

'She might when she hears that I am going to be living in Malta and that, in future, I won't be able to do anything to help her.'

Jack drained his glass and stood up. 'I think we'd better be getting back, don't you? You still have to break that piece of news to her.'

'I tell you what, Jack, will you have a look at the attic rooms before you turn them down?'

'No, I'm not interested.' Jack stuffed his hands in his pocket and hunched his shoulders. He wished Eddy would shut up about the attic rooms. He would like nothing more than to move in, to be closer to Vera, but what was the point of tormenting himself like that when she probably didn't give him a second thought?

She was nice and friendly, a good boss. They worked well together and she didn't interfere with the way he did things, but that didn't mean she cared for him in the same way as he cared for her.

'Those rooms could be made really comfortable, I promise you,' Eddy told him as they approached the shop. 'I meant it when I said you'd never need to have anything to do with Vera after work if you don't want to, not unless she needs your help with Dad. Will you just let me show them to you?'

'Only if it will stop you going on about them!'

'Great!' Eddy slapped Jack on the shoulder.

'Let's do it now before I tell Vera about my plans for the future,' he insisted. 'Since Vera is minding the shop we'll go in the back way so that she doesn't know what we're up to.'

The two rooms were much bigger and more airy than Jack had expected. At present there was an assortment of old empty boxes lying around and there were cobwebs everywhere.

'Clear all the junk and muck out, give the place a coat of paint, wash the windows and it will be a little palace,' Eddy told him.

'Certainly looks more promising than I had expected,' Jack agreed grudgingly.

'So we're on? You'll move in if Vera likes the sound of the idea?'

'I'll think about it, but don't twist her arm like you're twisting mine. Give her plenty of time to think about all the implications and let her make up her own mind.'

'You can ask her yourself if you want to,' Eddy told him. 'Once I've broken my news to her I bet she goes for the idea without any hesitation.'

Chapter Thirty-three

Before he left Liverpool to make his home in Malta, Eddy Quinn insisted on lending a hand to clear out the attic rooms. Between himself and Jack Winter they transformed the two neglected rooms above the shop.

Vera had agreed to their plan after Eddy had told her that his wedding to Rita was off, and that he was going to live in Malta. She even took an interest in how the rooms were to be decorated. She suggested that there should be white ceilings and white woodwork to make the place light and bright. She chose an attractive striped wallpaper for the larger of the two rooms and told them to use plain cream emulsion paint on the walls in the smaller one, which would be used as a bedroom.

'I'm really enjoying this,' Vera had told Jack when they left Eddy to mind the shop while they went off to Paddy's Market to look for some second-hand furniture.

Jack's mother gave him some curtains, and some sheets and blankets for his bed, as well as a great many other bits and pieces for his new home.

The result was cosy and comfortable. Vera was also impressed when Jack added a bookcase for the collection of books he brought with him from his lodgings.

'All you need now is a couple of nice rugs to make it even more homely,' Vera told him.

'My mum offered me some, but I told her I didn't need them.'

'Well, you do, so you'd better see if she still has them,' Vera said.

Michael Quinn completely ignored what was going on. He didn't question what was happening as all three of them tramped up and down the stairs a hundred-and-one times with all the decorating equipment. Nor did he show any interest when they carried in the furniture. He didn't even ask who was going to occupy the newly decorated and furnished rooms.

By the time the place was ready for occupation, Jack was eager to move in. Yet he waited for Vera's invitation to do so, even though he knew he didn't need it.

When Eddy had first proposed the idea, he had been unsure if he wanted to go along with it. The thought of being in such close proximity to Vera concerned him. He was afraid he would find it stressful to be living on the premises, knowing how he felt about her; not being able to tell her he loved her, desired her and wanted to marry her; not sure if she saw him as anything more than an old friend who, by sheer chance, was managing her father's shop.

After several sleepless nights in his digs he convinced himself that he should move to Scotland Road. It would be no harder to conceal his true feelings than it was now, when they were working side by side in the shop, he assured himself.

As it was, he reasoned, once Eddy had left he would worry himself to distraction if he had to come back to New Brighton each night, knowing that he was leaving Vera there on her own.

At the last minute, however, he had second thoughts and determined that as soon as he arrived at the shop the next day he would tell Eddy that he couldn't do it. He wouldn't give him the true reason, that it was because of the way he felt about Vera. He'd find some excuse or the other. After all, he told himself, he was under no obligation to take on the responsibility for Michael Quinn so why should he let himself be conned into doing it simply so that Eddy could start a new life in Malta?

But when he arrived at the shop, Vera seemed so delighted that he was ready to move in that he changed his mind again immediately. Since she was in his thoughts night and day, how could he have ever, even for one minute, contemplated disappointing her, he asked himself.

He would never forget the look of happiness on her face as they talked over their living arrangements. He could see that she'd planned everything in great detail and he began to speculate that perhaps she did care about him more than he thought.

He wouldn't build up his hopes, but he could dream. If there was even the slimmest chance that his friendship with Vera might develop into a full-blown relationship he'd do everything in his power to help it along.

Benny accepted the new arrangement without comment or showing any real interest. It was July

329

and his examination results weren't due for a while. He was hoping for high marks, but worrying in case he didn't do as well as he anticipated.

Eddy and Vera had discussed between themselves what the next step ought to be for Benny. But when they tried to talk to him about his future he was evasive and uncomfortable. He insisted that he still had no idea what he wanted to do with his life.

'Well, a lot depends on what your exam results are like, doesn't it?' Eddy challenged him.

'To some extent it does,' Benny admitted, avoiding Eddy's penetrating stare. 'The better my marks then the more openings there will be.'

'What sort of openings?' Eddy probed. 'You keep saying that you haven't a clue what you want to do! Surely you must have some idea about how you want to earn a living?'

'Yes, I have, but I don't think it's possible, so there's really no point in talking about it,' Benny muttered.

'What sort of stupid answer is that?' Eddy said irritably.

'If there's something you really want to do, Benny, then why don't you tell us what it is?' Vera urged. 'You never know, we may be able to help you.'

'Look, Benny, I'm leaving Liverpool in a couple of days' time,' Eddy told him, 'and I'd like to see your future settled. If you have something in mind that you want to do then, like Vee said, let's hear it.'

Benny looked uncomfortable and fiddled with the pen he was holding.

'Come on, spit it out,' Eddy said impatiently.

'Well, if you really want to know I'd like to stay on and take my Higher School Certificate. Then, if I get good marks, I'd like to go to university.'

'Bloody hell!' Eddy ran his hand over the top of his head. 'You don't want much, do you, kiddo?'

'Well, you did ask,' Benny defended, his face turning beetroot red.

'I know I did, but this wasn't the sort of answer I was expecting to get. Whew! Have you thought it through, whacker?'

'Of course I have! I've thought of nothing else for months.'

'Did you know about this?' Eddy asked looking at Vera.

She shook her head. 'This is the first I've heard about it. Benny has been studying very hard, though,' she added as an afterthought.

'Studying is one thing, keeping him in food and clothes and putting a roof over his head until he gets through that lot is another.'

'He has a home, here.'

'Yes, but there's more involved than just having somewhere to live. He'll need food, clothes, money in his pocket and heaven knows what else. I could go on forever. If he stays at school and gets his Higher School Certificate and goes to university, well, all that's going to take another five years at least. Bloody hell! It doesn't bear thinking about! No,' Eddy shook his head. 'It's out of the question.'

'Does it have to be?' Vera argued, 'We agreed he already has a roof over his head, and as long as the shop is providing us with a living there's enough money to put food on the table. He can take that for granted.'

'What about clothes? The trousers and jacket he's got on at the moment are at half-mast! The collar on his shirt is fraying and it's so damn tight that it's almost choking him.'

'It's the end of term,' Vera pointed out, 'I thought he would be leaving school in a couple of weeks so I've put off buying him new clothes until I know what he intends to do next. There was no point in buying him a smart suit if he was going to be a labourer down on the docks, now was there?' she stated tartly.

'Docker, him?' Eddy gave a short sharp laugh. 'He's got brains for something better than that, even if he can't stay on at school.'

'Then I'll kit him out with whatever he needs. I've already told you, Eddy, we're not on the bread-line. We can manage comfortably as long as we've got the money coming in from the shop, remember.'

'And is it?'

'Of course it is. Jack is a first-class repairer: we're doing more business now than we've ever done.'

'You are at the moment, but what happens if Jack packs the job in, or asks for a rise, or is off ill?'

'You've made pretty sure that Jack won't leave. That was why you helped him decorate those two attic rooms, wasn't it?' Vera smiled.

'No, I did that so that I knew there was someone here on call should you ever need help with the old man. It was to put my own mind at rest, knowing that I was going to be living so far away from you in future.'

Vera looked at him in bewilderment. 'Shall we leave this discussion for the moment, give ourselves time to think over all the implications?'

'Yes, if that's what you want to do,' Eddy agreed.

'So that's it, is it?' Benny asked, his voice raw with disappointment.

'No, not at all. We do need to think about it, though,' Vera told him in a mild, firm voice.

Later, when they were on their own, Eddy said, 'Why not see if we can persuade Benny to give up this hair-brained scheme . . .'

'No.' Vera reached out and laid a hand on his arm. 'Let's give him a chance, Eddy. You are doing what you want with your life so why not let him have the same opportunity?'

'Do you know what you are saying?' he blustered. 'Do you realise what a rod you would be making for your own back?'

'That might be so, but I'm sure I am doing what Mam would have done if she was alive. Doing this for Benny will be a tribute to her memory.'

Eddy's face softened. 'It's a wonderful thought, Vee, but don't forget you'll have to do it all on your own. I won't have any money to spare to be able to help you in any way. In a couple of months' time I'll have a kid of my own to support.'

'I know that, Eddy, but there's no need for you to worry about Benny.'

'I'm afraid I do. I won't be here to share any of the burden with you.'

'That doesn't matter. We'll manage, Eddy! We've done so all these years while you've been hoarding every penny you earned so that you could marry Rita Farthing and get a place of your own.'

'Yes, but Benny was only a young kid then. He didn't need all that much, but now . . .'

'I understand what you're saying,' Vera told him quietly, 'and I do know exactly what I am taking on. But I want to see Benny do well more than anything else in the world.'

'Isn't sacrificing your own life to take care of Dad enough for you, Vee?' he said, his gaze sharp and direct. 'Isn't it time that you had a life of your own? Time you found yourself a soul mate, married and had kids of your own to look after?'

'Benny is as close to me as any child of my own could ever be,' she told him firmly. 'My mind's made up, Eddy, so it is pointless saying any more. I've not said one word against what you are planning to do with your life so don't criticise me.'

'I can't help feeling that you aren't fully aware of what you are taking on,' he persisted ruefully.

'Look Eddy, I've wished you well in your new life, so can't you do the same for me?'

He stared at her long and hard as if intent on persuading her to change her mind. When she returned his gaze unwaveringly, he pulled her towards him and hugged her. 'Our Benny's a lucky little bugger,' he told her emphatically. 'I only hope he appreciates all you are giving up to do this for him.'

'I'm positive he will understand,' Vera told him confidently.

Eddy still looked uncertain. 'You're quite sure that you'll be all right?' he asked. 'What with this and Dad, you're taking on an awful lot.'

'I'll be fine, Eddy. Remember, from now on I'll have Jack here to help me if I need him.'

On the day when Eddy finally said goodbye to them all, Jack added his own reassurance.

'I'm as comfortable as a pig in clover. I've got a cushy flat and a good cook to feed me three meals a day. There's nothing at all for you to concern yourself about, Eddy. Rest assured I'll keep an eye on things here. I'll be on hand should Vera need any help, night or day, so you have nothing at all to worry about.'

'Thanks, whacker! It means a hell of a lot to me!' Eddy told him, slapping him heartily on the shoulder.

Chapter Thirty-four

For the first couple of weeks after Jack Winter moved into the attic rooms over Quinn's, he and Vera were walking on eggshells.

Both of them were scared of saying or doing anything that might embarrass or offend the other. Then, as time passed, the old comfortable familiarity that had been established after Jack came there to work reasserted itself.

It seemed perfectly natural to take their meals together in Vera's living room. When he was well enough, Michael Quinn sat down at the table with them. Benny sometimes joined them, but even though his exams were over he still spent a great deal of his time in his bedroom.

At first Jack had worried that this was because he was there, but Vera assured him it wasn't.

'Benny has always preferred his own company. He likes to sit and read rather than talk to people.'

'Doesn't he ever go out with lads of his own age?'

'He has one or two friends, but they don't live around here.'

Jack pulled a face. 'No, not many Scottie Road types go to grammar school, or want to go on to university. Do you think he'll ever get there, Vee, or is it all pie in the sky?'

'We'll have to wait and see,' Vera said quietly.

'I think he will,' she added confidently.

When the School Certificate results came through, they were all amazed at how well Benny had done. He had top marks in all of the seven subjects he'd taken.

'The headmaster asked if I wanted to sit for my Highers,' Benny told them.

'I hope you told him that you intended to do so,' Vera said quickly.

Benny's face brightened. 'You really mean that I can stay on?'

'You know you can. We discussed all this with Eddy when he was here.'

'I know, but I thought you might have realised how much was involved and changed your mind.'

'When I say something, I mean it,' Vera confirmed quietly.

Michael Quinn received the news with a shrug of his shoulders. 'Whose going to run the shop, then, if Benny is staying at school?'

'Jack will, of course, the same as he's been doing for a long time.'

'Jack?' He looked puzzled.

'Jack Winter. He lives here now, up in the attic rooms.'

'I don't think I've ever met him.' He gave her a crafty stare. 'Is he one of ours or is he one of the enemy,' he hissed.

'He's the best friend and worker you've ever had,' Vera told him.

'Then why have I never seen him around or had a chance to talk to him?'

Vera didn't bother explaining. Sometimes she felt saddened by her father's oblivion of all that was happening around him. She knew that at one time she would have felt exasperated or quite angry, but not any longer. Jack had managed to persuade her that the best thing to do was either to ignore these lapses of memory on her dad's part, or simply laugh about them.

More and more she wondered just how she would cope without Jack's support. His caring nature and his ability to remain calm no matter what happened, gave her the strength to cope with all the many day-to-day problems with her father.

There was no doubt in either of their minds that her father was sinking into a world of his own. His attacks were now happening less, but he seemed to be retreating further and further back into his past.

Sometimes he asked constantly for Annie and looked for her in every room in the house, even in the shop. When he couldn't find her he railed against both Vera and Jack. He claimed that they were deliberately trying to stop him from seeing her.

'Don't tell him that she's dead,' Jack advised, 'that might only upset him more.'

'So what can I do to stop him from looking for her?'

'Tell him that she has gone away for a few days and that she will be back soon.'

Vera did as he said and she found that Jack was right. Not only did this console her dad, but it actually seemed to please him and make him more cheerful.

'I'm marrying Annie as soon as she gets back,' he kept telling Vera, and there was a happy, contented look on his face.

Everything seemed to be going so smoothly that Vera could hardly believe her good fortune.

Benny returned to grammar school in September and again spent all his time closeted in his bedroom, studying. He never discussed what he was working on with either her or Jack. Vera assumed this was because he knew they probably wouldn't understand what he was talking about.

The shop was doing well and she and Jack had developed a system that worked smoothly.

At Jack's suggestion, the two of them started going out to the pictures once a week.

'You need a break, a bit of a treat,' he told her, 'and so do I.'

At first she had demurred, saying she couldn't leave her dad, but Jack had scotched this excuse right away.

'I've had a word with Benny and he'll listen out for him.'

Vera looked concerned. 'Are you sure he'll hear him? Benny gets so engrossed when he's studying . . .'

'He will. He's promised. He knows if he lets us down he won't get any money.'

'You're paying him?' Vera didn't know whether to feel angry or not.

'If you called in a stranger to sit with your dad you'd expect to pay them, wouldn't you?' Jack pointed out. 'Well, this is the same. It's a way for

Benny to earn some pocket money for himself. He was quite keen to do it, I can assure you.'

It took Vera a few days to come round to the idea, but the more she thought about a trip to the pictures the more attractive it seemed.

Finally she gave in and agreed. 'But we'll only go if Dad has had a peaceful day,' she stipulated.

Jack nodded understandingly and readily agreed to her terms.

He insisted that Vera should be the one to decide which picture they should go and see.

'I don't know what sort of thing you like,' she pointed out. 'Suppose I pick something that you find isn't to your taste?'

'Then I'll sit and look at you all night instead of the screen,' he told her with a cheeky grin.

She didn't answer, but she felt her cheeks burn. The trouble was, she suspected that he was telling the truth. It was becoming more and more obvious that his feelings for her were growing deeper.

She felt the same way about him, but she was afraid to admit it, even to herself.

It's only because we're living under the same roof and spending so much time together, she kept telling herself. He cares about me in the same way that I am fond of Benny. I'm always going out of my way to do things for him and make his life more comfortable. It's the same with Jack.

In her heart of hearts she knew this wasn't the case, though, it was much more than that. When she went to bed at night she listened for every movement from the room directly above her, knowing that Jack was sleeping there.

She even began to take more care about her appearance. Sometimes he noticed the changes. If he commented on them, she was thrown into a tizzy and blood rushed to her cheeks.

When they started going to the pictures together, she tried to look her best. Sometimes it was a different hairstyle, a new blouse, a change of lipstick. Whenever he noticed these things it made her feel pleased, but self-conscious at the same time.

She tried to hide her disappointment when Jack said he would be going to Wallasey to spend Christmas with his mother.

'I haven't seen her for ages, not since I moved in here, so I owe it to her. I'd much rather be staying here with you, mind. It will be quiet for you, all on your own. If there is any trouble with your dad, send Benny across for me and I'll come back right away. OK?'

When she came downstairs on Christmas morning she was disappointed to find that Jack had already left the house. On the table were several gift-wrapped presents, one of them with her name on it. Inside was a bottle of perfume. She opened it hesitantly, all the time remembering how much she had hated the smell of the California Poppy scent that Di Deverill had used.

The first whiff took her breath away, it was so strong. She dabbed a spot of it onto the back of her wrist and this time the smell was so delightful that she was captivated.

She checked the label and vaguely remembered seeing an advertisement for this very perfume. It had been so expensive that she'd laughed to herself, wondering what sort of people could afford to buy such luxuries.

Benny sniffed the air appreciatively as he came into the room and grinned knowingly. She handed him the small slim package Jack had left for him and watched his face transform as he unwrapped it and found a fountain pen inside it.

'Gosh! I never thought I'd own one of these,' he gasped. 'It's a real beauty! It has a nine-carat gold nib!'

The package for Michael Quinn contained a large bar of chocolate, something he never ate, but he seized on it with glee. 'Rations!' he exclaimed with obvious relief. 'Thank God, they managed to get this past the enemy.'

For the rest of the day he wrapped and unwrapped his present, slyly eating chunks of it when he thought no one was looking.

Vera and Benny exchanged amused smiles. 'It doesn't look as though he intends to give us a taste of it,' Benny commented.

Jack didn't return until New Year's Eve and Vera felt desolate. The house seemed so empty without him. She missed having him to talk to. Although she opened up the shop each day there were very few customers and she felt she'd never known such a long week in her whole life.

Jack was surprised at the spread she prepared for them on his evening home.

'I put off cooking the turkey until I knew you would be here,' Vera explained.

'You shouldn't have done that,' he remonstrated.

'That makes me feel guilty. What did you have on Christmas Day?'

'Bread and water,' Benny told him with a grin. 'Dad was all right, he had his chocolate!'

'Didn't he give you a piece?' Jack laughed.

As Vera went back into the kitchen to get on with last-minute preparations for dinner she could hear them laughing about what had happened.

For a moment she felt angry, but then common sense took over. What harm was there in it? They didn't mean it unkindly, and it was good for Benny to have another man around the place to talk to and share things with.

As she washed up after their meal, leaving Benny to teach Jack how to play the new game of *SORRY* that she'd bought him, Vera thought what a wonderful day it had been. Even her father had been dressed in his best suit and had sat at the table with them. She felt that they had been like a real family.

The only one missing was Eddy. They'd heard from him several times. He'd found a good job and had settled down well in Malta. He and Maria now had a baby boy and they'd named him Jacques.

It means Jack in English, he'd written, *so you can tell Jack Winter that we've named the baby after him.*

Even though it was New Year's Eve, Michael Quinn went to bed early, too tired to see 1935 in.

'I shouldn't imagine he will be able to sleep through all the noise, not when the bells and the ships klaxons start sounding,' Vera said when she came back downstairs. 'Benny said he'll stay up there with him until he has settled.'

'We'll hear him if he calls out,' Jack assured her. 'Come and sit down, I've got a present for you.'

'You've already given me a gift,' she protested.

'Yes, but this is another one. A very special one. Sit down in your dad's armchair and close your eyes!'

As she did so, from somewhere came the sound of music. She gave a sigh of pleasure as the strains of Henry Hall's Orchestra filled the room.

'You can open them now.'

On the table was a wind-up gramophone and beside it a small stack of records.

She clapped her hands in delight. 'Oh, Jack. It's absolutely marvellous!'

'The records are all your favourite bands and singers,' Jack told her smiling. 'As well as Henry Hall, there's Geraldo, and Glen Miller. Now you can listen to them whenever you want to.'

'How do you know they're my favourites?'

'They're all songs from pictures we've been to see!'

'Really?' She looked up at him wide-eyed, her cheeks pink with excitement.

'Truly!'

'I don't know what to say. Thank you doesn't seem to be enough!'

'You could give me a kiss,' he murmured softly.

They stared at each other for a long moment. She could feel her heart pounding. It was so loud that she wondered if he could hear it too.

Then, without knowing how it happened, she was in his arms. As their lips touched she felt a thrill of pure happiness spread through her, knowing that at last she had found love with a man she could trust. It was as if every nerve in her body was on fire.

They kissed again, eagerly, hungrily, enjoying the exquisite experience, something they'd both dreamed about for so long.

'I love you, Vera Quinn. I always have, ever since we were little kids,' he told her softly, stroking her hair.

He knew from her response, from the way she'd kissed him, that she felt the same way about him. He now wondered why they had waited so long. He had known what his feelings for her were from the first moment he'd walked into the shop.

Vera gave herself up to the sheer delight of being in his arms. She was sure it had been fate, as well as old Sam Dowty, that had brought them together.

Then, suddenly, memories she'd tried so hard to forget came flooding back. She struggled to free herself from Jack's enveloping arms. Tears brimmed in her eyes and her face was twisted with anguish as she shook her head and pushed him away.

'No, this mustn't happen,' she whispered. 'Please, Jack. There are things you don't know about me, terrible things. I can't even start to tell you!'

'Hush, hush! He pulled her back into his arms, holding her tight, smoothing her hair back from her brow. 'Everything is all right.'

'You don't understand . . .'

'But I do, Vee. I know all there is to know about you.'

Vera laughed bitterly. 'You only think you do, Jack. There are things in my past that even to this day I can't talk about.'

'You don't need to. I know all about what happened.' His lips rested on her sweat-soaked brow. 'Eddy told me. Everything! I know all about Bill Martin and what he did to you, so you don't have to say another word. OK?' he said gently.

Vera stared at him in amazement. 'Eddy told you? How on earth did he come to do that?'

'Does it matter? I know all about what happened and it doesn't matter. All I want to do is make you happy for the rest of your life. If you want to talk about it then I'll listen, but you don't have to.'

She shuddered and buried her face in her hands, as if unable to meet his eyes.

'I love you, Vee, with every fibre of my being. Please tell me you love me too.'

'Oh I do!' she breathed. 'I can't even start to tell you how much.'

Jack's lips covered hers in a kiss so sweet, so tender, that once more she melted into his embrace, cocooned in his love for her.

For a brief second, as the pressure of Jack's arms tightened, she stiffened. Then, with a blissful sigh of surrender, she let her own strong feelings of love sweep through her and take control. Jack knew everything about what had happened and yet he still loved her.

'We were meant for each other,' he whispered, 'time has proved that. Our being together is a wonderful beginning for the new year.'

Vera nodded. She felt as if she was bursting with happiness. 1935 was just dawning and she going to see her most treasured dreams coming true.

Chapter Thirty-five

The New Year brought so much happiness into her life that there were times when Vera felt that either she must be dreaming, or the bubble of euphoria that enveloped her would suddenly burst. She found it hard to believe that she deserved so much contentment or that it really could be true that Jack Winter loved her so deeply.

Since she and Jack had admitted their feelings for each other it was as if they had opened a door to another world. Everything had changed. The sun seemed to be shining even when it was cloudy; the early morning frost on the rooftops glittered more brightly; the wind was bracing, rather than dank and chill, as it swept in from the Mersey. She even saw people in a different, more compassionate light.

Never before had she felt so close to anyone as she did to Jack. It was as if their innermost thoughts and moods intermingled: they knew what the other was thinking without having to resort to words.

Every day revealed some new facet of their feelings for each other. She had always known that Jack was tall, friendly and good-looking, but now she discovered how deeply caring, thoughtful and generous he was, too.

Jack thought that he had already discovered

what a wonderful, loving person Vera was. He had seen how she was ready to sacrifice her time, and even change her way of life, to ensure that those nearest to her had all the care and attention she could possibly give them. Now he found that these endearing traits were more and more centred on him. She lavished so much affection on him that he was overwhelmed by the fact that anyone could care so much about him.

They had such strong feelings for each other, and delighted so much in their new-found love, that they could hardly keep their hands off each other.

When she brought a cup of tea through to the shop for him at mid-morning the moment their hands touched they found it wasn't enough. The desire to kiss was so powerful that their arms went around each other intuitively, and their lips automatically met.

Murmuring sweet endearments they would retreat back into the living room out of view of passers-by. He would hold her in his arms, kissing and caressing her for so long that by the time he went back to his work in the shop his cup of tea was often stone cold.

Several times, Jack tried to tell Michael Quinn that he wanted to marry Vera. Sometimes the answer was a smile and a nod, at others a raised fist and a threatening, low growl.

Neither of them were sure whether he realised what Jack was telling him or not. Even Vera seemed to be unable to make her father understand their intentions.

'There's only one way. We'll simply have to go ahead and get married,' Jack said resignedly. 'Thank heaven you don't need his permission to do so.'

'You're right, but I would still like to have his approval. Sometimes he doesn't even seem to know who you are. Yet, he did when you first came to work here.'

Jack gathered her into his arms, trying to pacify her as tears rolled down her cheeks. 'That was quite a long time ago,' he said softly.

'It means my dad is getting worse,' she said sadly.

'I'm afraid so, Vee. The only good thing is that he's much calmer these days. It's weeks since he's had one of his awful attacks and taken refuge from everyone.'

She sighed. 'His memory is failing, though, so perhaps that's why. He doesn't know you, or what is happening from day to day. He seems to be forgetting all about being in France and only remembers the things that took place before the war even started. Sometimes he seems to think that Benny is Charlie.'

Jack nodded in agreement. 'If it means he is no longer plagued by dreadful memories then surely it's all for the best?'

'You don't think we should let the fact that he is deteriorating stop us from getting married?'

'No, of course I don't.' He took her in his arms, his lips warm and demanding. 'Life goes on, Vee. We've got to accept that things change, whether we want them to or not.'

*　　*　　*

Vera remembered Jack's prophetic words when she discovered that Michael Quinn had died in his sleep at the end of March in 1936.

He looked so peaceful when she took his breakfast tray up to him that, for a moment, Vera thought he was still asleep. It was only when she touched him gently on the shoulder, asking him to sit up and eat his porridge before it went cold, that she realised what had happened.

She ran back downstairs and through to the shop to ask Jack to summon a doctor, even though she knew that it was too late for anyone to do anything more for her father.

Benny was so upset, that he seemed to be incapable of doing even the simplest task. White-faced and shaking, he stood staring down at his father as if he couldn't take in what had happened.

Vera put an arm around his shoulders and gently moved him away from the bed. 'Perhaps you should go off to school as usual,' she suggested, hoping it would bring him out of his trance.

'Are you sure, Vee? I don't want to leave you here on your own. Are you sure that there isn't anything I can do to help?'

'No, I can manage, truly I can. Jack will be here with me, remember,' she added as he still hesitated.

'Thanks, Vee.'

She knew she'd made the right decision when she heard the relief in his voice and saw the colour slowly ebb back into his face.

'If you leave now you will only have missed

about an hour. Explain to them what has happened and they'll understand.'

He grabbed his satchel, then paused in the doorway, looking bewildered. 'You are sure you can manage, that you don't need me to help you with whatever has to be done?' he persisted.

'Quite sure! Now go or you will be really late. Jack will help me sort things out.'

The next few days were wearying and traumatic. Vera kept wondering how on earth she would ever have managed without Jack's help. He was not only a tower of strength, but he seemed to know exactly what to do.

'I'll send a wire to Eddy. I'm sure he will want to come back to England for his dad's funeral.'

Michael Quinn had been so central to their lives, Jack thought, as he helped Vera organise things. Even though for a long time he had played very little part in running the shop, or doing anything connected with the home, his presence had dominated every decision taken.

His demise was going to cause a noticeable gap and an enormous upheaval. It was important that Eddy did come back to Liverpool, Jack thought worriedly, so that they could plan what was going to happen in the future.

Vera decided that the funeral should be low-key. It was such a very long time since her father had mixed with people socially that she didn't expect many neighbours to attend. Most of his old boozing companions had either moved away from the area or had died.

It was a sombre occasion. A handful of their long-standing customers came to the funeral, but none came back to the house afterwards. They were morose and tongue-tied. There was very little reminiscing. It was as if a chapter had ended and they all wanted to get on with their lives.

Eddy, Benny, Vera and Jack returned home alone to a cold meal that she'd left ready. Because he felt it ought to be settled while they were all together, Jack broached the problem that was uppermost in his and Vera's minds.

'Can we discuss what is to happen about the shop, Eddy?'

'The shop was leased to your father,' Jack pointed out, 'so can we take it you are quite happy if the landlord agrees to transfer the tenancy?'

'Do whatever you like. If you want to stay on here, Vera, then of course you can ask for it to be put in your name, if they will do that.'

Vera hesitated. 'Actually, I was thinking of asking if they would transfer it to Jack. Without him being here there would be no business.'

'So you're going to use blackmail to keep him here, are you?' Eddy grinned.

She shrugged lightly and glanced across at Jack. 'Something like that,' she admitted.

'How do you feel about that, Jack? Do you think it is a good idea for it to be in your name, and then you promise to keep the business going?'

'I've got an even better suggestion,' Jack told them.

'Go on, let's hear it then,' Eddy prompted.

'Why don't we ask if the lease can be transferred to Mr and Mrs Winter, since we will both be running the business?'

For a moment there was a stunned silence, then Eddy burst out laughing.

'You crafty devils! Are you trying to tell me that you two are thinking of getting married?'

'Well, I am,' Jack grinned. 'I'm not sure if Vera is going to accept my proposal or not, of course!'

'Was that a proposal?' Benny asked in surprise. 'I thought you had to go down on one knee when you asked someone to marry you.'

'That's the old-fashioned way,' Jack told him sombrely. 'This way you take them by surprise and they say yes before they know they've done it.'

'It looks as though we've reached a decision, then,' Eddy said, his voice tinged with relief. 'I shouldn't think there will be any problem, the rent's always been paid on time.'

'Our Vee hasn't given Jack an answer yet,' Benny pointed out.

'Well, Vee? Is it "yes" or "no", or have you kept us all in the dark and it's a forgone conclusion,' Eddy joked.

'I'll give it my consideration,' Vera told them, 'but there are certain conditions to be agreed first.'

'Well, we're waiting!' They all looked at her expectantly.

'I'll say yes, providing we can get married while you are still here in England, Eddy,' Vera said firmly. 'I want both you and Benny to be there. I've set my heart on having one of my brothers as our best man and the other one giving me away.'

There was utter silence as Benny and Eddy looked at each other uneasily.

'What's wrong with that? Don't you like the idea?' she asked in surprise.

'I've got to get back, Vee,' Eddy explained, apologetically. 'I've only got ten days off and I have to allow for travelling time out of that.'

Jack and Vera exchanged amused glances.

'Shall I tell him or do you want to do it?' Jack asked.

'We were already planning to get married. We'd even set the date,' Vera told him. 'There's plenty of time for you to attend our wedding before you go back to Malta.'

Eddy gave a long, low whistle. 'What can I say? You're one step ahead of us, I can see that.'

'It will be a very quiet wedding,' Vera warned them. 'We don't want any fuss, but we do want both of you to be there. It means a great deal to me.'

'Won't people think you are rushing things, Vee?'

Vera frowned. 'I don't understand.'

'Well, I mean you two getting married so soon after Dad dying,' Eddy said awkwardly.

Vera shrugged. 'Does it matter what other people think? Nobody worried about Dad when he was alive. No one even came to visit him, and the few outsiders who turned up today for his funeral were there more out of curiosity than for any other reason.'

'You're probably right,' Eddy muttered. 'We've settled that point, but there are one or two other things which we ought to sort out.'

'Such as?'

'Well,' Eddy hesitated and looked uncomfortable. 'There's the future, for a start.'

'We've already said that the shop should be in both our names.'

'That was the lease. I'm talking about the actual business.'

'I most certainly meant that both the lease and the business should be in joint names for Jack and me,' Vera confirmed sharply. 'You haven't any objections, have you? Don't tell me you've suddenly changed your mind and decided you want to come back here to run it,' she said sarcastically.

'No! I'm definitely not coming back. My future lies in Malta! I was thinking about Benny.'

'Benny? You don't think he wants to become a cobbler, do you?' Vera exclaimed.

Eddy pushed a hand through his hair. 'I'm not explaining myself very well. Who is going to look after Benny and where is he going to live until he finishes his studies and gets a job?'

'He'll stay here with us, of course!' Jack assured him.

'That means things will go on exactly the way they are now.'

'Yes, and we'll continue to run the business as usual,' continued Jack. 'There won't be any changes at all, not unless you want us to make some.'

'Except my name,' Vera interrupted. 'I will be Mrs Winter.'

'That, of course, is an extremely important

change,' Jack agreed, pulling her into his arms and kissing her tenderly.

Eddy shook his head, a look of bewilderment on his face. 'I can't understand this,' he said. 'You two want to get married and start a life of your own, yet you are prepared to stay here, go on running the business, and give Benny a home as if nothing has changed.'

'Well, it hasn't, except that Jack and I will be man and wife,' Vera pointed out.

'I know, but will such an arrangement work?' He looked from one to the other, perplexed.

'Of course it will work. Why ever shouldn't it?'

Eddy waved his arms, embracing the room and all of them. 'Are you sure that this is what you want, Vee? It's all the same as before. That's not the right beginning for a marriage. This place is so full of bad memories. Jack should be taking you right away from here, to make a fresh start in a home of your own. You've had years of being a slave to this family, looking after us all, especially when taking care of Dad. It's no life for either of you if you stay here, carrying on in exactly the same way.'

'It's only for a short time, until Benny has finished his education,' Jack pointed out. 'Once he's got a job and a life of his own then we will be free to change things . . . that's if we want to do so.'

'That's all very well, but that will be several years away,' Eddy persisted.

'We know! By then we may have built the business up and be making a mint.'

'In Scottie Road? I doubt it!'

357

'Don't worry about us, Eddy,' Jack told him. 'We do know what we're doing. Vee and I have talked it through very carefully. If your dad hadn't died when he did we would have been getting married this week anyway.'

'What more can I say?' Helplessly, Eddy looked at Vera.

'Nothing at all,' Vera assured him. 'Except to wish us well.'

'I'll certainly do that. You deserve every bit of happiness that comes your way.'

'And that's exactly what I can look forward to with Jack at my side,' Vera told him confidently.

Vera and Jack's wedding took place on Easter Saturday, 11th of April 1936. The sun was shining and it was unusually warm for the time of year.

Vera wore a cream woollen dress with a matching coat. Her hat was as blue as her eyes, which were sparkling like brilliant sapphires.

They only had eyes for each other as they exchanged their vows, every word underlying the intensity of their feelings for one another. Both Vera and Jack seemed to glow with happiness and fulfillment.

Afterwards, when they posed for a photograph, Vera's face was wreathed in smiles as she stood with her arm linked through that of her handsome husband. Jack was gazing back at her as if there was no one else in the whole of the universe. Eddy was standing on one side of her, and Benny alongside Jack.

'Why don't you take some time off? Come back

to Malta and spend a week with us,' Eddy suggested. 'Maria would love to meet you, and you'd be able to see Jacques, too.'

Jack and Vera both shook their heads. 'Thank you, Eddy,' Jack told him. 'It's a nice thought, but we're not ready to go on a spree like that, not yet. We have a business to run. Perhaps in a few years' time, after Benny has graduated.'

'I hope you will, it's an open invitation, remember. I don't suppose I'll be making another trip back here. Maria is expecting again,' he explained. 'More expense. You know how it is!'

'No we don't, not yet at any rate,' Jack grinned broadly. 'All that is still to come, but don't worry,' he added, squeezing Vera's hand, 'I know we'll get there, given time.'